CW00495142

IMPURITY

A thrilling murder mystery full of devilish twists

RAY CLARK

THE BOOK FOLKS

Published by The Book Folks

London, 2019

This book is a work of fiction. Names, characters, businesses, organizations, places and events are either the product of the author's imagination or are used fictitiously. Any resemblance to actual persons, living or dead, events or locales is entirely coincidental.

ISBN 978-1-913516-99-4

www.thebookfolks.com

"They very commonly construct for themselves a life-romance, a personal myth in which they are the maltreated hero, which secret is the key of their battle against despair."

William Bolitho

Prologue

Leeds, West Yorkshire. Twelve Months Ago.

"All set?" he asked as he held her coat open.

She nodded and slipped into the garment. He put his hat on as they left the restaurant.

Sarah had presented it to him before they went out for the evening.

"I still can't believe you bought this. What possessed you?" he asked.

Sarah glanced up and adjusted it. "It was you. The minute I saw it I fell in love with it. As I knew you would."

He laughed. He had to admit, it was comfortable. The grey Australian leather hat resembled a Stetson with a narrower brim. Two studded holes sat on either side of it, with a braid circling its base. A six-pointed gold badge graced one side of the crown.

Despite being early December, the weather was mild. Gardener carried his topcoat over one arm, held Sarah's hand with the other. The couple were enjoying a relaxing evening together before the onslaught of Christmas left them with little, if any, time for themselves. They passed courting couples whispering and giggling to each other. At the intersection with Boar Lane, a large group of youths spilled out from a pub. They headed toward The Corn Exchange in search of one of the city's many nightclubs.

"What it is to be young," commented Sarah.

"We're still young."

"I know, but we're not going to a nightclub, are we?"

Her comment amused him, and he laughed.

"What's funny?" asked Sarah, chuckling herself.

"We're only young in mind, these days."

They both laughed again. Gardener wrapped his arms around Sarah, lifting her up, swinging her round. He recited the lyrics to an obscure pop song, which would be the nearest they would come to a club tonight.

Sarah giggled. "For God's sake, put me down. You'll put your back out."

As soon as she'd spoken the words, Gardener took a step back, and cried out in pain. He put her down, placing both hands on the base of his spine.

"Stewart! Are you all right? I warned you."

As Sarah bent closer, he leaped upwards and grabbed her around the waist.

He nuzzled his face into her neck and growled as he bit her. He kissed her – a long, lingering kiss he wished would last forever. The curves of Sarah's body aroused him. He never tired of running his fingers over her smooth skin, a testament to the strength of their physical relationship. They made love as often as when first married, twenty years previously.

"I have another surprise for you when we get home," she said.

"Have you now?"

"It's not what you're thinking, but you can have that as well."

Gardener laughed. "So, what is it?"

"You'll have to wait and see."

Gardener's curiosity was piqued, but he decided not to press any further. He raised his head, took her hand, and led her across Duncan Street. They were heading towards the intersection of Briggate and Boar Lane. They passed a busy McDonald's, heading for the NCP car park next to the now-closed travel agency.

As they turned the corner, hand in hand, they were completely unaware of the skirmish that had brewed between two men.

"Get the fuck off me!"

The couple stopped. The smaller of the two men held his victim by the throat up against the shop window, repeatedly crashing him into the glass.

Sarah gripped Gardener's hand tighter, to warn him against becoming involved.

Gardener's police instincts spurred him to action. "Come on lads, break it up." He pulled at the smaller man's shoulder. As the man turned, Gardener observed a misshapen forehead and a cluster of foreign bodies attached to his skin, like barnacles.

"You keep your face out of my business," said Warthead, in a cockney accent. Gardener raised his hands. "I'm not really interested in your business. I just think you could pick a better time and place."

"You ain't listening to me, are you? Get the fuck out of here."

It suddenly occurred to Gardener how quiet everything had become. A bustling city had been reduced to a ghost town. No people, no traffic. Realizing the situation was approaching dangerous, Gardener reached for his warrant card.

"I wouldn't if I was you."

The detective was unexpectedly staring down the barrel of a gun. Where it had come from, Gardener had no idea.

"Stewart!" Sarah cried out.

"Sarah, it's okay," he said over his shoulder to her, before turning back to Warthead. "Put the gun down."

"I told you to stay out of my business. Looks like I'm going to have to sort out both of you now."

Gardener glanced back at Sarah, pleased to see she had the good sense to keep her distance. He needed to keep Warthead under control until backup arrived.

The taller of the two men, still pressed against the window, took advantage of the distraction. He brought his right fist upwards, catching Warthead directly under the chin.

Gardener heard the crack as both upper and lower jaw connected. The hard blow dropped Warthead to one knee.

Surprised his attack had given him the upper hand, the taller man paused, giving Warthead enough time to react. Warthead raised the gun and pulled the trigger twice, blowing the left side of the man's face off. The force of the shots threw him against the shop window, which shattered under the impact. Blood and brain tissue decorated the wall and pavement.

"Bastard!" shouted Warthead as he stood.

Gardener launched forward, trapping Warthead's left arm with his own. He then forced his chin upward with his right hand.

"Put the gun down, now!"

"Go to hell."

He twisted Gardener around and shoved him against the shattered shop window. Stuck against the metal frame that had held the window, a piece of glass dug into Gardener's back. The sudden pain made him act quickly. He brought his right knee up between his assailant's legs, crushing his testicles. The man sunk a little, but still maintained his grip. He wheezed into Gardener's face, a mixture of bad breath and stale cigarette smoke.

The gun went off. Sarah screamed as Gardener felt the breeze of the bullet. It passed his nose and blew a hole through the brim of his hat, which flew into the air. Gardener hit Warthead full in the face, dropping him. The gun went off again as he hit the ground.

Sarah shrieked.

Gardener turned in time to see his wife collapse, clutching her stomach. "Sarah!" he shouted, stepping over his attacker to reach her as she lay face down on the pavement.

A small crowd gathered from the nearby McDonald's, eager to see what the commotion was about. He kneeled down, gathering her up into his arms.

"Oh God, Sarah. Speak to me, please?"

She opened her eyes, trying to crane her neck to see her stomach. He followed her gaze. A large red stain spread across her abdomen where the bullet had entered.

"Don't move, love." He placed his hand on her stomach, trying to stop the flow.

"Oh, God, Stewart, it's hurting!"

"I'm sorry." He pulled his hand away, panic-stricken, fumbling inside his suit for his phone. Then he remembered. He left it at home. They were having a night out. He wasn't on call.

He raised his arm, staring at the blood covering it. Sarah's blood.

Dread passed through Gardener as he realized the enormity of the situation. With little knowledge of first aid, he knew he couldn't help Sarah.

He raised his head, searching the crowd. "For God's sake, somebody call an ambulance."

He gazed into Sarah's eyes. "You'll be all right, Sarah. We'll call an ambulance for you, get you to hospital."

"Stewart," her voice lower now, "it's hurting me."

"Try to keep still, love. You're going to be fine."

Gardener glanced around desperately. Warthead had disappeared. He was left with only a crowd of youths, and people in cars slowing down to see what was happening, but no offers of help.

It was midnight in the centre of Leeds. His wife had been shot; every minute she spent on the pavement, bleeding, was another minute wasted. And all he could do was watch and wait.

His eyes welled with tears. His stomach knotted. "Sarah, please don't leave me."

He held his wife's gaze, watching her life drain away. He refused to turn away. He was not going to shout at some bastard in the crowd for not phoning the emergency services quicker. He was not going to see if anyone else could help him, or whether or not there was a doctor around.

He knew they had little time left together. He held her tight, determined to remain strong for her, comfort her, as he said he would during their wedding vows.

"I love you, Sarah."

She tried to reach up to touch his face. As her hand touched his skin, he felt how cold she was, how lifeless.

"I will be all right, won't I?"

Her words were carefully pronounced, spoken with insecurity.

Gardener choked. "Sarah, you're going to be fine. The ambulance is on its way. We're going to get you to hospital. You're going to be fine." He fought hard to stop his tears.

He heard a siren in the distance, the answer to his prayers. A flickering flame of hope burned in his heart, in anticipation that she might yet be saved.

"Ambulance is coming, mate," said a youth, tapping him on the shoulder.

Sarah reached up to him again, crying out in pain before she managed to speak. "Stewart, promise me something."

Gardener felt as if his own life were extinguishing. He searched her face for a sign she would be able to hold on, gently caressing it with his bloody hand.

"Anything. I'll do anything."

"Look after Chris. Please look after our son, my darling. He needs you."

"Oh, Jesus. Sarah, don't talk like that."

She winced, her breathing shallow. "Stewart..."

She gripped him tighter than he thought possible, staring at him intently.

"Stewart, please help me... Stewart?"

Sarah died in his arms as the ambulance arrived: her dying breath spent saying his name.

The crew had to physically restrain Gardener in order to take over. He stood, raising his hands to his head.

"No. Please, God, say it's not true."

Gardener fell to his knees, screaming.

Chapter One

Leeds. Present day.

A wintry breeze brushed across Detective Inspector Stewart Gardener's face as he studied the building. Three storeys tall, Victorian and imposing, it had been converted from a house to a group of small flats leased out by an unscrupulous landlord charging extortionate rent while maintaining a low profile.

The street lighting revealed rotting window frames, cracks in the outside walls, and brickwork in need of re-pointing. Fallen roof slates lay scattered amongst the debris in the front yard. A girl passed by one of the front windows, gently rocking her baby.

Gardener pushed open the paint-blistered front door, only to be shouldered backward by an ashen-faced young constable as he tripped and fell forward out of the door.

The PC landed on his hands and knees, and started to retch.

"Why me?" muttered Gardener to the night sky. Three concrete steps led to the door. He jumped down and hauled the constable up by his collar.

"Stop contaminating my crime scene."

He dragged the young PC over to a small brick wall separating the crime scene property from the one next door and leaned him over it. "Stay there until you've finished."

Gardener turned back to the house and entered. There were no lights on. Peering up the staircase to the second floor, he heard a mixture of voices filtering down from the other landings. A child cried. Someone complained loudly about the mess.

He grabbed the handrail, took a single step, and crashed straight through as the timber crumbled.

"Jesus!"

He reached his arms out for protection as he fell forward. His right hand punched through the broken staircase, ending up next to his foot. His hat fell off as he struggled to pull free. Bracing himself, he dragged his hand out. The wood came away in splinters, scratching his skin.

His mood approached nuclear. He'd been called out to a crime scene on his first night off in two weeks, pulling at least a fourteen-hour shift every single day. He prodded the wall, hoping to find a light switch. His patience diminished rapidly when he couldn't.

"Is it too much to ask to have some light around here?"

He smiled as the scene was illuminated.

His grin soon disappeared as a voice on the landing boomed out.

Chapter Two

"Who's there?" demanded the hard-faced woman charging down the stairs. Her attire was a yellow cotton dress with a floral print that had probably been the height of fashion when the house was built. "You can't come in here, it's a crime scene."

Gardener picked up his hat. "You don't say." Slipping it back on, he said, "I know it's a crime scene."

"Then you'll know you can't come in here. We're waiting for someone."

Gardener pulled his warrant card from his pocket and held it up to her.

"That's me."

He didn't think he'd ever met anyone quite as offensive as the squat little woman. He could easily imagine her as the sentinel to the abode of the damned. Her dyed hair was black and wiry. She reminded him of an alligator he'd once seen in the Florida Everglades – its face and body fat, and squat. Beady brown eyes peered down at him above a snub nose and a wide mouth filled with sharp, pointed teeth.

She folded her arms. "You took your time, didn't you? Have you seen the mess up there?"

"No." Gardener made as if to search his pockets. "And it looks like I'm all out of crystal balls, so I'll have to do it the old-fashioned way."

"I don't like your tone."

"The feeling's mutual. And you are?"

"Olive Bradshaw. The landlady."

Gardener glanced around, now that he could actually see. The peeling paper exposed walls covered in green mould, streaked with black lines. An offensive smell of mildew permeated the passage.

Horrified at the degradation, he asked, "You actually charge people money to live like this?"

She was about to speak when she saw the young constable wandering back in from the yard.

The PC's complexion was pale, his expression grave. His uniform bore an orange stain across the front from the brick wall Gardener had bent him over.

"I suppose he's just vomited all over my steps."

"No," said Gardener. "I managed to save you from that. Though I shouldn't think it would make much difference." Before giving her the chance to reply, he faced the constable. "Have you finished?"

"I think so."

Gardener turned to the landlady. "Where do you live?"

She pointed to the room in the corner of the ground floor.

"Well, get yourself back in there and stop walking all over our crime scene."

He addressed the constable. "Go with her and take a statement. When you've finished, stand by the front door and see that she doesn't leave."

"I knew something like this was bound to happen," continued Olive Bradshaw. "I only went to bingo. I had heard the commotion before I went out, never thought I'd come back to this. Who's going to pay for it to be cleaned? That's what I want to know."

Gardener ignored her and continued up the stairs.

Chapter Three

On the way up, Gardener passed a girl cradling a crying child. She threw out a venomous jibe, which he ignored.

The top landing was about eight feet square. The threadbare carpet must have been original, as its colour was hard to distinguish. He noticed a cupboard door in the wall to his right.

To his left, another ashen-faced constable with watering eyes barred entry into the room behind him.

Filtering out was a strong, overpowering odour Gardener couldn't place. It smelled of blocked drains and rotten garbage.

"What is that smell?"

The PC pointed to the room.

"Is there a body in there?"

"If that's what you can call it."

"What would you call it?"

He hesitated before offering. "A mess!"

"Who found it?"

"The landlady. About half an hour ago. Maybe a bit longer, sir."

"What's your name, son?"

"Benson, sir. Paul Benson."

Benson had curly ginger hair with brown eyes. His smooth voice and pleasant manner indicated he was either a little shy or he felt intimidated in the presence of a senior officer. His face bore the scars of teenage acne. Gardener estimated his age as early twenties. Benson appeared to be standing up well, considering what he'd apparently seen.

"Take me through what happened."

"The desk sergeant took a call. The landlady was complaining about an offensive smell.

He asked her if that was all and she said no. She wouldn't go into detail but she couldn't open the door, and she needed us, quickly."

"So, you came straight away?"

"Yes, sir. We could smell it as soon as we entered the premises. Me and Rick Johnson. He's the one you probably passed by on the way in, being sick."

"We met briefly."

"Anyway, we came up here. The landlady was still trying to push this door open." He pointed to the room behind him. "I persuaded her not to go in. She gave us grief, but did as I asked."

"Have you been in the room?"

"No, sir. Just poked my head round the gap in the door from where she started to open it."

"I'm still here," shouted the girl on the stairs. "About time you all fucked off and let us get some sleep."

Gardener glanced over the banister at her glaring up at them.

He addressed the constable while still staring at the girl. "Go down to her flat, take a statement. Don't let her mess you around. I don't care how late it is. Keep her in there."

Paul Benson nodded and did as he was asked.

Gardener turned to the apartment door. The lock was intact, no damage to the woodwork.

As he pushed on it, he felt resistance. He pressed harder, sliding his head through the gap to see inside. His eyes went wide with horror as the door opened.

"Jesus Christ!"

Chapter Four

As Benson approached the girl with her baby, standing before the doorway to her flat, she glared at him in disgust.

"How many more of you lot are there? I'm trying to get me fuckin' kid to sleep. People been paradin' through here all night. Don't care for how much noise you make."

Benson studied the girl, startled at her appearance. He figured she was no more than seventeen. Her long black hair sat matted and unwashed upon her head. She sported a purple bruise under her left eye, uneven teeth, and puncture marks on her arms. She wore scruffy faded denims and a ripped black T-shirt. Appalled by her unkempt appearance and rancid odour, Benson took an involuntary step back.

"I need to take a statement from you, miss."

"You'll be lucky," she replied. "Seen what time it is?"

"Look, it won't take long. What's your name?"

"Why?"

"Don't give me any grief. The boss man up there's in no mood for games."

"Really? Who does he think he is, Dirty Harry? What's that fucking hat all about?" she mocked.

Gardener's voice from the landing above stopped her in her tracks.

"Are you going to get that statement, Benson, or do I have to spend all night in this human cesspool?"

Benson opened his mouth to reply when Gardener spoke again, much louder.

"You can tell her if she doesn't cooperate, I'll nick her for obstruction and have her down the station so fast, she'll think her feet have been spit-roasted."

The girl's expression changed. "Nicki Carter," she said sullenly. "Has anyone told him about police harassment?"

"Have you been here all night?"

"Yeah."

"Give me five minutes and a statement and I'll leave you in peace."

Chapter Five

The flat bore all the characteristics of the rest of the building: shitty carpets, warped wood, peeling wallpaper. No doubt the room smelled under normal circumstances, but he doubted it could compete with the decayed remains on the carpet.

The corpse had somehow disintegrated inside the clothing. A bubbling brown mess remained, which leaked across the floor. It was basically a skin sack hugging a skeletal frame. The brown gunge was still secreting its way through the clothing. Gardener's brain worked overtime trying to assess the cause of such a rapid deterioration.

A few things came to mind. Acid, paint stripper, or possibly even a poison of some kind. The most prominent question by far, though, was whether or not it was something contagious.

One floor below, there was a young baby to consider. The child would be far more susceptible than any adult. He sighed. Two solid weeks without a break or a partner, and now a riddle the size of the Dead Sea Scrolls. He had no choice. He would have to return to the front door, stop anyone else from entering the building. The crime scene had probably been contaminated already. He needed to make a call.

There were two distinct directorates within the Crime and Response service – each with its own bronze, silver and gold command structure. Response had already worked. The uniforms had attended. Gardener was Crime, and bronze. His Detective Chief Inspector, based in the control room, was silver. They were twenty-four seven.

Gardener called DCI Briggs and declared a Hazchem incident.

Within thirty minutes, the boys in the suits arrived and cordoned off the house. They distributed paper overgarments for everyone at the scene. They collected stepping plates and clear tenting from the van, and began the process of sealing the building up.

Gardener felt completely helpless. The whole process was now on a go-slow. He wouldn't be allowed near the crime scene until it had been cleared. Lord only knew what time that would be.

Chapter Six

Outside, Gardener studied a group of people whispering to each other across the street.

He wondered if any of them had seen anything. He seriously doubted it. No one ever did.

He sighed and peered down the street. To an outsider, Rawston appeared as a reassuring scene of frost-covered, two-up-two-down, back-to-back terraced houses set against the background of a thriving textile industry. Reminiscent of an Ealing Studio's B-movie, the close-knit community would spend the night indoors huddled around the fire, wrapping presents for their broods of children safely tucked up in bed, surrounded by the mouth-watering aroma of chestnuts roasting in the grate.

To him, the maze of buildings concealed a new breed, representing the filthiest scum the city offered. The enterprising drug pusher, attempting to build his empire by adding more clients to an ever-growing list of depraved addicts who'd stop at nothing for the next fix. Then came the perverts, the child molesters, and porn kings trading black market videos, magazines, and DVDs in an effort to satisfy an insatiable appetite.

Merry Christmas, Stewart, thought Gardener.

Chapter Seven

Staring at the rundown building, Gardener wondered what the hell was going on.

"Bout ya?" said Detective Sergeant Sean Reilly, poking his shoulder.

Startled, Gardener nearly jumped out of his skin. "Jesus, Sean." He relaxed a little. "I'm sorry. I was miles away."

"So I noticed."

"How's it going?" Gardener shook his partner's hand.

Reilly couldn't have timed things any better. Gardener needed to bounce ideas around.

He always found his partner's solid frame a measure of his personality, someone he could rely on in a crisis. The Ulsterman stood six feet six, his mouse-coloured hair long overdue for a trim. His probing brown eyes told you he wouldn't believe a word you said until you exhaustively convinced him you were telling the truth. They were a complement to his hard-and-fast interrogating techniques. He worked well with Gardener, allowing them to use the hard-man, soft-man approach to their advantage. He wore, as usual, a brown leather bomber jacket and jeans.

"Well enough," said Reilly. "Not sure I can say the same about you."

"Have Laura and Feargal come back with you?"

"They're staying another week, what with it being nearly Christmas. I don't blame them. I wish I could have stayed."

Gardener respected Reilly for two things. A family man, Reilly enjoyed an excellent relationship with his wife and son. After Sarah's death, it had been Sean Reilly who knocked him back into shape, forcing him to return to work. Gardener felt indebted to his colleague. That aside, he was also excellent at his job.

"I'm pleased you didn't," said Gardener.

"Why don't I like the sound of this?" Reilly glanced around.

"It's a major problem. We can't go in." Gardener pointed to the door behind him.

The rest of Gardener's team had arrived. He gathered together Detective Constables Colin Sharp, Frank Thornton, and Bob Anderson. They were accompanied by a young woman Police Constable by the name of Robinson, and a number of operational support officers he'd never seen before.

"Thanks for coming out. I don't intend to keep anyone longer than necessary. Briefly, a call came in around half past ten. The landlady found one of her tenants dead. Two PCs arrived before me to secure the scene. The deceased is male. He hasn't been shot, stabbed, strangled, kicked to death or had his life taken by any other means known to man. What I found were decayed remains on the carpet. You wouldn't think it was human from the condition. Somehow the body disintegrated inside the clothing."

"When you say disintegrated…?" prompted Thornton.

"Just that, Frank. It's a sack of skin holding the skeletal frame together. The brown gunge was still oozing its way through the clothing when I last saw it."

"Any idea what caused it?" asked Reilly.

"No," said Gardener. "Which is why I've had to call Silver and declare a Hazchem incident."

"That's all we need," moaned Anderson. "Judging by the smell that's wafting through that front door, I'd say he's been there for days. Doesn't look like that adds up, though, with the expression on your face."

"The landlady went to bingo at half past six. Apparently, he was fine then. Four hours later, he was spread out all over the floor."

"Christ," said Reilly.

"You all know well enough that criminals have little consideration for anyone but themselves, least of all us," Gardener said to the group. "It's cold, it's late, and the people I've spoken to have even less respect for us than for the victim. Let's do what we have to, fast."

Shivering a little, Gardener blew into his hands. "We're in Rawston, so most of the community will still be awake.

If there are no lights on, don't knock people up. We can always call back in the morning. I want you to split up and do a house-to-house. You know the drill. You know what we're looking for. Keep it brief. If you pick up on anything, make notes, and we'll come back in daylight. The two PCs are in the house taking statements from the residents."

Gardener turned to his sergeant. "Sean, you and I will search the deceased's flat once Hazchem give us the all-clear."

He turned to the group. "Let's go."

Chapter Eight

Gardener glanced at his watch as the Home Office pathologist, Doctor George Fitzgerald, came out the front door carrying his medical bag and still wearing a scene suit and mask. His watch read five o'clock.

Gardener approached him. "Can you tell us anything?"

Fitz removed his mask, drew in some fresh air. "Not really, but you'll be pleased to know Hazchem doesn't think it's contagious. From what I've seen, it looks like all the proteins have broken down. There's nothing left. Nothing I can use to start my investigation."

"Don't suppose you know what might have caused it?"

"Not without further tests. Who found him?"

"The landlady. A woman named Olive Bradshaw."

"What time?"

"About half past ten. Claims she went to bingo around half past six, came back, and this had happened."

Fitz shook his head. "You can't do this to a body in a few hours."

Gardener stared up at the heavens. "Somebody has."

Fitz checked his watch. "Kevin Swan will be down shortly. His team is just finishing up. They're going to transport what's left to the mortuary. He's declared the scene safe, so you should be able to move things forward."

"At least that's something."

Fitz left.

An hour passed before the senior Hazchem officer gave Gardener the green light.

He'd been there six and a half hours, and hadn't moved a muscle.

He and Reilly donned scene suits and climbed up to the top storey. A stepping plate had been used for every stair. A few more on the landing led into the room. The building had been reduced to a deathly quiet.

Once inside, the Irishman held his nose. "Jesus!"

"If you think that's bad, wait till you see the victim."

Gardener studied the flat. On the floor behind the door sat a brown stain where the remains had been. Woodchip wallpaper, magnolia in colour and dirty, decorated the walls. The filthy nets and curtains and windows combined with the threadbare carpet created a general atmosphere of depression. Along one wall sat a stained and discoloured brown Dralon settee, which had seen better days. The springs threatened to poke through the cushions. A similar seat backed up to another wall, facing an old pre-digital TV. In the corner of a makeshift kitchen, pots and pans were stacked high, caked with stale food. Next to them lay a pile of discarded takeaway foils.

The bedroom stood equally as offensive. The paper had peeled and slid down the wall.

Filth caked the carpet, making it sticky. The unmade bed stank with the odour of stale sweat mixed with God knows what else. No curtains covered the window, but who was likely to see in when you were on the top storey?

The pair of them left the bedroom.

"Doesn't look like he's cleaned up in years," Gardener said. "I really don't want to spend any more time in here than I have to. We still need to sort through the witness statements. Let's crack on."

After an extensive search, the pair came up with nothing more than a few pornographic magazines and DVDs, most of them Dutch and German. Gardener kept them for the incident room exhibit store back at the station.

Chapter Nine

Gardener and Reilly returned to the station after eight. Most of the team were already processing information. Despite it being early, the building showed signs of activity. Phones rang constantly, keeping everyone busy. A handful of officers watched a small TV in the canteen, and a radio played in a tearoom close to Gardener's office.

Paul Benson and Rick Johnson appeared, coffees in hand. Gardener waved them to his office, where he found Reilly, also with a coffee and a half-eaten doughnut. He sat with his chair tilted back and his legs stretched across the top of his desk.

Detective Constable Colin Sharp stood in front of him, a thirty-something dedicated professional with a dark complexion, a deep, resonant voice, and premature balding. Sharp had obviously said something funny because Reilly's infectious cackle reverberated around the room.

"Here's the boss now," said Reilly, his feet still on his desk. "Would you care for a coffee?"

"From that machine? You must be joking."

Gardener turned to DC Sharp. "Come with me, Colin."

Sharp followed Gardener down a long corridor, acknowledging colleagues he passed along the way. Gardener couldn't help but notice that although the decorations were sparse, they had a comedian on the force. A long balloon and two round ones had been arranged as a phallic symbol above one of the doors. At the end of the corridor they turned left, entering the first room on the right.

"We'll run the investigation from here, which we'll also use for briefing and debriefing. There's sufficient trunking and enough power sockets for all the internal computers. I've also called in the HOLMES operators. We'll put them next door."

He faced Sharp. "Can you set up the white boards and start off the spider chart with the name Herbert Plum, which I believe is the name of the deceased tenant?"

Gardener left Sharp and returned to his office.

Reilly glanced up at him and nodded as he entered. "When you gonna fix that hat, boss?"

Gardener smiled. "When the time's right."

"It's been nearly a year. You've not seen anything?"

Gardener grew cold inside. His stomach turned over. Not a day went by when he didn't think about the bastard who had taken the life of his wife, Sarah.

"No. But I will."

The rest of the team rolled in. Gardener instructed them to head over to the incident room, and told them that he would be along shortly. When he arrived, the group was sitting conferring with each other, waiting for him to start. He could hear the HOLMES team setting up their equipment next door as he addressed the team.

"I appreciate all your efforts. It's been a long night. I'm not going to keep you up any longer than I have to.

Judging by the early witness statements, no one's seen anything, no one's heard anything, but that's nothing fresh. Most of the people you talked to will be lying. It'll probably take us a lot of hard work to ferret out the truth.

"You lads could do with a break. Get yourselves a coffee and something to eat. While you have a break, Sean and I will stay here and organize the HOLMES team and the operational support officers to go through the rest of the witness statements. I'll also update the spider chart.

"When you come back, we can make a start by trawling CCTV, if there is any around there. We'll have to do another house-to-house. Sean and I will go back to the crime scene and grill the residents more thoroughly. Any questions?"

Gardener glanced around. There were none.

Chapter Ten

A small gathering huddled at the site of David Vickers' grave on a cold December morning. His mother Lesley, dressed in black, held a white handkerchief up to her face. Her tears flowed freely, obscuring her view, the last she would ever have of her only son. Jim, her husband, held her close, as if afraid to let her go. His contorted expression reflected the pain that could only be associated with losing a child. His other arm was wrapped around his daughter, Susan. David's grandparents stared vacantly at the coffin, trapped within their own torment, oblivious to everyone else.

Two police officers and a press photographer had also come to pay their respects.

Despite being mid-morning, the air blew crisp and fresh. A film of white frost covered the grass. Glistening brown leaves crunched underfoot. Exhaled breath hung around the mourners' heads, reluctant to spread to the outside world, an unsafe place where perverts killed children.

As Jacqueline Bâlcescu finished the service, she stepped back from the open grave as a mark of consideration. Lesley fell to her knees and begged for her son's return. She promised she would not let anything happen to him again. She would look after him properly, if only the Lord would grant her another opportunity.

Jim reached down to her, tears in his eyes. He wrapped both arms around his wife, pleading with her, offering reassurance. Through clenched teeth, he whispered to her no one could have given David a better home. Their son couldn't have had a more considerate mother. She should not blame herself.

Jacqueline wanted to reach out and comfort Jim. His haunted expression was pitiful. His son's death had torn his family apart, and the only thing he could do was watch. She noticed a number of other villagers hovering at the gate, unwilling to intrude upon the family's suffering. At the other end of the cemetery, a couple walked their dogs, their heads turned in the direction of the funeral. Most of the villagers had sent wreaths and sympathy cards. Jacqueline had seen the cards, and though they meant well – as people always did – she perceived in the messages the unstated relief that it was not their child.

She heard a rustling sound behind her. Turning, Jacqueline saw Stewart Gardener kneeling over his wife's grave. He'd cleaned up the area around the headstone, placing fresh flowers in the small urn, whispering as he did so.

Gardener glanced in the minister's direction, nodding courteously, before returning his attention to Sarah's resting place.

Jacqueline turned back to the grieving family. She felt it was time to make her departure.

She walked around the edge of the grave toward Lesley. She pressed her handkerchief tight to her mouth, her eyes shut and her voice a series of choking, broken sobs.

"Is there anything I can do for you, Lesley?"

The bereaved mother turned to face the minister with imploring eyes.

"You can't... bring him back… can you?"

Jacqueline felt hollow inside. What was she supposed to say, "Yes, just give me a few minutes and I'll have a word with Him upstairs?" She may not have children of her own, but she was sensitive enough to appreciate the heartbreak Lesley endured through the loss of a child.

"I'm sorry. I wish I could."

Time seemed to stand still before Lesley responded. She answered quite simply, "Well, I'm sorry too. There isn't anything you can do."

The minister nodded and gave the lamenting mother a hug.

Lesley raised her head and stared at Stewart Gardener. Jacqueline noticed the sudden change in her expression as her eyes darkened.

"But there's someone who can!"

Lesley made her way around her son's grave and approached the detective before Jacqueline could react.

Gardener stood and gazed at his wife's headstone, oblivious to Lesley.

"Mr Gardener?"

He raised his head to her, startled. "Lesley. I'm sorry, I didn't want to intrude."

"Mr Gardener, I'm begging you. Please catch this monster..." She broke off, unable to continue as sobs took control of her once more.

Jacqueline walked over to the grieving mother, taking her hand. "Come on, Lesley, this won't help you."

"It will. Please. I don't want to interfere. I know why he's here," she said to Jacqueline, before turning back to face the officer. "I understand what you're going through, but I'm asking you, as a parent, please catch the animal who did this and put him behind bars. Please make sure he doesn't do it again."

Stewart Gardener gazed directly at Jacqueline. She sensed his torment, his inability to reply.

"It might be your son next time," said Lesley.

The comment cut deep. The colour in the detective's face drained.

Jacqueline noticed an immediate change of expression in his eyes. They were no longer warm, friendly. His eyes became impenetrable. He made no reply.

Lesley fell to her knees, grabbing Gardener's hand. Through her tears she pleaded, becoming hysterical. "For God's sake, Mr Gardener, catch him. Please! He's taken my son, please don't let him have any more! Oh, God, please Mr Gardener, please!"

Suddenly, Jim stood at his wife's side.

The press photographer saw an opportunity for a front page exclusive and took photos.

"Lesley, don't do this, lass!" He turned away from his wife, glancing at the officer. "I'm sorry, Mr Gardener, she didn't mean to say what she said about your lad." He gazed down at his wife, still sobbing on her knees. "Come on, girl, let's get you home."

Gardener reached down to her as well. "Let me help you, Jim."

"No, it's all right. She'll be right enough when I get her home."

Jacqueline heard the break in Jim's voice. He continued pleading with Lesley to leave Gardener, and let him take her home.

They were both now sobbing.

The rest of the family joined the mourning couple as Jim helped Lesley up. Together, they walked in silence to their cars.

Chapter Eleven

Jacqueline turned to Gardener. "I'm sorry about that."

"It wasn't your fault."

"You look like you could use a cup of tea."

Jacqueline thought Gardener seemed unsure of her offer at first. Then his face softened into the comely expression she was used to, the one she liked.

"Er, yes. I'd appreciate that," he replied. "Thank you."

She studied him for a moment. He had a tall, athletic frame – a little too lean, perhaps – with short, black, well-groomed hair and brown eyes. He wore a grey designer jacket, a blue denim shirt, and grey chinos. He held his hat in his right hand. His face was tired and drawn as if he hadn't slept properly. She knew what he did for a living. Perhaps his work was keeping him up. She couldn't help but admire him for the way he'd coped with his own recent tragedy. Not only had he kept himself together, but his family as well. Jacqueline gave him a warm smile.

After a quiet word with the other officers and the press photographer, Gardener and the minister turned from the grave. They walked back towards the vicarage – a short stroll down a pretty, tree-lined path, which had become a haven for squirrels.

Jacqueline hunched her shoulders up against the cold, rubbing her hands together. As they entered the house, she showed Gardener through to the sitting room, where the heating quickly took away the chill of the cemetery.

The burgundy leather Chesterfield, matching footstool, pure wool carpet, and fine collection of sculptures and paintings displayed Jacqueline's expensive tastes. A television stood in one corner, a stereo in the other. An array of potted plants decorated the room, adding a rich natural beauty to an already colourful space.

Jacqueline returned with a tea tray. She placed it on a small table and poured a cup for each of them.

"I feel as if I ought to apologize for what happened back there," she said, taking a sip of her tea, her cup clasped between both hands.

"There's no need."

"Nevertheless, there's a time and a place."

"She was grieving. That's something I understand only too well."

"It can't have been easy for you, losing your wife so recently."

"It was a year ago. You cope."

"Yes, but bringing up a son as well, I think you've coped marvellously." Jacqueline noticed that her compliment unnerved Gardener, made him blush.

"I'm lucky. My father lives with us. He's a widower as well."

"I'm sorry. I didn't realize you had lost your mother." Jacqueline could have cut her tongue out.

"It was a long time ago, now. My father knew what we were going through. His experience came in handy." Gardener sipped more tea. "To be honest, it was only meant to be temporary. It became a permanent arrangement due to a loophole in the mortgage agreement."

"What happened?"

"My wife dying didn't mean that the house insurance would pay off the mortgage. I had to keep up the payments anyway. Three months in and they were crippling us. Dad figured it out and offered to move in permanently, help us financially. My son's health and well-being were the most important things to both of us."

"No wonder Lesley's comment struck a nerve."

"I'd have preferred not to have heard it. Chris has been through so much as it is."

An expression returned to his eyes.

"I hope you catch the person responsible, for everyone's sake."

"I don't have anything to go on at the moment. What Lesley doesn't realize is that, until now, it hasn't been a murder inquiry."

David Vickers had been abducted. He'd said goodbye to his friends after school, but never made it home. Someone found his body a week and a half later on a piece of waste ground, naked, his school bag sitting next to him.

The post-mortem revealed puncture marks in his arms, and signs of sexual abuse. The results from the specialist toxicology report confirmed his body contained traces of a powerful sedative. He'd been dead twenty-four hours by the time he'd been found.

"But surely you are looking for someone?"

"A specialist team was set up to search for missing children. Two had disappeared before David, but no bodies were ever recovered. From what I've read, there were no clues as to who'd abducted them."

"I can see I'm making you uncomfortable. I'm just concerned."

Gardener glanced around the room. His eyes came to rest upon the portrait above the fireplace.

"A member of your family?"

"Good grief, no," Jacqueline smiled. "It's Alexandru Ioan Cuza, elected prince of the United Principalities of Moldavia and Wallachia in January 1859. I think."

"You're very proud of your heritage."

"Almost everything I own has been hand-made and passed down from my grandmother. I seem to have inherited her taste for traditional Romanian furniture, most of which I have in my bedroom."

"I wondered about the surname." He changed topics. "You've not put up your Christmas decorations yet."

"No. I really should make the effort, particularly this year. I have my aunt coming to stay with me."

"Is this her first visit?"

"No, we spend Christmas together every year. I went to her last year. It's her turn to come to me."

"What about your parents?"

"My mother died when I was ten years old. Breast cancer."

"It seems we have something in common. Your father?"

"I haven't seen him for years."

"Looks like I'm making you uncomfortable now." Gardener checked his watch. He finished his tea and rose from the chair. "I must be going. Thanks for the tea. I've enjoyed our chat. Maybe I'll see you again."

"I hope so. Before you go, may I ask another question?"

"Go ahead."

"Why the hat?"

He smiled. "I'll tell you another time."

As Gardener left, Jacqueline couldn't help but think he had been distracted in her company. She suspected part of the problem was David's funeral.

Once again, village life in the close-knit community of Churchaven had been rocked to its foundations. David had been the third child to disappear.

After the first – a girl – had gone missing, parents had been unsettled by the possibility their child could be next. For a while, they had closely monitored the security of the children.

Their guard eventually slipped, despite the culprit still being at large.

A second child disappeared, another girl. Her school bag had been found on wasteland a week later, her purse inside still containing her dinner money.

The Residents' Association called an emergency meeting in the village hall, which had been chaired by a volatile member of the community. He was intent on inciting the gathering to take the law into their own hands.

Jacqueline had observed the tumultuous emotions of her fear-stricken neighbours see-saw out of control. She envisaged the birth of a vigilante force set on hunting down the depraved killer. She remembered seeing a police presence. At least half a dozen officers had shown up to answer questions, offer advice, and generally bolster the confidence of the parents that they were doing everything they could to find their missing children.

Jacqueline thought about the harrowing trauma David must have been subjected to in the kidnapper's hands. What kind of a person was capable of such a despicable act?

Could it be someone from her own parish?

Chapter Twelve

By the time Gardener and Reilly arrived at the mortuary, they had been on duty for twelve hours with no sleep and little in the way of breaks. Navigating the weekend lunchtime traffic through the centre of Leeds had been a nightmare. Their patience wearing thin, they made their way through the empty building, their footsteps echoing loudly down the corridors.

They found Fitz in Theatre 1, which was long and low-ceilinged with bright strip lighting. Four steel gurneys, each occupied, lined the walls. Fitz stood at the sink removing his gloves and mask.

"I thought I might have seen you two before now."

Gardener noted the pathologist's agitation. He liked that in Fitz, his no-nonsense attitude.

He always told you what he thought, despite your rank. Gardener recalled the first time they'd met. On being introduced, George Fitzgerald had asked the young, fresh-faced Gardener to go to the boot of his car and collect a brown paper parcel. When Fitz opened the package, it contained a human heart. Gardener had felt nauseous for the rest of the day.

"Such a long day when you have nothing to do," Reilly joked.

"Nothing to do? I think I've been on my feet as long as you two. And I reckon I've put more constructive hours in."

"In that case, you should have plenty for us."

Fitz hesitated – a bad sign. The pathologist put on a fresh set of gloves. "You'd better follow me."

The two detectives followed Fitz down the hall to another examining room. The decaying corpse had been sectioned to solitary confinement.

"I've never seen anything like it. Whatever attacked the body is still eating away at it." Fitz removed the sheet and pointed at what was left.

To Gardener's horror, the body had deteriorated since the previous evening. He struggled to convince himself that, only twenty-four hours earlier, it had been a living human being.

A few strands of hair dangled helplessly on the skull. Lingering remnants of once healthy tissue clung to the bones, no longer pink but brown, almost black. An eye gawked accusingly at the two detectives from the base of the cranium. A pair of false teeth perched precariously between the mandibles. Gardener leaned over for a closer examination and caught sight of a finger bone floating within the liquefied area where a hand used to be. The foul smell assaulted his nostrils.

"Fuck me!" said Reilly.

"I told you."

Gardener wondered what could have caused such complete destruction. He turned to Fitz. The man was tired. His normally tall, lean frame stooped. Fitz's wrinkled complexion, combined with the exhaustion in his face, easily gave away his sixty years. The pathologist's half-lens glasses, still speckled with blood, perched lower down his nose than they should be, on the verge of falling off.

"Can you tell me anything?" asked Gardener.

"The only fact I have at the moment is the skeleton belongs to an elderly male, approximately sixty years of age. I can't do a normal post-mortem. As you can see, there's nothing left. All the major organs had been completely destroyed before I could make an inspection. His brain, heart, liver, lungs, kidneys, all gone. There's nothing but bones and mush. Extensive degradation due to proteolysis."

"Which means what?"

"All the proteins have broken down. I've taken tissue samples for analysis."

"You've no idea what caused it?"

"None. Because of the advanced putrefaction, I had to work pretty quickly. I've taken hair samples, which can be tested for drugs, and I managed to acquire some urine. Hopefully, toxicology will tell us something. I would have liked at least one major organ to work with for histology."

"What about acid?" Reilly asked.

"It's possible, but acid usually leaves a residue on the bones. Most acids leave something of themselves behind. For example, if sulphuric acid had been used, the bones wouldn't have dissolved. There would have been an insoluble coating of calcium sulphate, which would show on the bones as a strange, off-white, almost yellow colour. But acid doesn't usually leave bones. I remember the case of John George Haigh in 1949."

Oh, God, thought Gardener, here he goes.

"He's probably the most celebrated of the acid murderers. He had an acid bath at his factory in Crawley, Sussex. Dropped a Mrs..." Fitz paused, sucked in breath, "Durand-Deacon in it. If a human body is submerged in acid, it will be completely digested, bones and all. Haigh's mistake was that her body wasn't fully immersed. A little bit of the feet were left above the level of the compound.

"One of the doctors investigating the case found a gallstone on the ground outside the factory where Haigh had dumped her sludge. He also discovered the remnants of the bones of the feet and believe it or not, her false teeth. They were identified by her dentist, and Haigh was convicted."

"That's all very entertaining, Fitz, but we're investigating this body, not some woman who was killed while you were serving your apprenticeship."

Fitz snorted. "It's not an acid, in my opinion. Whatever it is, it started on the inside and worked its way out. It's dissolved all of the soft tissue, but not the clothing or the bones. It's a new one on me."

Fitz's last comment worried Gardener. As far as he knew, the pathologist was probably the best in the country. He had over thirty years in the specialist area of anatomic pathology. Gardener trusted him. If he said he'd never seen anything like it, and he didn't know what caused it, they were in trouble.

"Is it homicide?"

"In my opinion, yes. What's happened isn't natural. If it is natural, there is no recorded case."

"Any ideas on the unnatural substance?" asked Gardener.

"Not at the moment, no."

"What about an estimated time of death?"

Fitz shrugged before answering. "Judging by what the landlady said last night, he was still alive between half past six and eight o'clock. Yet he was almost completely destroyed by half past eleven."

"So, whatever it is only took three hours to do its work."

"Yes."

"Jesus Christ." Gardener stared at Reilly.

He turned back to Fitz. "Have you any ideas? Is it a chemical?"

"Without the results of the analysis on the samples, I can't tell you anything. Just give me a day or two and I'll send my report through. Hopefully, I will have something more concrete for you."

"Any opinion on the type of person we should be looking for?"

"You really need a profiler for that. For what it's worth, I think it's someone with high intelligence. Whatever the assailant used is probably very specialized."

Fitz paused.

Gardener could tell there was more.

Apprehensively, Fitz added, "It took three hours for the body to reach a state of decomposition which normally takes three months."

Fitz replaced the sheet over the remains. "I wish you the best of luck, Stewart. I think you're going to need it."

Chapter Thirteen

Back at the house in Rawston, Gardener mounted the stairs cautiously, warning Reilly to do the same. He knocked loudly on Nicki Carter's door. She answered immediately, forcing Gardener to wonder who she'd been expecting. He could tell from her expression it wasn't him.

She was wearing the same clothes she had on the previous evening. Of course, so was he. The only difference was, he hadn't been home yet.

"What do you want?" she asked.

"To talk."

"I've already spoken to you lot."

"No, you made a statement which told us where you were. Now we need to build up a picture of the deceased. It's our job, remember? Can we come in?"

"I suppose so."

She didn't actually invite them in, she simply left the front door open and skulked off. The flat contained two rooms. One had been sectioned into nothing more than three cubicles accommodating a bathroom in one corner and a kitchen in the other. A small bed struggled for space with a bookcase along one wall. The other room, the living room, gave a view of the terraced housing in Rawston around them. Both rooms stank of baby and damp. A threadbare carpet covered the floor, and peeling wallpaper and nicotine-stained paintwork the walls. She owned very little in the way of furniture. Nicki Carter offered them a seat.

Gardener chose to stand.

"Will it take long?" she demanded. Her manner and her broad Yorkshire accent, in which she had a habit of dropping H's and reformulating words to suit the dialect, annoyed Gardener.

"As long as it has to."

She lit a cigarette, sighed, and slumped down heavily on the sofa. A cloud of dust billowed up around her.

He loathed cigarette smoke, but it was her flat.

"Where's your baby?"

"With me mother."

"What can you tell us about the man upstairs?" He picked up a photo of Nicki, her baby, and a third woman, perhaps her mother.

"Is he dead?" She exhaled a cloud of smoke.

Gardener glanced in her direction but didn't speak. He figured his expression would be enough to answer her question.

"I didn't like him. What's it all about?"

Nicki started as Reilly spoke from the other side of the room. "We'll ask the questions, if you don't mind."

"Come on, Nicki. What happened in the flat upstairs is serious. It's our job to investigate. It doesn't matter whether any of us like it or not. We need to work together," said Gardener. "We'll ask you a few questions, then we'll be out of here. All we're after is a little cooperation. Now, you said you didn't like him. Why was that?"

"He were so high and bloody mighty. Thought he were above everybody. Look at this place. It's hardly the Ritz, is it? Used to prance around as if he owned it. Professor Plum I used to call him, of Tudor Mansion." Nicki snorted laughter. "A big, fat, ugly slob who thought he were important."

"Why do you say that?"

"Do you know what he used to call us, all of us? 'My dear.' Slimy bastard. Is he dead?"

Gardener ignored her question. "So, we've established you didn't like him. Why?" He replaced the photograph and strolled over to the window, his back to Nicki.

"He were a pervert."

Gardener turned to face her. "Clarify that statement."

"He flashed at me once."

"Where?"

"Up there on the top landing. It were ages ago." As she finished her cigarette, she lit another with the stub of the first. "He were drunk. Bloody fond of a drink, he were. Always comin' home late, pissed, causing a racket, shoutin' and bangin' into things. Used to hammer on me friggin' door as he went past, thought it were funny to wake the baby. Anyway, he did it this night. She were at bingo…"

"Who?" Gardener asked.

"Olive Bloody Bradshaw." Nicki Carter leaned forward but remained seated, her expression angry. "You wanna ask her about him. There's summat goin' on between 'em, if you ask me. Well, this Friday night he comes home drunk, as usual. It were about midnight. Starts bangin' on the door. I couldn't hear what he were sayin' because I had the telly on. Did it about three times. I got up in the end. When I opened the door, he were halfway upstairs. I asked him what the bloody hell he were playin' at, and he just turned round, had his cock in his hand, said I could play with that if I wanted and just started laughin'. Bastard!"

"Did you report it?"

"What's the point? What would you lot have done? It were my word against his. By the time you lot had got here he'd have been asleep. He'd have denied it anyway."

"That's not the point, Nicki. We can't do anything if you don't tell us."

The girl stood up and walked into the kitchen. She came back with a can of lager. "Do you want one?"

"No, thank you. We're on duty."

Sitting back down, she took a long drink, and followed it with a guttural belch. "Nasty bastard as well; had a right temper. Cornered me on the stairs once, outside me flat. I were rushin', gettin' the baby ready to take to me mam's. As I got outside, he were rushin' by the door. We bumped into each other."

Gardener noticed the expression on her face, a mixture of fear and disgust. He could tell she hated Plum but suspected it went deeper than one or two isolated incidents.

"He dropped a brown paper bag, and a load of porn mags fell out," she continued. "I picked one up, see, to have a laugh. I could just imagine him, sat up there most nights playin' with himself over these mags. Went bloody mad, he did. Pushed me up against the door. All he did were stare at me, didn't say nothin'. Picked up his mags and pointed a finger at me, then carried on upstairs."

Nicki fell silent again.

Gardener glanced over at Reilly busy taking notes.

"I don't mean to be rude," she spoke up, "but I've got to be somewhere."

"So, last night, you were here all night?"

"Yeah."

"Did you notice whether or not he had any visitors?"

"Can't say as I did. But then, I spent half the night tryin' to calm me son down."

Gardener changed topics. "Who lives in the flat next door?"

"Not sure."

"You're not sure. What does that mean?"

"It means, I hear the door opening and closing every now and again, but I never see anyone. It happens at odd hours as well."

"You've never seen anyone," Gardener pressed.

"No. You'll have to ask Olive Bloody Bradshaw about that as well. It's her house." Nicki glanced at her watch.

She seemed agitated. Gardener was surprised she'd been so forthright with her information. He still suspected her hatred of Plum went deeper than she was letting on, which may or may not have a bearing on the case.

"Okay, we'll leave it at that for now. I may want to ask you some more questions later, though. If you do remember anything, give me a call." He passed her a card. She jumped quickly to her feet, following them both out onto the landing.

"Oh, one more thing," said Gardener. "Which pub did he drink in?"

"The Black Bull, I think, a couple of streets away."

Gardener nodded. "Thank you for your time. If you do remember anything, no matter how trivial, give me a ring."

He stopped her as she went to close the door. "I think you're hiding something. I will be back."

Nicki didn't respond. She locked the door behind and leapt down the stairs two at a time, leaving them standing in front of her apartment.

Gardener turned to Reilly. "What do you think?"

"I think we need to speak to Olive Bradshaw."

Chapter Fourteen

"You'd better come in."

The eye-catching decor and level of hygiene in Olive Bradshaw's flat pleasantly surprised Gardener as he entered. It created a remarkable contrast to the other flats, the building's exterior, and the neighbourhood itself. He wondered what possessed her to live in a crumbling, derelict, plague-infested area like Rawston.

He noticed her residence was bigger. The living room was one large open space, into which she had crammed an eccentric number of personal belongings. Queen Anne chairs carefully coordinated around Wilton rugs. The woman was obsessed with trinkets.

"Would you like to join me and my sister Mabel for tea, Inspector?" She pointed to a chair at the table. Once seated, she picked up a brass jug and started polishing it.

Mabel had a petite frame and a relatively smooth complexion. She clasped her cup with arthritic fingers. She wore her blue rinse hair in a tightly packed bun, and wire-rimmed spectacles.

"Thank you, I'd love a cup."

Reilly nodded his agreement.

To Gardener, not only was Olive Bradshaw's flat a complete contrast, so was her attitude – giving him the impression of a Jekyll and Hyde personality.

Olive passed them both a cup of tea using a Chinese bone tea service.

"Biscuit?" She pushed a plate towards him.

"No, thank you." Eager to move on, Gardener decided to open the investigation with an apology, suspecting it would appeal to her better nature. If she had one. "I'll have the mess upstairs cleaned up as soon as possible."

Olive nodded her approval, rubbing the jug vigorously. Gardener noticed the brassware in the room outnumbered every other trinket. The collection included plates, jugs, bowls, candleholders, and pine surround mirrors, all of which sparkled.

"So, how can I help you, Inspector?"

"You can start by telling me a little about yourself and the setup here."

"What do you want to know?"

"Just some general information, etcetera. How old are you?"

"I'm in my golden years, Inspector."

"You mean diamond, don't you, Olive, love?" offered Reilly.

She narrowed her eyes, shooting him a withering stare.

"Married?" asked Gardener, quickly.

"No." She paused, before adding, "I'm saving myself."

Gardener's eyes met Reilly's, pleading silently with him not to follow that comment.

The Irishman smirked and continued with his notes.

"How long have you lived here?"

"About five years. It was my brother's house to start with. He'd always suffered with asthma, and as he got older, it got worse; didn't it, Mabel?" She nodded to her sister. "Anyway, he asked me if I'd like to come and live here. In return for doing a bit of caretaking and looking after his affairs, I was allowed to live rent-free."

"Is he still alive?"

"No, Inspector," said Mabel. "Our Maurice died a year back now. Poor love had a stroke."

"I'm afraid I've let the place fall into rack and ruin," continued Olive. "Grief is a funny thing. Anyway, we're selling up now, aren't we, Mabel?"

Her sister nodded.

"She's just sold her house in Burley-in-Wharfedale," Olive informed Gardener. "We're both living here temporarily until the sale goes through." By the time she finished, Gardener's cup sat empty. Mabel cleared all the dishes, washed, and replaced them at the table.

"And Herbert Plum?"

"I'm not sure I know that much."

"You'd be surprised," said Reilly.

"Anything would be useful," Gardener added.

"He was about sixty. A big man, not very house-proud. His clothes were clean enough, always washed them at the launderette." She glanced at her sister. "You know the one, Mabel, on Dewsbury Road. Small shop, mucky windows, smells. Her who always takes her dog to bingo runs it. Don't like her myself. Too secretive." She turned back to Gardener. "Anyway, he washed his clothes there. Never ironed 'em, mind. Well, what man can?"

She smiled at Gardener before continuing.

"He was always polite, always said 'Good morning, my dear.' Knew his manners, he did. Brought up properly. Not like kids these days. I blame the parents, myself. They're always hanging about on street corners now, up to no good. It's about time your lot brought the bobby on the beat back." To Mabel she said, "Mrs Watson's eldest is in trouble again."

"Craig? He's never been any good, that one. Never amount to anything," Mabel replied.

"Can we stick to the point, please?" Gardener asked.

"Oh, I'm sorry, Inspector. Where was I?"

"Trying to establish some facts about Herbert Plum. What did he look like, Miss Bradshaw?"

"I've got a picture somewhere."

She left the table and went into another room. Gardener studied the impressive range of oil paintings. Little could be seen of the wallpaper. Each wall had a theme: country scenes, stormy seascapes, old world inns, and animals and children.

"Here we go," Olive said as she returned. She sat and passed him a photo. Four people posed at a seaside resort. Olive and Mabel, each holding candy floss, stood between two men.

"That's our brother on the left. Herbert is on the far right."

"When was this taken?"

"A few weeks before our brother died. He'd taken us all to Scarborough for the day."

Gardener stared at the photo. Portly, Plum stood at around sixteen stone. His brown hair was combed from left to right across his head, streaked with flecks of grey. His small brown eyes stood out in a fat, round face.

"I'd like to take this with me."

"It's the only one I have, Inspector."

"All I want is a copy, you can have it back."

Olive nodded. Gardener passed it to Reilly, then pressed on.

"How was he with the other tenants?"

"As I said, always pleasant."

Gardener noticed her glazed expression. "You weren't aware of any disagreements, then?"

"None that I know of. Why? Has someone said something?"

"I spoke to one of your other tenants earlier, Nicki…"

The snapping alligator reared its ugly head, cutting him off. "You don't want to listen to her! She's got too much to say for herself, that one! I don't know who she thinks she is. Barely sixteen with a baby, on the social. Pinching everything she can get from the state. Visitors at all hours! I've heard 'em, creeping down the stairs. You don't want to go listening to her, she's no manners. She's no example for that baby. She takes drugs!"

"Do you know that for certain? Have you actually seen her taking them?"

"I don't have to. I've seen her arms."

Gardener was beginning to build a picture of contradiction, something he didn't relish, despite it happening with almost every case.

She continued her tirade. "It's shocking the way they take these drugs nowadays. No respect for their bodies, or anyone else. It wouldn't have happened in our day. We'd have had it knocked out of us, and no mistake. I think I'll have words with her." She glanced at her sister. "When I think of the problems that filth causes, it makes my blood boil. It really does. Mrs O'Connor's daughter's into drugs, you know? Still, she's going to pay the price. Used a dirty needle last year, now she's got that HRT thing. Serves her right, that's what I say."

"Let's get back to Herbert Plum. Where did he shop?"

"He wasn't very well organized. Never did a weekly shop, just picked stuff up when he needed it. He always used the Co-op, round the corner. And I've often seen those takeaway delivery vehicles in and out of here."

"Did he walk, or did he have a car?"

"No car. Walked most places."

"What about employment? Any idea where he worked?"

"Couldn't tell you. He was usually up early and out the door, so he must have had a job of some description."

"You never thought to ask?"

"It's not my business. So long as he pays his way."

"And did he?"

Gardener caught a slight hesitation before she answered.

"Well, he wasn't always on time with his rent. I often had to give him a polite reminder. Maybe he didn't earn much, but..."

"But what?" Reilly asked.

"I've caught him down the bookies a few times. I have the odd flutter myself. You know, the Grand National, the Derby. That sort of thing."

"Do you think his money went on the horses before anything else?"

"It's not for me to say, but he did lead a frugal life."

"It's one explanation for overdue rent. Was it a regular occurrence?"

Again, she hesitated. "At first, he never missed. But of late, I had to remind him every week. I don't particularly like chasing my tenants. Still, I won't have to do it much longer."

"Which betting shop did he use?"

"The only one I know about was William Hill on Dewsbury Road."

"Any family, visitors, phone calls?"

"No family that I know of, and in the two years he'd been here I never saw one visitor. I felt sorry for him. I don't like to see nice people on their own. I had one a few years ago. Dead a week before I found out." She placed a hand on her chest. "Such a shock. I only found out then because he was late with his rent, first time ever. Come to think of it, he lived in Herbert's flat. Ever since then I've made a point of checking my tenants regularly. I often used to go and have a cup of tea with Herbert. A gentleman. I shall quite miss him."

Even though he was late with the rent, thought Gardener. "Which reminds me, does anyone live in the flat next door to Nicki Carter?"

"No. Someone did about six months ago," she replied. "When he moved out, I started using it as a storeroom. Very handy if you can pack up your boxes and put them somewhere."

Gardener studied the room. God alone knew what she had packed away because it still seemed full to him.

"Did Herbert Plum have any references when he came here?"

"I don't ask for references, Inspector. This is Rawston. We take people as we find them. Always have."

A small scuffle outside the front window drew their attention. A gang of youths chanted and cheered as they walked by the front of the building.

Olive Bradshaw stood up, staring out at them.

"Just listen to that one. He wants his mouth washing out with soap!"

She glanced at Gardener. "You lot should take a keener interest in him. Peter Atkins. I know his mother well. All the same, that family. Think nothing of airing their dirty washing in public. I've had words with her over the years, I can tell you."

She turned to her sister. "He's just come out of prison. Who is it that told me? Ron Franks, down the shops last week. Apparently beat his girlfriend up."

She resumed her conversation with Gardener. "Black and blue, she was. No good will come of that one, you mark my words. He'll be back behind bars soon, if you lot are up to it."

She peered at Gardener's hat. "He has a hat similar to yours, Inspector. If you don't mind my saying, it looks unusual. What's the story behind it?"

"A long one," he replied. "With regards to your statement last night, there are a couple of things I want to establish. You say you went to the bingo, around six-thirty?"

"That's right."

"And returned when?"

"About ten-thirty, as I said."

"Can anyone verify your movements?" He noticed her glance at Mabel. "Apart from your sister."

"Of course, the people in the bingo hall, for a start."

"Which is where?"

"Dewsbury Road."

Where everything else is, thought Gardener. "Do you know the name of the ticket seller?"

Olive Bradshaw folded her arms. "Certainly do. A woman named Molly Simpson, lives on Queen Street, number twenty-three. You can check out my story with her, seeing as you think I'm guilty."

"I didn't say you were guilty."

"No, but you're thinking it."

"Do you read the tea leaves, then, Olive?" Reilly asked. "Or is it just minds?" He could tell by her expression she wasn't amused.

"When was the last time you saw Herbert alive?" Gardener continued.

"Friday afternoon, I think. Mabel and me were out doing a bit of shopping. He was at the Co-op."

"How did he seem?"

"Fine."

"Did you speak?"

"No, but he waved. We were on the opposite side of the road, about to cross. He was leaving. He had a carrier bag with him."

"Which direction was he heading? I take it he wasn't coming home?"

"No, he was probably going for an afternoon tipple. Looked like it, anyway. Heading toward The Black Bull."

"Did you see anyone close to the house as you left?"

"No. Passed a few people further down the street, but we knew them all."

Gardener made a note of their names so he could cross-check back at the station, before rising from his seat. "Well, thank you for the tea."

He threaded his way around the antique furniture. "You've been most helpful."

"Anytime, Inspector. If you could see to it the room is cleaned up as soon as possible, I would be most grateful."

"I will."

"I know I'm selling up, but I don't want anyone talking about me when I'm gone."

"Dread the thought," replied Gardener. He opened the door to leave, and stopped in the doorway. "Just one more thing. How many keys were there for the room?"

The question made her think. After a short pause, she answered, "Three. I have a master; he had the other two."

"Are any of them missing?"

"Well, I've still got mine."

"Okay. I'll check and see where the other two are." Gardener paused before asking, "And you're sure he had no visitors?"

"Not that I know of. Why do you keep asking?"

"Curiosity, Miss Bradshaw. There was no forced entry. In my opinion, Herbert Plum was not only murdered. He actually knew his killer."

Chapter Fifteen

Six-thirty on a Saturday evening and the incident room stood full, not a prospect any officer relished. Gardener assembled his team quietly and efficiently. They listened while he went through the contents of the pathology report he'd only recently received.

It noted the recorded condition of the body as expected: advanced state of decomposition. Fitz placed the time of death between seven and eight o'clock in the evening. DNA from the victim's hair matched a comb taken for evidence by Scenes of Crime. Plum's dentist identified his false teeth.

The sixty-year-old skeleton contained evidence of osteoarthritis in some of the joints. Most hard tissue still remained, but all soft tissue had broken down. A liquid analysis contained traces of sodium, potassium, calcium, phosphate, chloride and amino acids.

Fitz had been unable to find any proteins. Not even a trace. The pathologist's conclusion stated the body's state was consistent with 'complete rapid proteolytical decomposition'. The cause of death was unknown.

"Doesn't tell us much," said Briggs.

Briggs had held the senior position for a little over a year, having transferred from Liverpool. Gardener had been in line for the promotion when the position became available, but Sarah's death had removed the possibility. Gardener didn't have a problem with that, but he suspected Briggs did. As a result, their relationship had improved very little in the past year.

Gardener returned to the path report. "Cause of death unknown. Anyone have any theories?"

"I thought it was acid at first," Anderson replied. "But Fitz has blown that one."

Gardener stared at the findings, mystified. "What kind of a compound can destroy your entire insides in the space of two or three hours?"

"There's a lot of dangerous stuff out there, boss," said Reilly. "Back in Northern Ireland, we have terrorist groups that specialize in killing people with a mixture of lethal cocktails. I've seen the remains of some of those people. I've never seen anything like this, though.

"I came across a bloke in a warehouse once, bit of a mess. He'd crossed one of these groups. Held back some money he was supposed to have been collecting for them. When they caught up with him, they trapped him, kept him locked up for days. Then they cut him all over with razor blades. Only small cuts, mind."

Gardener noticed Reilly's eyes glaze over as he talked.

"Once the cuts had been opened up a little more, they covered him in manure. The smell was the least of his worries. You see, manure is usually full of nasty little things called gas gangrene bugs. Once they're inside, you're in trouble. The terrorists walked away and left him to rot. I found him a few days later. His whole body was in an advanced state of gangrene. His limbs were black. He'd actually started to fall apart at the seams."

Gardener exhaled a long breath, trying to imagine what Reilly had described. "Well, it's not gas gangrene, but whatever Plum was subjected to was probably just as lethal."

DC Thornton, Anderson's partner, took a sip of coffee. "It would certainly narrow down who to look for. Surely, it's medical. A doctor? A chemist? It has to be someone who knows what they're doing."

"I'll go along with that," Gardener said. "It wasn't a random killing. It was planned. Whoever did it knew whom they wanted and where to find him. Despite the internal mess, it was a precision kill. Swift, accurate, little time wasted. There was no forced entry, no signs of a struggle. He knew his killer."

"Makes you wonder what we're chasing," said Colin Sharp. "It was pretty extreme."

"I think our killer wanted to inflict pain. They wanted revenge. Have you any idea what Plum must have gone through? What kind of pain he felt? The change his body went through? Was he still alive while it was happening to him?"

"Jesus Christ!" said Briggs. "He must have been on fire inside. And that's another thing. How did it get inside? Was he made to drink it?"

"Who knows?" said Gardener. "So, we have a sixty-year-old man, lives on his own. Has no relatives, no visitors, no phone calls, yet his death, and what he did with his life, are a big mystery.

"You all have a photo of Plum and a copy of the path report. I want answers. Who was he? Where did he work? Find out his last movements. I want to know Herbert Plum better than I know myself. Keep the report to yourselves, but use the information to your advantage. He wasn't just killed, he was obliterated. I want to know why."

Gardener turned to Anderson and Thornton. "You two are going to love this. I want you to cover every sex shop in the area with his picture. Plum's flat contained pornographic books and DVDs, and a variety of sex toys suitable for both males and females. Find out where he bought them."

"Can we watch them first? We might be able to tell you ourselves," replied Thornton with a grin. An anaemic, six-foot rake of a man, with grey hair, which was never quite free of dandruff, Thornton was so thin he continually reminded Gardener of a POW.

"Nothing would surprise me, Frank."

Laughter circled the room.

"All right, calm down. It's all very suspicious. Plum was a sixty-year-old bachelor. From what I've seen, he had an active sex life."

"Wish I did," shouted a voice from the back.

Gardener smiled and continued. "He had books, DVDs, and toys. What could he possibly use them for if he never came into contact with anyone?"

He suddenly thought about Olive Bradshaw.

"From the people I've spoken to, it would appear he and his landlady were conducting a relationship of sorts. One of her lodgers suggested as much. Olive Bradshaw claims he was often late with the rent, but she didn't appear to have had a problem with it. Which further compounds the theory. She claims she was at the Bingo Hall on Dewsbury Road between six-thirty and ten-thirty.

"Someone check that out, please. There were lots of nods and glances to each other when we interviewed her and her sister. Told me they knew more than they were letting on. If they know more, I want to know more. I want the answers to three serious questions. Who killed Plum? Why? And with what?"

Sensing the briefing was over, the team started to leave.

Returning to the pathology report, Gardener read the list of items recovered from the crime scene, noting an entry for something called Papaverine.

"Just a minute, lads, before you go. There's a record of something called Papaverine in the path report. Who found the pills, and where? Any idea what they're for?"

"I did," said Steve Fenton. "They were in a bedroom cupboard. No idea what they do, sorry."

"Don't worry about it," replied Gardener. "I'll ring Fitz now."

Gardener left Reilly to deal with any queries as he went back to his office and dialled the pathologist. It rang six times before Fitz answered.

"Fitz? It's Stewart. A small problem you might be able to help me with."

"Go on."

"I'm looking at an entry on the list of items recovered from the crime scene. Small bottle of pills, they're called Papaverine. Any idea what they are?"

"I shouldn't think you need them. You're still a young man."

Gardener's interest piqued. "So, what are they?"

"A sexual stimulant. Normally supplied by doctors to help with a failing libido."

"Thanks, Fitz. I'll keep in touch."

As he replaced the receiver, he sat back in his chair. The mystery deepened.

Chapter Sixteen

Gardener glanced at his watch. It was a little after eleven o'clock. He made himself a green tea before bed even though he knew it wouldn't help. A complete jumble of thoughts stirred in his mind. Apart from last night's gruesome discovery and the troubling encounter at the cemetery, he found himself thinking of Jacqueline Bâlcescu. He liked her; found her reassuring.

He enjoyed her company and, aside from today, their conversations never felt awkward. He could tell she was a well-educated woman with expensive tastes, who knew what she wanted out of life.

They had much in common.

He found her wide, sensuous smile inviting. He liked her chestnut-coloured hair with its healthy sheen in its short, fashionable bob. He appreciated the fact she wore little to no makeup.

He even found the chip in her tooth an attractive feature.

He saw her around the village regularly. Over the last few months when visiting Sarah's grave, they had spent more time together. He'd begun to wonder whether or not he should move on with his life, which always brought on a sudden pang of guilt. Sarah had only been in her grave a year. During that time, he'd paid little heed to other women and the feelings they stirred in him.

Now he found himself consciously aware he had feelings for the female minister.

Those emotions confused him. He and Sarah had enjoyed an excellent rapport. They shared a fun-filled life together. Their combined tastes blended so well the relationship felt like it didn't need to be worked at. It simply fell into place. They had frequently disagreed. What married couple hadn't? Sarah's impulsiveness often amused him. She often came around to his way of thinking, however. He was the level-headed one, after all. Above that, though, he felt the closeness of their relationship came down to the mutual trust and respect they had for each other.

Their bond had been so close that the two were almost one. Then the two had become three.

He took a sip of his tea, the memory replaying in his mind as clearly as if it were yesterday.

He'd planned to meet Sarah for lunch in the local park. He'd arrived later than anticipated. He caught her watching longingly as the young mothers entertained their children on the swings. She'd cried as she'd told him.

He remembered the world seemed to stand still while he considered what she'd said.

Excitement took over, and he picked her up and swung her around. The two of them giggled and whooped.

As he turned, an old couple halted in their walk to observe the young couple's celebration. He told them his news. They congratulated each other and then swapped childhood stories. The old couple departed without him ever finding out who they were.

As he continued to reminisce, he fondly recalled how strong and independent Sarah had been. All she ever wanted out of life was to please her family. She centred her existence around their happiness. She would not want him to be unhappy or guilty or confused. Sarah had been a great believer in 'life goes on.' If he wanted to risk building another life for himself and their son Chris, she would have encouraged him.

It occurred to him that he could be overreacting to simple, friendly gestures. As a minister, Jacqueline's job meant she had to be pleasant to everybody she met. He thought her eyes, her smile, her body language all said differently. He admitted he could be wrong. It could simply be that he'd reached a period of desperation after a year of self-isolation, and mistaken her attitude toward him for something else.

He rubbed his face, tried to clear his mind of those thoughts. He turned his attention to the multiple child disappearances on his patch.

He wondered about the two girls. Had they, too, been murdered like David Vickers? If they had, where were their bodies?

The fact David's body held traces of a powerful sedative brought a different perspective to the case. The drug, coupled with the abuse he'd suffered, pointed to the probability he had been abducted by a paedophile. Perhaps even a ring.

Did they have the girls? He'd heard about girls being shipped out to the Middle East and forced into prostitution. Perhaps that's why no bodies had ever been found.

His feelings went out to their parents. He remembered the comment Lesley Vickers had made.

What would he be doing if it had been Chris, and not her son? He grew cold at the thought, realizing it could so easily have been. The boys attended the same school. Chris knew David well. When it had all come to light, Gardener questioned Chris. Chris didn't remember seeing anyone suspicious hanging around the school. No one saw the boy leaving with an adult, or talking to a stranger. No one had come forward with any information at all.

He thought about the Rawston incident and, in particular, the public. They expected the police to find criminals, to come up with all the answers. All while they preferred anonymity. They went around with blinkers on, blocking out the world around them. Until, of course, it happened to them. Then they accused everyone else of doing what they'd been guilty of in the first place.

Gardener heard the same statement from everyone he'd ever interviewed in that situation.

"Somebody must have seen something."

He agreed. Somebody must surely-to-God have seen or heard something the night Herbert Plum died. Killing a person in such a manner without attracting attention stood next to impossible.

Gardener sighed and drifted into the kitchen. He left his empty cup in the bowl, before turning out the lights and heading for bed.

Chapter Seventeen

Gardener lost his footing and stumbled. He stood alone in the centre of Leeds, enshrouded by a thin, spectral mist. Flustered, he peered through the fog in a desperate attempt to figure out where he was, and where Sarah had gone. They had been together in a restaurant not a moment ago.

His surroundings seemed unfamiliar. A group of crumbling warehouses on the verge of collapse stretched out in front of him. Their grime-encrusted facades presented a stark image of impending doom. Office blocks stood adjacent to the warehouses, in the same state of deterioration. Turning his head, he stared down Bridge End, over the River Aire. He ran to the bridge, peeking through the railings. The water ran unseen through the impenetrable shroud.

As he retreated, the scenery changed. He found himself at the corner of Duncan Street, facing Briggate. His parents strode toward him. His father checked the time on his pocket watch while his mother chattered incessantly next to him. His spirits lifted. It felt good to see his mum again. They walked right by him, oblivious to his presence. A car passed dangerously close to his mother. For all the world, it seemed like it would hit her. But it didn't.

He then clearly heard his mother lecturing his father about an unpaid TV license bill. Mum should let that drop. Dad had only done it once, a long time ago. Surely she was over it now?

He called out to her. She ignored him. Panic overcame him as he suddenly spotted blood on her, a red trail running from a wound below her ribcage. He put his hands to his face to block out the vision. He had been here before and had no wish to return. He knew where it would end.

In the hope of a different outcome, he lowered his hands to find his parents had vanished. The clock above the jeweller's on the opposite side of the road struck midnight. Gardener stood confused. He shouldn't be here. He should be at home in bed with Sarah. As the clock chimed, a gunshot rang out. His world came to a sudden, terrifying halt. He ran toward the source of the shot, afraid of what he would find.

Sarah emerged from the mist, clutching her abdomen, blood coursing through her fingers. "Help me, Stewart," she pleaded, both the sound of her voice and her expression pitiful.

"Oh, God. Sarah!"

His wife started to fade, signalling the end, as it always did.

"No!" he screamed long and loud.

Still screaming, he fell out of bed, shouting. "No, please God! No! Don't take her away from me. Not again..." His body shook from the sobbing. "Please, not again."

He reached out for the lamp on the bedside cabinet, switching it on. Lifting the frame that contained Sarah's photo next to it, he placed the picture next to his heart. Wrapping both arms around his body, he slumped against his bed, drawing his knees up to his chest, hugging the photo, crying softly.

Even after a year, her loss was still painful. He had the nightmare on a regular basis.

Every morning, he'd reach out for her, hoping she'd be there. She never was. He never thought it possible to miss someone so much.

"Sarah," he whispered, "I never meant it to happen." He lifted the photo to gaze at her. "I know you didn't want to go. I'm so sorry." More tears followed as he held the photo tight. "I should never have made you. You died because me of me, Sarah. How will you ever forgive me? How can I ever forgive myself?"

He lowered the photo into his lap and continued weeping, staring idly at the ceiling, realizing he never could. He knew he would carry the guilt of his wife's death to his grave. He felt responsible because of an inability to turn his back on something that had nothing to do with either of them.

Chapter Eighteen

Gardener made himself tea. The expansive kitchen was long and wide, lit mostly by strip lighting positioned underneath the fitted units. Beige and magnolia tiles covered the walls and floor. Scattered around the kitchen sat constant reminders of Sarah: several small clay-figure animals she made herself. A wall clock in the shape of a tulip he bought her during a weekend in Amsterdam. He'd never liked it, but he couldn't part with it now. Spook, Sarah's cat, joined him at the kitchen table. A fluffy, white half-Persian, she meowed continuously and was constantly grubby because she rarely preened herself.

Stooping, he stroked Spook. Sarah had loved the cat when she'd found her three years ago. The stray had wandered into their garage, half emaciated, full of fleas. Their first meeting had been a shock to both of them. The cat had jumped out from a bundle of rags, startling Sarah. She eventually won the animal over and nursed it back to health. She chose to call it Spook because of the incident in the garage.

He filled a saucer with milk. "I suppose if I'm having one, you'd better, too."

The kitchen clock chimed four-thirty. No chance of sleep now. Gardener took a sip of his tea and wandered through to the living room and the dark oak bookcase in the corner. As he scanned the shelves, he smiled to himself at the number of horticultural encyclopaedias his father had. There must have been a copy of nearly every gardening book in print.

He admired his father for his dedication to something that was not only a hobby but also his living. He himself had shown no interest in following his father's footsteps as a landscape gardener. Even now, he refused to enter the greenhouse at the bottom of the garden.

He selected a book of his own. He studied the cover. He'd waited a year. Perhaps it was time.

He walked into the kitchen and through the connecting door into the garage. He switched on the lights. The extra room was like any other. Along one wall stood a worktop, with a vice attached. He'd put a shelf above it, housing a variety of bottles of all shapes and sizes. They contained every nut, bolt, and washer known to man. Gardening implements and machinery fought for the right to a bit of space. One of the family vehicles permanently lived on the drive.

At the back of the garage sat a hi-fi stereo system with a pair of speakers he had bought at a fire-damaged sale in an auction room off Boar Lane. No one wanted the speakers because they gave the impression they were beyond help. He'd paid ten pounds for the pair. They were the best he'd ever heard.

He put his tea down, switched on the hi-fi, and selected a CD from a pile. *More Than A Feeling: The Greatest Rock Anthems Of All Time*. He put the CD into the machine, and pressed play.

He walked over to a grey dustsheet covering the focus of his interest in the far corner of the garage.

"I've waited a year for you."

He pulled the dustsheet off. In front of him rested a 1959 T120 Triumph Bonneville – wrecked, of course. It had seen better days. The tyres were bald. The exhaust rusty and hanging off. The seat chewed by rats. The badge on the fuel tank was missing, the tank itself worn down to bare metal. There was no front number plate. The headlamp was smashed. Before their time together was through, he figured he would find a number of other problems.

It was the last thing Sarah had bought him before she died, the present she referred to when she said she had employed the help of his father. Sarah knew he wanted a Triumph Bonneville for as long as he could remember. He'd never found the right one, nor the right time to buy one.

His father found the bike in a breaker's yard when he had been searching for spare parts for a friend. The owner hadn't even known it was there. Malcolm told Sarah. She made an offer.

His father picked up the bike that fateful afternoon, waiting until they had gone out before smuggling it into the garage. Sarah knew Gardener would have devoted most of his spare time to the care of the bike.

He knew the restoration of the bike would be therapeutic for him. It would help him to think. He collected his tools and went to work.

He removed the seat first. He stared at it for quite a while, wondering not only where he would be able to buy a new one, but how much it would cost him. He also started wondering about the case. Considering what little he had learned so far, Gardener realized he had his work cut out for him. A lot of questions needed to be answered.

Chapter Nineteen

Jacqueline moved around her aunt's kitchen with ease and confidence. She knew every inch of the large farmhouse better than her own. She'd lived with the old lady for the better part of her teenage years, until the time she had started her training to become a minister.

To her knowledge, the room's interior had never changed; it was long and angular with pine-finished units and a polished timber floor. A variety of copper pans hung from ceiling beams. A mixture of live plants and dried flowers enhanced the decor.

The kettle came to the boil as the clock struck ten. Pips on the radio signalled the start of the morning news. Jacqueline finished making the tea. Her taste buds tingled with anticipation as the aroma of freshly baked bread and pastries permeated the room. She selected a couple of cakes, put them on plates, and placed them on the table with the tea. She sat and poured herself a cup. She clasped it in both hands, sipped her tea. It tasted good. She felt good.

The farmhouse – passed down to her aunt Anei from Jacqueline's grandmother Irina – had always generated a feeling of inner security. Aside from her own house, she knew of no other place that provided a safer haven. Except perhaps in Stewart Gardener's arms. She flushed at the thought.

The back door opened and her aunt Anei came in from outside. She immediately rubbed her hands together, blowing into them.

"It's cold."

"Which is why I'm here. You shouldn't be working outside at your age."

Her aunt smiled, washing her hands at the sink before taking her seat at the table.

"Hard work never harmed anyone. I have worked all my life outside. It's what I know."

She rose and stepped outside the back door again. Anei returned, dragging a wooden box in with her.

"I know you have," said Jacqueline, nibbling on a piece of cake. "But it doesn't stop me worrying. You're seventy years old now. You should be taking life a little easier."

Anei smiled warmly at her niece. Jacqueline noticed the glint in her eyes. She knew what her reply would be. Despite her concerns and voiced opinions, nothing would change.

"I'm as healthy as you. You are staying for lunch, yes?"

"I'm not sure I should, you always make me eat too much." Jacqueline found it almost impossible to resist her aunt's cooking, mostly traditional Romanian, home-grown. "What have you made?"

"Transylvanian soup. Your favourite!"

Jacqueline's eyes narrowed. "Not much chance of resisting that, is there?"

The soup had been made with green peas, small slices of white ham, green garlic, tomatoes, and parsley. Anei always insisted they eat the dish traditionally, with a wooden spoon. She said it tasted better. Anei reached down into the box, pulling out a variety of different vegetables, all of which she had harvested within the last hour, judging by the fresh soil.

"How do you manage to grow so much stuff in winter?" Jacqueline said, amazed.

“You can grow anything you want any time of the year. If you have the touch.”

“Surely you’re not going to eat all those.”

“Not all of them.” Anei set some aside on the table, then slid the box toward Jacqueline.

“It’s no use passing them on to me. I’ll never eat all of them, either.”

The news on the radio finished, and a country song followed. Jacqueline recognized the singer as Glen Campbell.

Her aunt put the vegetables away, then sat back down, taking a sip of her tea. “Maybe not, but you have parishioners. I’m sure some of them will be glad for something extra, especially in this economy we are having. A ‘recession,’ they keep saying on the news. People are facing hard times. A little help goes a long way.”

“No one knows more about hard times than you.”

Her aunt didn’t reply straight away. The minister noticed the pause. She sensed a slight change of mood, fearing where the conversation would lead. “Venin! Those poor children. I have read the papers. I know what goes on.”

Jacqueline reached out and placed her hands over Anei’s. “You shouldn’t upset yourself over newspaper reports. You of all people should know how ruthless others can be. Your family survived a World War, not to mention a hazardous trek across Romania to escape the clutches of the Nazis.”

“I can’t help myself. Children should not have to suffer at the hands of men. People should not be allowed to live in a world when they are so cruel to children.”

“I know. I had to bury the child. His parents were so grief-stricken. I have no idea how they are going to cope with the loss.”

“And then they find a body in a flat!”

“A body?”

Anei fished a broadsheet newspaper out from under the table and passed it towards Jacqueline. The story ran centrally at the bottom of the second page, short and precise.

Body Found in Rawston Flat

The identity of an elderly man whose body was discovered in a flat in Rawston last Friday has today been revealed by the West Yorkshire Police. Landlady Olive Bradshaw said, "The flat was occupied by Herbert Plum, last seen alive at 6:30 p.m." A spokesman for CID said: "A post-mortem has been carried out by a Home Office Pathologist." No other details are available. The police inquiry is continuing. No date to open an inquest has been fixed.

"That's awful!" Jacqueline laid the paper on the table. "Well, perhaps now we have the right man on the case, we'll see some results, and these people will get what they deserve."

"They never get what they deserve. If the crime were left in the hands of God, the punishment would be just." Anei rose from her seat and placed her cup on the draining board.

"All we have are the police. They are only human. Their hands are tied."

"Yes, I know. I'm sure most of them feel the way we do. It's worse for the police. They have to deal with the results. We only read about them."

Jacqueline's thoughts returned to Saturday morning in the cemetery. She had faith in Gardener. Whoever was responsible would be punished accordingly if he had anything to do with it. "I'm sure Stewart will do his best."

"Stewart?"

Jacqueline smiled. "Oh, he's just someone I know."

"Sounds to me like you know him well. He's the right man for the job, is he? And you know him well? Are you hiding something from me?"

"God forbid I should even try," replied Jacqueline, a little flustered.

"You are my little girl. You came to live with me when your mother died, God bless her. There's nothing I don't know about you. You look different this morning. Brighter. There is a spring in your step. I heard you singing in the kitchen. Beautiful voice. You don't need to tell me anymore." Anei waved her hand in dismissal. "Come with me while I attend to my family. Tell me about this man, Stewart. If you want to."

Jacqueline joined her aunt in the conservatory, which was connected to the kitchen. The only furniture in the glass-enforced room was a cane two-seater settee and a small heater. The furniture shared the space with a variety of plants and flowers. Anei Bâlcescu had a passion for nature. Jacqueline figured her aunt knew more about plants than anyone living. It was not uncommon for Anei to while away her evenings in the conservatory, surrounded, as she put it, by her 'family'.

As she watered, the old lady continued their conversation. "You like him, no?"

"Is it that obvious?"

"It is to me. And why shouldn't you? You're a beautiful young woman. You've had a terrible life. Now you should take your pleasure. And if this policeman can provide it, then you have my blessing."

"I'm afraid he doesn't know how I feel. More to the point, I don't know how he feels."

"Tell him." Anei's reply was matter-of-fact.

"What about the church?"

"The church will not deny you your happiness. We all go through life missing out because we lose the nerve to simply ask. Or say what we mean." Anei turned to face Jacqueline. "Don't become one of those people."

The minister knew there was a lot of truth in what her aunt said. It still wasn't easy to tell someone your true feelings.

A sad expression crossed Anei's face. "I myself must now practice what I preach. There is something I would like to do for Christmas. I know we are planning to spend the festive season together, but I would like us to go home, to Romania. Only for Christmas. To see my homeland. I have not seen it since I was a baby. I want you to see your heritage, too. My sister would have wanted this for us."

Anei reached up towards the shelves circling the perimeter of the conservatory. To her pride and joy, her Venus flytraps. There were a dozen in total. As far as Jacqueline knew, Anei was the only person other than her late grandmother who knew the secret to cultivating the carnivorous plant all year round. In Anei's eyes, no other plant compared.

Jacqueline hesitated before answering her aunt's proposal. "If that's what you want."

Chapter Twenty

"Mrs Janet Soames?"

"Yes."

Gardener could see very little of the woman save for a pair of accusing eyes staring through the small gap left by the safety chain between the door and its frame.

"Detective Inspector Stewart Gardener and Detective Sergeant Sean Reilly, Major Crime Team." Gardener held out his warrant card for her inspection.

"Yes."

He couldn't quite determine whether her reply was an answer, a question, or confirmation that she'd accepted who he said they were. "You called the station this morning. You have some information about David Vickers?"

Behind him, Reilly rubbed his hands together and exhaled a long breath, mumbling to himself.

Gardener didn't hear his partner's comment, but he could guess what it was. Janet Soames closed her front door and slid back the chain. Gardener turned and surveyed the area. The Soames' residence was a large, two-storey house with a white facade, leaded dark oak windows, and a front door to match. The grass was trimmed, with an assortment of colourful gnomes, a fishpond, and a bench. He imagined it was peaceful in summer, despite being opposite a school.

The door finally opened. "That's better," she said. "Could I trouble you for identification again, please?"

Both men held out their warrant cards.

"Please, come in," she said, satisfied. She led them through a long hall into a highly polished, tiled kitchen, offering a seat at the small round table and chairs. Reilly sat down. He produced a notebook and pen.

"I'm sorry about keeping you at the door, but you can't be too careful, can you?"

Janet Soames sat opposite Reilly.

Gardener smiled, removed his hat, placed it on the table. From his inside jacket pocket, he produced a photograph of David Vickers and passed it over. He'd obtained it from Lesley and Jim when he'd interviewed them.

"Can you confirm from the photo, Mrs Soames, that we're talking about the same boy?"

She adjusted her glasses. "Yes, that's the boy. I'm not sure what I can tell you, though."

Janet Soames had a soft voice with a clipped accent. Gardener estimated her age around mid-fifties. She had bleached blonde hair, the roots of which were dark brown. Her face was long and drawn, and she wore too much makeup. She was dangerously thin.

"You'd be surprised," replied Gardener, concerned by her constant fidgeting. She was clearly uncomfortable.

"I used to see him every day," she continued. "Leaving school. He was a beautiful child. Blond hair, lovely complexion, well-mannered. He once asked my husband if he needed any help to carry his equipment from the car." She paused.

Reilly took up the conversation. "What do you and your husband do for a living, Mrs Soames?"

"Photography. We take pictures of old castles and stately homes in England and Europe. Then we go across to America and sell them. In frames, of course."

"Well now, that sounds a grand way to earn a living. I wouldn't mind having a pop at that myself." Reilly gave her a reassuring smile. Gardener recognized the tactic for what it was. A pleasant diversion, a clever way to encourage her to open up.

"Have you ever been to Ireland?" he asked her.

"My husband has. We're both hoping to go next year."

"Well, you be sure to give me a call. I'll point you in the right direction for some lovely places. You'll not go far wrong."

Janet Soames smiled.

Gardener resumed. "You were saying, Mrs Soames. You saw David Vickers every day. What was unusual about the day he went missing?"

"He was with someone."

"Adult?" inquired Gardener.

"More a youth. Nineteen, maybe. To be honest, I took him for his brother."

"They looked alike?"

"I couldn't say whether they looked alike. The youth wore a baseball cap. But they chatted away quite happily, which is why I thought they were related."

"Can you remember anything else about him?" asked Reilly.

"Only what he was wearing. He had jeans and a pair of boots. What do they call them? Tan colour, builders wear them..."

"Rigger boots," answered the Irishman.

"Yes, that's it. He also wore a black leather jacket. There was something on the back. It looked like a golden bird. There was some writing as well, but I wasn't close enough to see what it said."

"Had you ever seen him before the day in question?" asked Gardener.

"Not that I can remember."

A rattling sound in the direction of the back door drew Gardener's attention. He watched an overweight black cat squeeze its way through the cat flap.

"Any distinguishing features? Did he have a limp? Was there anything odd in his manner?" asked Gardener.

Janet Soames thought for a moment before replying. "It all happened so quickly. And it seemed so natural. The younger boy didn't seem troubled. In fact, the youth held a carrier bag in one hand. He was trying to eat fish and chips with the other, which is why I thought they might be brothers."

"But you hadn't seen the teenager before?" pressed Gardener. "Had you ever noticed anyone else collecting David Vickers. An adult?"

"No. Sometimes he was with friends, sometimes he was on his own."

Gardener frowned. A twelve-year-old boy leaving school without supervision, particularly after two teenage girls had gone missing, was asking for trouble.

"Where were you when you saw them?"

"The living room. I'll show you."

The room was big and bright and smelled of pine. Aside from a blue Dralon Chesterfield suite, the only furniture it contained was a bookcase and a coffee table. There were no net curtains at the windows, which let in the full light of daytime.

"I was here, by the chair."

"What happened?"

"I was using the vacuum cleaner, when I noticed the two of them walking past the gate, together."

Gardener noted a hesitation, a quiver in her voice. She was holding something back.

"And?"

"Past the school bus."

"Did he normally catch the school bus?"

Janet Soames paused again. "I think so."

"But not this time?" persisted Reilly.

"I don't think so, no." Gardener saw the tears forming in her eyes.

"Is there anything else you can add to what you've told us?"

She wiped her eyes with a tissue, and brightened a little. "Yes. The youth had a carrier with the name of the fish-shop on it. Barker's." She pointed to her left. "It's about half a mile from the school in a block of small shops on the right. If they went in there, maybe Mr Barker can tell you something."

Gardener passed her his card. "Thank you, Mrs Soames. You've probably been more helpful than you realize. If you think of anything else, please ring me."

The two detectives crossed the room. Before leaving, Gardener turned. "One more question. Can I ask why you haven't told us before now?"

"My husband and I have just come back from America. Well, Sunday actually. It's taken till now to catch up on the newspapers."

"Would you recognize the youth again?"

"The jacket, yes. I didn't see his face."

"Maybe we should talk to the neighbours. Do you know them well?"

"The old couple next door, the Watsons, might be worth visiting." Once again, she pointed to her left. "They're retired now so they're home most days. I feel sure they might be able to help.

The couple on the right I'm not so sure about. The Mallards. They're both teachers, but the school is in Halifax."

"You never know, Mrs Soames. One of them might have been at home. Thank you once again for your time. Like I said, if you think of anything else, just call the station."

Outside, the Irishman turned to Gardener. "A teenager luring kids away. I wonder if he had anything to do with the missing girls. We might strike lucky with the jacket."

"That's what I was thinking. But why did he change sex with his victim this time? And if he did take the girls, what's happened to them? I've read all the interviews. As usual, no one's seen anything. He must be bloody sure of himself if he has taken all three!"

Janet Soames mentioned how well-mannered David was, which fit in with what he'd discovered from the parents. He had never missed school, was liked by his teachers and peers, as well as the neighbours. He earned pocket money by tending to odd jobs for them. He wasn't sports orientated, more a bookworm. He had a computer in his room, his games being challenging adventures as opposed to shoot-em-ups. He used to help his father, Jim, on weekends, in the small DIY shop they owned in Churchaven. The boy was definitely not the outgoing type, so how had the youth lured him away? It must have been more than a promise of fish and chips.

Gardener sighed. "Two cases with no leads to suggest a connection. Two children are missing, a third is dead, and no one can help. We find a decomposed corpse that looks as if it's been dead three months, but really only dead for three hours. We can't find out anything about him, what he's been killed with, or who killed him…" – He turned to his partner and scowled – "…and now I've a gut feeling that something is seriously amiss. I really don't like where this is heading, Sean."

Chapter Twenty-one

"I'll have a pint of the black stuff, thank you very much."

The landlord reached up and removed a clean glass from the shelf. As he poured the Guinness, he stated, "Not seen you in here before."

"No. I'm meeting someone. Place comes highly recommended."

"Pleased to hear it."

Reilly pulled up a barstool. From his vantage point, he had an unobstructed view of the whole pub. The bar was long and straight, running almost the full length of the room. Opposite the bar in the far corner, leading to the toilets – and the so-called beer garden – was a pool table. Of the twenty or so people in The Black Bull, only half were seated. The rest lined up at the bar, except for four playing pool. The jukebox cranked out a sixties number by The Monkees.

"Got any sandwiches?"

"One or two, nowt special, mind. Beef, ham, cheese and pickle, corned beef..." He left the sentence unfinished as if he'd lost interest.

Reilly sipped his pint, sizing up the publican. He was small and bald, aside from a few wisps of grey hair, which snaked along his pate. His eyes were black and soulless, much like his attitude. His teeth were false. A Band-Aid held his glasses together in one corner. He was dressed in an old grey woollen cardigan with tweed trousers. Reilly wondered if he'd left his slippers on.

Further down the bar, a pot-bellied pensioner cackled in delight, squeezing the backside of a woman half his age.

"Made your mind up, yet?" questioned the landlord.

"Not yet, no."

"Suit yourself. What brings you round here, then?"

"I'm looking for someone. I'm told he drinks in here."

"Who might that be?"

"Herbert Plum."

The Irishman noticed the landlord stiffen. Although slight, it was enough to arouse Reilly's curiosity.

"Never heard of him. Now, if you don't mind, I've got other customers to attend to. If you want that sandwich, give us a shout."

The landlord shuffled down to the other end of the bar. Reilly wasn't so naive as to think he could have walked straight in and obtained the information with ease. He hadn't expected such an abrupt change of attitude, however. The publican conversed with a couple of customers, but still threw occasional glances in his direction.

The detective checked his watch, wondering where his partner was. He left his stool. On his way to the toilets, he glanced at a few black and white pre-war frames hanging on the wall, of what he surmised to be Rawston and the surrounding area. On his way out, he was greeted by a reception committee. The four pool players.

The man Reilly assumed to be the ringleader stood with his arms folded, his cue neatly tucked across his chest. Although he was big, he was out of shape, with a beer belly that somehow managed to defy gravity. His visible skin was heavily tattooed. Of his three colleagues, Reilly considered only one of them a possible problem: a barn door of a man, cracking his knuckles, probably more at home on the rugby field.

"Gentlemen," said Reilly, nodding his head.

"We don't want your sort round here."

The ringleader had spoken. Reilly made some quick observations. No one else seemed willing to back up the four. The people sitting at the nearby tables made a hasty exit, expecting trouble. The landlord conveniently turned his back. The music stopped.

"What sort?"

"Perverts!"

Gardener walked through the front door, dressed in a black sweatshirt, jeans, and trainers. He chose to sit at the bar. He gave Reilly a slight, almost imperceptible nod.

"If I was you, I'd be a little more careful when you're addressing people you don't know," Reilly said, his tone even.

"What?" the tattooed man asked. He glanced around at his colleagues, pointing towards Reilly, and laughed. His grin revealed uneven, tobacco-stained teeth.

"Some people are easily offended." Reilly paused. "Now me, I've been around a bit. I've developed what you might call a 'thick skin'. But I draw the line at being called a pervert."

The atmosphere grew heavy. From the expressions in their eyes, Reilly could see that two were reluctant to become involved. Gardener was still ignoring the publican, who seemed content to disregard the brewing trouble.

"Shouldn't hang around with other perverts then, should you?"

"I don't," replied Reilly. "I said I was looking for him."

"Come on, Craig, let's leave it."

"Now that sounds like good advice to me, Craig. So, I'm going to go over there and finish my wee drink. I suggest you go back to playing pool. We'll let this little matter drop, and no one will come to any harm."

Maintaining eye contact, Reilly pushed his way past the man.

"Sean!" Gardener shouted suddenly. As Reilly turned, the ringleader was raising his cue, ready to bring it down across the detective's head. All hell broke loose.

Reilly brought his right arm up, wrapping the cue up and yanking it toward him, out of the way. He slammed his left fist into the tattooed man's face, then followed through with a knee to the man's testicles and a right uppercut to his jaw. He then snapped the cue across his knee and hurled it the length of the bar, narrowly missing the landlord as he frantically made a phone call.

Gardener rushed past Reilly, shouting, 'Police!' It made no difference. One of the remaining two pool players took a swing at the senior officer. Gardener avoided the blow by raising the barstool he'd brought with him, smashing it into the man's face.

The pub might as well have been in the middle of the football ground for all the noise that erupted. Two women at the bar screamed, encouraging the pool players. Glasses were smashed. Tables were overturned.

A pair of hands grabbed Reilly, one on his shoulder, the other hooked into his belt buckle. The next thing he knew, he was airborne. He crash-landed on the pool table, immediately rolling off and taking a pool ball with him.

He pulled himself to his feet, glancing around. Charging towards him was the rugby player, his face a contorted grimace of rage. His hands clenched into tightly-balled fists; his eyes vacant of emotion. Reilly took the only option open to him.

He launched the pool ball with an accuracy that relied on luck more than judgment. He heard the crunching of bone as the rugby player dropped to his knees. A guttural howl escaped his lips, along with teeth and blood, which spilled out onto the floor.

A man suddenly slammed down on the pool table in front of Reilly. The Irishman pulled him up by his collar, punched him hard in the mouth, then threw him over the side of the table.

He supposed he should have tried harder to impress upon them who he was, but by now he was enjoying himself.

As Reilly turned, he saw Gardener take a hard punch to the face. Kicking a chair out of his way, Reilly climbed over a body to reach the barbarian who had floored his superior officer. The giant turned fast. Using all his weight, he barged into Reilly, knocking him off balance. He landed beside the body he'd climbed over.

The last thing he expected was to be helped to his feet. He drew his fist back but momentarily held it, surprised at the sight of a riot squad officer trying to restrain him. Surveying the pub, he realized it was almost empty. Only the landlord and two customers remained, all of them horrified.

"Where the hell did you come from?"

The riot officer ignored his question, choosing instead to read him his rights.

Reilly held up his hand. "Hold it, I'm a police officer. So is he." Reilly pointed to Gardener, who was nursing his swollen cheek. The officer let go but waited for identification. Once satisfied, he checked to ensure the ringleader and the rugby player had been escorted from the premises.

Chapter Twenty-two

"What the bloody hell did you two think you were doing?" demanded Briggs. Apart from the fact that Briggs was the

DCI, no one argued with him because he was physically overbearing. His huge chest rose and seemed to keep on rising as he took a breath. Little could be seen of his face due to his thick black beard and moustache. Briggs was a few inches shorter than Gardener, but nevertheless, his authority – and the fact he spoke extremely fast without fluffing any of his words – gave him a decided advantage.

"Defending ourselves," replied Gardener, taking a sip of water and wincing.

"Defending your-bloody-selves? Against who? The Fantastic Four? A couple of blokes playing pool, and you go in like you're auditioning for 'Lethal Weapon 6' and trash the place!"

"It didn't happen like that!" shouted Reilly.

Briggs glared at Reilly with an expression that would have killed a crow in mid-flight.

"Well, you would say that, wouldn't you? You were responsible. You're a walking one-man war zone, Reilly. You ought to carry a government health warning. According to the landlord, who by the way is putting in a claim, you walked in, ordered a drink, and then went over to the pool table.

He's no idea what happened next, but whatever it was, it sparked off a riot."

"Sean's right, it didn't happen like that."

"I'm surprised at you, Stewart. I can understand it from the Urban Guerrilla, but not you. You've obviously been under a lot of pressure lately. Maybe you came back to work too soon."

"You're out of order there, sir," said Gardener, infuriated by the suggestion.

"All I did was ask about Herbert Plum," said Reilly. "The landlord didn't answer, and when I came out of the toilets, the pool players were waiting for me. We didn't get a chance to explain who we were before they were on us."

"That's exactly what happened, sir. We were only doing our job." Gardener stood up and walked around Briggs' desk, depositing his cup in the bin. An elongated silence descended upon the room. Briggs sighed. "I just wish you'd tried restraining yourselves a little more."

After another silence, Gardener asked, "What are you going to do?"

"About you two? Nothing. But there will be an inquiry. Questions will be asked, but we can cross that bridge when we come to it. On the subject of Plum, have you made any headway?"

Gardener sat down again, dejected. "We didn't get a chance."

"Well, I did," said Briggs.

That piqued Gardener's curiosity. "How?"

"Craig Sutton." Briggs glanced at Reilly. "That was the bloke you knocked unconscious."

"He talked?"

"Sutton's well known. He's been busted a couple of times for possession. He also has a record for handling stolen goods. Nothing heavy, he hasn't got the guts. Looks like you did us a favour, Reilly. He was wanted for questioning in connection with the stolen paint from that warehouse near The White Rose Centre last week. He was seen driving the getaway van.

"So, we traded a bit of information. Turns out that Sutton was also involved in another incident in The Black Bull last week, with Plum. Our friend Plum had a bit of a drink problem. After a bloody good session, he loosened his tongue, offered Sutton's woman a part in a film. Said he had the right contacts, all she had to do was give him the nod."

"What kind of film?" inquired Gardener.

"'Artistic' was how Plum put it, Christ knows why. Have you seen Sutton's girlfriend? I know looks are only skin deep, but she must have been born inside out. Anyway, she was offended. She told Sutton, who threatened Plum."

"No wonder he wasn't too happy to see us," said Reilly.

"Still doesn't tell us much," said Gardener.

"No, but you might like to know Plum was in there regularly, with a colleague. Craig Sutton doesn't know anything other than his name. Bernard Thornwell. Sutton had the impression they worked together. Unless…"

"Unless what?" asked Gardener.

"…unless they were partners," finished Briggs.

Gardener didn't buy it. "Not Plum's style. He was definitely into females."

"Well, whatever it was," said Briggs, "I want you to concentrate on finding Thornwell. He might be the key to the investigation."

Chapter Twenty-three

Gardener brought his car to a halt outside the pathology lab. Switching off the engine, he sat motionless for a moment, reliving the events of the previous two days. As the case unfolded, it was proving more complex.

A house-to-house inquiry of Rawston revealed very little. General opinion proved that Plum had neither been liked nor disliked. He was simply one of the millions who shuffled by inconsequentially. He was someone you acknowledged, then promptly forgot. According to the turf accountant and his landlady, he had a money problem. He'd died owing them both. Shop assistants had seen little of him. Those who had couldn't remember what he'd bought.

The seedier side of the investigation revealed Plum had not purchased his pornography in Leeds or the surrounding areas. Seeing as he had no computer, it was unlikely he'd bought anything online. Gardener assumed he had sent abroad for it. There were enough outlets, all of them too difficult and time-consuming to chase down.

Plum had no bank records, no building society accounts, no legal documents of any kind. He had neither contributed to the Inland Revenue nor National Insurance. He had no pension, and his bills had been paid with cash. Gardener could find no employment details. He had no medical records, and only one dental document, for a pair of false teeth supplied twenty years previously, also paid for in cash.

So, where and how did he earn his money?

Gardener returned to The Black Bull, where he found the landlord more cooperative than Reilly had. Thornwell's description bore a resemblance to Plum's. He was a similar age, portly built with thinning grey hair, beard, and moustache. He walked with a limp. He only used the pub occasionally, with Plum. Never by himself.

The landlord said he had not seen Thornwell since before the brawl. He also confirmed what Briggs had said about the incident involving Craig Sutton and his girlfriend. The landlord hadn't been sure what it was about, but Sutton had been extremely angry, taking a pop at both. What Sutton had declined to tell Briggs, which had been overheard by the landlord, was Sutton telling both men if he saw either of them in the pub again, he'd kill them.

Later in the evening, the landlord also heard Sutton saying, "It isn't over. I'll get even with them. Both of them!"

So far, Gardener had been unable to find Bernard Thornwell. He and Plum had socialized together, very possibly worked together. Now one was dead, the other missing. The mystery deepened. Gardener was awaiting copies of both men's birth certificates. Reilly was still digging for information. The team was still investigating. An appointment with Fitz beckoned.

Gardener was hoping for something positive. He left the car, nursing his still swollen cheek.

Gardener found Fitz at his desk. Unlike most pathologists, he kept a tidy office. Folders were neatly stored, easily accessible. On a shelf behind him sat a MIDI hi-fi, currently playing a CD from an opera. He had a computer on his desk and a fresh cup of coffee. Apart from a couple of prints and a framed photograph of his wife, the only other item decorating the walls was a plaque, which read: "Hic locus est ubi mors gaudet succurrere vitae. This is the place where death rejoices to teach those who live."

"What happened to you?" asked Fitz, glancing up.

"It's a long story," replied Gardener.

"It must involve the Irishman, then." Fitz finished playing with his computer and turned his attention to Gardener. "How's the case progressing?"

Gardener briefly took the pathologist through what he had learned.

"Come with me." Fitz took a sip of coffee before leading Gardener through to Herbert Plum's corpse. The vile smell was still prominent.

"I've examined the bones thoroughly. See here?" Fitz held one aloft. "They're hollow, no bone marrow present. And take a look at this." Fitz picked up a magnifying glass, directing Gardener to the skeleton's trachea.

"What am I looking for?"

Fitz used a long needle to pinpoint the exact location. "The third cervical vertebra has slight damage. That pinprick is the mark of a syringe, which could mean that the killer has some medical knowledge. Although on this occasion, they've gone too far and hit the bone."

"What were they after?" Gardener straightened, following Fitz as he returned to his office.

"At the moment I'm only guessing, but I suspect the jugular vein." Fitz sat down behind his desk. "The jugular carries blood from the brain to the heart, where it's pumped around the body. There, it mixes with the rest of the body's blood. Inject the vein with a lethal compound, and within minutes, the entire body is contaminated."

"Could it be a poison?"

"I don't know. The vast majority of fatal poisonings are suicidal or accidental. Less than six percent of homicides are due to poisoning. I've discussed the case at length with Professor Matthew Stapleton, probably the country's leading toxicologist, up in Edinburgh. I considered aconitine, a poison widely used in ancient times. Mainly in Greece and Rome for the elimination of political enemies. The Greeks called it 'Stepmother's Poison'. It has the same effect as a depressant on the central nervous system. Symptoms include numbness, increase in body temperature, vomiting, visual disturbance, and quite a number of other unpleasant side effects..."

"But?"

"It's not capable of destroying the body. It could be a mixture of a few poisons causing a severe reaction. Antimony is another, made famous in the trial of George Chapman for murder in 1903." Fitz leaned forward, a little excited. "Chapman was a sinister character with experience as a barber-surgeon, which had led to the speculation he was Jack the Ripper…"

"Fitz!"

"What?"

"Can we stick to the point? I've got Briggs breathing down my neck. I need facts."

The opera CD finished. Fitz pressed the play button again. He gave Gardener an expression of disappointment. Fitz loved nothing more than to share his encyclopaedic knowledge.

"I'm not convinced it's a straightforward poison. I'm not aware of anything on the market that's capable of destroying a body." Fitz paused. "Matthew Stapleton is researching poisons and their effects for me. The only speculation I'm prepared to make is the injection into the jugular. I've studied it at length. From the angle and the position of the puncture wound, I'd say your killer is left-handed."

Gardener considered the possibilities of such an action.

"How do you manage to inject a person in the neck? It's not as if they're going to stand there and cooperate, is it?"

"Not unless your assailant is extremely powerful, or heavy. Or very, very quick."

Craig Sutton entered the detective's mind. He met the requirement of being strong enough. But was he left-handed? Did he have any medical knowledge?

"Even so..." Gardener stopped, another train of thought distracting him. Sutton was a known drug dealer.

"What?" Fitz asked.

"An easy way to get someone to cooperate would be to drug them, yes? If they're almost out of it, you can do anything you want to them."

Gardener left Fitz thinking about his statement. On his way out, he heard the pathologist mumble something about time and accuracy.

Chapter Twenty-four

Gardener was staring into the window of the Leeds United supporters shop in The Merrion Centre. His mind wasn't on the reason he was here – to try and find a Christmas present for Chris.

Football was a world away from when he was young. It was all about money now. The prices they charged for season tickets were horrendous: add that to what he could see here, and it soon reached extortion. He'd heard recently that there were different levels of membership and even if you were a Gold member it didn't guarantee tickets.

A voice from behind distracted him. "Stewart?"

He turned. "Jacqueline. Nice to see you. What are you doing here?"

"Same as you, I suspect. Christmas shopping. It's amazing how it creeps up on you."

She paused, staring at his cheek. "What have you done to your face?"

"It's nothing, really," he replied, touching it. "It's not as bad as it looks."

"You look tired. Is everything all right?"

Gardener smiled. "Just a few sleepless nights."

He was a little self-conscious and she must have picked up on it.

"I was about to have a coffee. Please say you'll join me."

He checked his watch. "I shouldn't, but I will."

"Good!"

She led him out of the building to a small, cosy café opposite a bookshop at the edge of an arcade. Despite being December, the weather was mild. She suggested they sit outside. Gardener agreed. Jacqueline went inside, emerging shortly afterwards with a latte for herself and a decaf for him.

The atmosphere in the arcade was tranquil. A few people browsed in the bookshop. A couple of Japanese tourists stared eagerly into the window of the camera shop next door.

As she sat, they both leaned forward, went to speak at the same time, then leaned back and stopped, also in unison. They shared an awkward laugh of embarrassment in an effort to disguise their discomfort.

"You first," said Jacqueline.

"Not at all, ladies before gentlemen, and all that," Gardener replied.

"I was going to ask you what you'd been buying?"

"I was about to ask you the same." He laughed again. "I'm struggling to buy a Christmas present for Chris. He loves his football. He's hoping to play for the school. Anyway, I've managed to find a copy of the new FIFA game for his Xbox." Gardener paused, taking a sip of coffee. "What about you?"

"Trying to choose something for my aunt. It's not easy to buy for the person who has everything."

"Tell me about it. I have the same problem with my dad." He took another sip of coffee, then stopped to observe the brew. "This coffee is good. It's not something I usually drink. Anyway, you're spending Christmas with your aunt. Bet you're looking forward to it."

Her expression changed. "There's a lot to do before then."

He wondered about her defensive answer. In order to break the tension, he glanced at a young couple emerging from the bookshop, holding hands, gazing intently at each other – unaware of everyone else around them.

"Are you doing anything tomorrow night?" she asked him.

Gardener hesitated. "I've nothing planned, no, and I'm not on call."

"How would you like to join me for a meal… at my place?"

The question took him unawares but he answered suddenly, without further thought. "I'd love to. What time?"

He noticed another pause from her before she answered. "Eight o'clock?"

"Fine. I'll bring the wine," said Gardener, slipping into the spirit. "You do drink wine, don't you?"

"Of course I do."

"Any preference?"

"I'll leave it to you. Lidl have a pretty good range: reasonably priced."

Sarah came into his mind and his insides turned at the thought of what he was doing. But it didn't stop him.

"Okay. Eight o'clock it is." He checked his watch again, then finished his coffee. "I'm really sorry, but I have to go. Cases don't solve themselves. I'll see you tomorrow at eight."

"It's a date," replied Jacqueline.

Chapter Twenty-five

An elderly gentleman dressed in a Santa Claus suit staggered drunk through the centre of Leeds, blissfully unaware of the freezing cold wind.

He negotiated crossing The Headrow in a disorganized series of blunders, swaying as though at sea, narrowly missing traffic.

He was observed by a courting couple huddled in a doorway, hungrily devouring a Burger King takeaway after a night on the town.

On New Briggate, he sang to himself as he lurched across Mark Lane.

A vagrant observed him trip through an archway which led onto the grounds of St John's Church.

No one saw him leave.

Chapter Twenty-six

Gardener opened the kitchen door and shouted down the garden path to his father. A persistent chill hung in the air, but the early morning mist was beginning to clear. Although it was only eight o'clock, the old man had been in his greenhouse since seven. Gardener was not surprised. His father was, by habit, an early riser. He heard the faint reply and shivered before closing the door.

Walking back through the kitchen, the mouth-watering aroma of grilled bacon set his taste buds on edge. Although Gardener preferred a healthier diet, he felt he needed to indulge every now and again. He walked through the living room into the hallway. At the foot of the stairs, he bellowed for Chris to hurry up.

Malcolm was standing by the sink as Gardener returned to serve. "You can't beat a bacon sandwich." The old man was drying his hands. "What a life. An hour in the greenhouse, and then back in for breakfast!"

"Rather you than me," said Gardener. It wasn't that he had a dislike of plants. It was more the overpowering odour he couldn't stand. Quite apart from the fact that he saw the greenhouse as his father's domain, his own private sanctuary.

He placed sandwiches and ketchup on the table as Chris entered the room, casually dressed in a Reebok tracksuit with trainers. Chris switched on the radio. Gardener cringed as the brash trap music bounced around the kitchen. "Oh, come on, Chris, give us a break!"

"What's up, Dad? Too old for this stuff?"

"No, I'm a music lover. So, come on, turn it down."

"Okay," sighed Chris.

"There's a good lad. You know it makes sense," mocked his dad, smiling.

"Oh, I get it. Use your authority to cover your age."

Malcolm laughed. Gardener saw the funny side. He realized Chris was growing up fast. Another three years and he would be sitting his GCSEs and very probably making his own way in the world. But he was still his son, and as such, he regarded him as his little boy in a lot of ways. He understood, however, that his son's maturity was fast creating a new level to their relationship. Something he had to accept as much as Chris.

"So, what do you fancy doing today, son?"

"You're not working?" asked Chris, taking a huge bite of his sandwich and a slurp of coffee.

"There's a few things I need to do, but Christmas is coming, so I'd like us to spend a bit of time together. And don't fill your mouth so full!"

The phone ringing interrupted their conversation. Gardener wiped his lips with a napkin before answering.

"Stewart, it's Alan."

"Something wrong?" Gardener felt his stomach clench.

"We've had a call from the priest at St John's Church in the centre of Leeds. Father O'Hanlon. He's found a body on the grounds. Sounds like a carbon copy of Plum."

Gardener sighed. "Same MO?"

"Exactly."

Gardener glanced apologetically at Chris, realizing his son knew what was coming.

"I'll be there as quick as I can. Will you call Sean for me, please?"

Chapter Twenty-seven

Gardener negotiated the early morning traffic with mixed feelings.

He was concerned for the victim's identity and for the fact the death was so public. That meant he might have to deal with the press. Not a prospect he relished.

As he approached New Briggate by the side of the Primark store, he stopped at a roadblock that had been set up. He signed the log and was cleared. Driving through, he turned left into Mark Lane. The entrance to the church was blocked by a couple of PCs. A crowd of onlookers had gathered, a fair number of them the uncompromising face of journalism. Two junior officers kept them at bay. He drove past the loading bays on the left to a parking bay on the right.

He left the car and slipped into a scene suit at a station set up next to a shop near the church grounds. The nosy counter assistant almost broke her neck in an effort to catch him, but a young PC put paid to that. In the distance, at the entrance to the church, he heard questions being directed at the officers. Staring at the scene, Gardener noticed the mist had cleared. The winter sun was trying to penetrate his mood, but it did little to dispel his cold feeling of dread.

Behind the building, he could quite clearly see the corpse guarded by another PC.

He heard a car pull up behind his. A door slammed. Following the protective suit ritual, Reilly joined him. Together they entered the church grounds and made their way to the body.

Gardener knelt down. The deterioration of the corpse was more advanced than Plum's had been, suggesting he'd been dead longer. The end result was still a bag of bones in a loose fitting skin-suit. Reilly knelt alongside him.

"Sean, go over to the main gate, oversee security of the site. Make sure anyone who has a camera is forbidden to use it. If they give you any grief, throw the book at them."

Reilly nodded and left without saying anything.

Gardener flipped open his mobile and called the station. He requested his team, along with the biggest tent they had. Apart from Fitz, he wanted a scientist from the Forensic Science Service. He also wanted CSIs, photographers, and a PolSA – police search advisor – team for a fingertip search.

Before closing the call, a quick glance upwards revealed a clear sky. There had been no rain overnight. He asked the desk sergeant to put a call into the Met Office weather centre, demanding accurate information on temperatures, rainfall, and wind speeds over the next few hours.

Chapter Twenty-eight

When his team arrived, Gardener gave them their instructions. He asked for a tent around the body, as well as an inner cordon on it. He wanted an outer cordon around the scene.

He introduced himself to Mike Sanderson, the PolSA team leader, before he and Reilly paid the priest a visit. Father O'Hanlon was young and efficient, careful but confident with his answers.

He spoke with a southern Irish lilt. Confirming he'd arrived at the church at approximately seven o'clock that morning, he stated he didn't notice anything at first. He'd used the front entrance, however. From that angle, the body would have been difficult to see.

The cleaner arrived an hour later, informing him of what she'd found. She also noticed a vagrant on the grounds, perched on a low stone wall near the kiosk. Father O'Hanlon had investigated the body before raising the alarm.

Gardener asked a number of routine questions, concentrating on the priest's daily duties and his whereabouts the previous night. Father O'Hanlon said he left the church around ten o'clock. He hadn't noticed anything suspicious. He hadn't inspected the grounds either. The cleaner was unable to add anything constructive. Reilly took down the details, and both detectives returned to the scene.

Chapter Twenty-nine

Back outside, Gardener noticed scene tape stretching around the circumference of the small marquee. He and Sean Reilly stepped inside, stared down at the corpse. Fitz turned and stood to greet them. "We must stop meeting like this."

"The MO looks the same. Don't suppose you can give me an estimated time of death?" Gardener asked.

"Difficult to say. Probably around midnight."

"Are we declaring a Hazchem scene?" Reilly asked.

"Not this time," Gardener replied. "At least not until it's safely back with Fitz."

Gardener rose, stepped outside the marquee, and surveyed the area. Beyond the railings around the grounds of the church, people had come to a standstill, trying to watch what was happening. The PolSA team search was underway, scouring the nearby bushes and the surrounding area. The CSM, Steve Fenton, shouted to Gardener: he'd found something.

As Gardener approached, Fenton held out a syringe. Gardener produced a plastic bag from his inside jacket pocket. Fenton dropped it in.

"Any more?" he asked.

"Not so far."

Gardener sealed the bag and took it back to Fitz, who was still inside the marquee. He passed it over. "Can you analyse it today?"

"I'll do my best. It could be tomorrow before I get the results. It may not tell us anything. In fact, it might have nothing to do with the body."

"I'm well aware of that."

"I'll take it back to the lab. There's nothing more I can do here." Fitz stood up. "Can I have what's left of the corpse as soon as you've finished?"

"Of course. I won't be much longer."

Gardener and Reilly returned their attention to the body. "What's happening, Sean? A week ago today we found the first. We barely know anything about him. Now we have another, same MO. There are two missing children, another dead. Every avenue we explore is a virtual dead end. If you ask me, someone is carefully controlling the situation."

"We'll need to find some answers soon, boss. Those press boys will not be giving us a break. Not now."

The officers stepped outside. Gardener noticed the gathering journalists still jostling the two uniformed guards. One of the undertakers approached him. "Can we move the body yet, sir?"

"No. I'll give you a shout when we've finished." Gardener turned to Reilly. "I want another word with the priest."

The second meeting was fractious. When Gardener asked about any drug-related problems, Father O'Hanlon appeared outraged. He vehemently asserted there had never been a problem in his parish. He'd refused to accept a syringe had been found in the grounds of his church, claiming it had to be connected to the murder.

Chapter Thirty

Outside, the press hounded the uniformed guards. By now, the television cameras had joined them. The medics and the undertakers were unsettled. The two senior officers walked back to the marquee.

Once inside, Gardener produced a fresh pair of gloves. He made a systematic search of the body whilst doing his best to hold his breath. Underneath the Santa suit, the victim had worn a plain black shirt and underpants. All the clothing was stained and smelled disgusting.

"Check the shirt pocket, boss. Something bulging," said Reilly.

Gardener kept the clothing separated. Reilly extracted the sodden wallet, which squelched as he opened it. Amongst the contents were money, possibly a business card – illegible – and a couple of credit cards. Reilly held up a Visa card and sighed.

Gardener's heart sank as he read the name. "B Thornwell."

The Irishman kept the wallet and the cards. Gardener let the clothing fall. The watch around the skeletal wrist was engraved with Thornwell's name. Gardener stood up.

"Like I said, Sean, control. Someone has a lot to lose, for one reason or another."

Reilly turned to his superior officer. "Craig Sutton?"

"It's possible," replied Gardener. "But it's all circumstantial."

"We have enough to talk to him. He has a motive. We have reasonable suspicion."

"Oh, God." Gardener held his nose. They stepped outside.

"Looks like our man has something to say," Reilly smiled.

Gardener spotted an old vagrant standing by the smokers' kiosk. He had his hands inside the pockets of his aged, tattered duffel coat. He wore jeans, trainers, and a Panama hat. He watched the two detectives curiously.

Although he didn't want to, Gardener couldn't help but stare at the man. He noticed the vagrant's skin was dark and wrinkled, and difficult to put an age to.

The vagrant coughed before speaking. "I assume you'll want to speak to me now, sir?"

Gardener was astonished. The vagrant's voice was velvet smooth, the accent BBC English. His manner suggested a well-educated person. "Who are you?"

"Bob Crisp, sir."

Reilly turned to Gardener, smiling. "Is he serious?"

"I assure you, sir, the name is genuine." The vagrant smiled.

"Why would I want to speak to you?" asked Gardener.

"You'd like answers."

The SIO sighed, placing his hands in his pockets. He scrutinized the area again. He wasn't particularly happy that the TV cameras were there. Satisfied that no one had broken the barrier, he returned his attention to Bob Crisp, unable to decide if he was genuine. Either way, he did not want to waste any time with him. The man could be a potential witness, though, which was something he could not ignore.

"Look." Gardener glanced at his watch. "I don't have time for riddles and puzzles, or to play games. If you know anything that you think will help, tell me."

A pair of anxious undertakers came to within a few feet of the marquee. Gardener turned, raising a hand. "Give us a couple of minutes." They backed off, but Gardener could see they were unhappy.

"You should make time, sir," said Crisp. "'Half of our life is spent trying to find something to do with the time we have rushed through life trying to save.'"

"I've heard enough!"

Reilly placed his arm on Gardener's. "Give him a chance, boss. He reminds me of old Seamus back in Ireland. It sounded like rubbish at the time, but there was a lot of wisdom in his words."

"Your colleague is very perceptive. I have but three things to say, as you are so short of time," Crisp said.

A fracas at the gate diverted Gardener's attention. TV reporters and journalists were growing agitated. He noticed Father O'Hanlon talking to them, and wondered if that was a wise move. Bob Crisp's voice broke his thoughts.

"You, sir, are troubled. You have the look of a man who has lived through tragedy, although you display a very different facade. If you are not careful, tragedy will seek you again. I sense you are about to embark upon a new lease of life. Think very carefully."

Gardener's skin prickled.

Crisp pointed to the canvas covering. "Please, lift the flap."

Against his better judgment, Gardener did as he was asked.

Crisp gazed dolefully down at the body.

"'We owe respect to the living. To the dead we owe nothing but truth.' Though I have no wish to speak ill of the dead, Bernard Thornwell was a drunkard! Perhaps it eased his conscience, for I too would be a drunkard, should I have had his employer."

Gardener was transfixed by the surreal situation he was caught up in. Who was Bob Crisp? How much did he really know? He dropped the marquee siding. "You know who he works for?"

"Indeed, I do." Crisp pointed. "You have a wallet in your hands. Amongst the credit cards, is there a business card?"

Reilly held it up. Gardener glanced at it. "Derek Summers, Entertainment Agent."

An entertainment agent would account for the Santa suit, thought Gardener.

"Seek out Derek Summers, but beware. He is not a man in which to place your trust."

A thumping of feet grew closer. Gardener turned. A young constable had arrived at the scene, short on breath. "Sir, the press. They're getting out of hand."

"Why? What are they doing?"

"They say they have a right to know what's going on."

"Go back and tell them they have no rights until I say so." Gardener paused, turning to Reilly. "On second thought, Sean, perhaps you'll be more persuasive. Can you have a word?"

"Leave them to me."

As Reilly left, Gardener noticed Bob Crisp was on the move. "No. Wait, I haven't finished with you, yet. What do you know about Derek Summers?"

The vagrant hesitated before speaking. "Knowledge is power, if it's connected to the right person. I fear I have said enough. You are the detective."

Bob Crisp tipped his hat. Before leaving, he pointed to the members of the press. "You must talk to them, sir, despite your obvious dislike."

Gardener was confused, but he knew he could not keep the media waiting much longer.

He glanced around, checking out high vantage points. Flats, offices, apartments. It wouldn't take two minutes for some smart journalist and photographer to reach the high ground, giving themselves a bird's-eye view. If some clown hadn't done it already.

Gardener checked the crime scene. He breathed a sigh of relief. The canvas covering the area of the corpse also concealed the Santa coat from prying eyes and state-of-the-art telescopic lenses. He started walking towards the media. A couple of flashguns sliced through the grey morning.

As he reached the gate, he composed himself before talking. "Ladies and gentlemen, good morning. I'm sorry to keep you waiting." He spoke quietly, calmly, his demeanour clearly indicating if there were any interruptions, he would turn tail and leave them.

"At this moment, we have an unidentifiable male corpse. Cause of death has yet to be determined. We are awaiting the Home Office pathologist's report. Therefore, the death is being treated as suspicious. We are appealing for anyone in this area between 3:00pm yesterday afternoon and 8:00am this morning to come forward."

Cameras flashed. Chilled hands made notes.

"Male corpse, Mr Gardener?" asked one of the pack. "Any connection with the missing children?"

Gardener noticed heads rising from notebooks. TV cameras slid into close-up.

"No, the deceased is a male adult."

"Cause of death? How long?" shouted another.

"Too early to say," replied Gardener. "The police press office will issue any updates, or cover any further developments."

Another flurry of press activity followed. Gardener suspected the television news teams wanted one-to-one interviews. But he wasn't keen. Gardener shuddered as he turned away, ignoring further shouted questions. Reilly ambled up to him.

"Sean, get the uniforms to walk around the block a couple of times. I don't want the cameras here too long. The press will want some local colour, and before we know it, the place will be swarming with vagrants. It wouldn't take much for one of them to talk. The promise of a bottle of cider."

Reilly nodded and turned to the reporters. "Okay, gentlemen, that's all for now."

"What do you mean, that's all?"

"We've said all we're going to."

He raised his hand, indicating the interview was over, much to the chagrin of the reporters.

As he moved to rejoin Gardener, one of the journalists lunged forward. He carried a recording device in one hand, and his camera in the other. "Mr Gardener? Is it true you were one of the officers involved in the Roundhay Ripper Trial?"

Reilly spun on him, anger evident in his eyes. "I've told you, that's all for today."

Gardener turned as the camera flash went off in his eyes. He was about to say more when Reilly pushed past him.

"Give us the camera!"

Gardener cringed at the comedy of errors that followed. Reilly lost his footing, fell down the steps. Somehow, his hands ended up around the journalist's throat, and they both tumbled to the ground. Every camera present clicked in unison.

Gardener stared into the sky and sighed.

He could see the headlines now. "Police Brutality!"

Chapter Thirty-one

Gardener spent the rest of the afternoon in and out of meetings with his team, issuing instructions and trying to locate Derek Summers. He had to leave a message on the agent's answering machine. He left the station filled with thoughts of the evening ahead, narrowly missing a call from Janet Soames. The tone of her voice impressed a sense of urgency.

The desk sergeant promised to relay her message for Gardener to return her call.

Chapter Thirty-two

Gardener's route to Jacqueline's followed the meandering stream which bordered the western side of the village, allowing him to gather his thoughts and clear his head from the toil of the day.

The problems had, as usual, spiralled out of control. Thornwell's body on the grounds of the church, the mysterious vagrant, the press. The media coverage could, if not carefully handled, cripple them. Briggs wouldn't be pleased about the photos when they came to print. The fact they were nowhere near catching the killer made Gardener realize the pressure on him was mounting.

Craig Sutton's name cropped up again. Although the evidence they had was scant, he would still have to interview him officially. Two victims, both associated with Sutton in threatening circumstances, didn't necessarily make him a killer. He was definitely a suspect, however.

As for the vagrant, that was something else entirely. Bob Crisp's words had really aroused Gardener's curiosity. He sensed today's meeting wouldn't be their last. But who was he? What did he really know? Was he involved, somehow?

In an effort to really beat it out of his system, Gardener had spent an hour on the cross-trainer in the police gymnasium. He notched up a few miles, worked up a sweat, and left himself breathless. That, however, had been a waste of time. His head still buzzed, which was by no means the correct frame of mind for the evening ahead.

He'd thought quite a lot about the meal since Jacqueline had asked him. He still couldn't believe she had. Over the last few months, he'd found his attraction to the minister becoming stronger. Whether or not he was prepared to do anything about it was another matter. The thought of commitment scared him.

Approaching the lane which led to Jacqueline's house, he passed a middle-aged couple walking a spaniel. They nodded in recognition as they climbed the bank to the stream.

Gardener opened the gate to the vicarage. He had two bottles of wine and a box of Belgian chocolates with him. As he lifted his hand to knock on the door, the words of the mysterious Bob Crisp entered his mind. In particular, his parting shot. Be careful.

Chapter Thirty-three

Gardener took his place at the table at Jacqueline's insistence.

The dining room was sparsely furnished with a table and chairs and a matching writing bureau, all finished in dark oak. Adorning the walls was a selection of oils, mostly Romanian.

Jacqueline had worked hard setting the table, using fine china and candles. The choice of music wasn't to his taste, but she'd chosen it to create a romantic atmosphere. The Carpenters were reliving Yesterday Once More.

Settling in her company would probably take him longer than he'd anticipated.

Jacqueline returned to the room with a food trolley. There were two bowls of Transylvanian soup and a large bottle of wine in an ice bucket. She poured two glasses, sitting opposite.

"It smells delicious."

"Let's hope it lives up to the smell."

"Compared to my cooking, I'm sure it will." Gardener tasted it. He wasn't disappointed.

"Do you eat like this all the time?"

"Hardly! I'd be twenty-stone if I did. I only tend to eat such delicacies when my aunt is around."

"Did she cook it?"

"No, but it's her recipe."

Gardener set down his spoon and picked up his glass of wine. He thought a toast to friendship was fitting. Jacqueline agreed.

"So, how's your day been?" he asked, continuing with his soup.

"I had a lovely day. A young couple came to see me. They've been engaged for about two years and want to get married. He's had a recent promotion, and they'd like to start a family. They want to do things properly. They seemed to have a very old-fashioned view of life. I was really pleased," she said.

"I like to see young people getting their priorities right. Especially in the world we're living in. To most, if it doesn't have a monetary value, it's not important."

"I know," replied Jacqueline, breaking off a piece of bread and dipping it into the soup. "A throwaway world with falling moral standards. Which are responsible for a lot of problems."

Jacqueline paused and took a sip of wine. "Still, tonight isn't about falling standards. Tell me about your day."

Gardener laughed. "All my days are about falling moral standards." He finished his soup and sipped some more wine. The Carpenters were singing a cover version of an old Beatles song he recognized. His father was a huge fan. As he reflected on his day, he wondered how much he should tell her.

"I have two murders on my hands. The same killer, same style. No clues. I have disappearing children, another of them dead. It's been one problem after another, with no answers."

"David Vickers," Jacqueline reflected. "It must have been awful for him. I keep wondering what he must have gone through. Was he tortured? Locked away by himself, calling out for a mother who was unable to protect him in his hour of need?"

Gardener's stomach tightened as he noticed Jacqueline's eyes reddening. The subject was obviously a raw nerve. For both of them.

She reached for her napkin, wiping her eyes. "I'm sorry. I find any crime connected with children emotionally distressing. I don't think people who hurt children should be allowed to get away with it."

"You don't have to apologize for being upset." He wasn't sure what else to say. He was out of practice when it came to dating. "I feel as strongly as you do, particularly with having Chris around. He's growing up fast. I'll probably lose him to a college in the next five years. God forbid I should lose him sooner to some pervert who can't control himself. Worse still, a maniac I should have put behind bars."

Jacqueline poured them each another glass of wine before clearing the dishes. "Do you think there's a connection between the murders and the disappearing children? Particularly with the Father Christmas angle?"

Gardener paused mid-sip, a tingling sensation creeping up his spine.

"How do you know about Father Christmas?"

She hesitated before sitting back down. "I'm sorry, I shouldn't have said anything. I'm afraid ministers are no different from ordinary citizens. We gossip as much as everyone else. I saw Father O'Hanlon today. He was upset by the body on the grounds of his church. I'm sorry."

Gardener finished the glass. "It's okay. It'll be common knowledge soon enough, especially now the press is involved. But, to answer your question, I'm not sure. With what little evidence I've unearthed so far, I sincerely hope not."

Gardener paused. Talking about work was the last thing he wanted. He wasn't there to become tangled up in the logistics of murder with his date. "Let's try and forget all that. This kind of evening doesn't happen often for me. We should try to enjoy ourselves. It's nearly Christmas. I'm enjoying the meal and the company. One of the reasons I accepted tonight's invitation was because..." Gardener stopped talking, unsure if he should even say anything.

"Because what?" Jacqueline was smiling.

"Because I'd like to know more about you."

"I'm pleased you said that. I'll bring the main course through and we can go from there."

Chapter Thirty-four

"A meal fit for a king, so it was."

"Such a pity to waste it on the court jester," retorted Laura.

Reilly chuckled. They were sprawled out across the sofa in the living room, listening to a Clannad CD.

Laura jumped up and cleared away the takeaway cartons before returning with two beers. She cuddled up next to Reilly.

"How's Stewart? It must be hard for him. Christmas, the anniversary of Sarah's death."

"Something's bothering him. I wouldn't put it all down to Sarah's death."

Laura straightened up. "Why do you say that?"

"Little things. You know how professional he is. Nothing escapes him. The harder the case, the more he thrives on it. He doesn't seem himself at the moment, though. His temper is a little shorter. He's distracted. He's not thinking as quick as usual." Reilly sighed. He didn't like to see his friend so preoccupied.

"Are you sure?"

"Of course I'm sure. Take today. There was an incident on the grounds of a church. We met up with an old vagrant…"

"That would have been enough to distract him."

"I could tell he didn't want to be near him. In fact, the vagrant was no threat at all. Didn't even attempt to come near us. But there was a genuine fear in Stewart's eyes. The man clearly had something to tell us, but the boss man hung back."

"Did you ask him why?"

"No. The only reason I persuaded him to listen was because the vagrant reminded me of old Seamus."

"Old Seamus. I miss him."

Seamus was Laura's grandfather. When Sean Reilly was seven years old, he and his family had moved to the beautiful golden coastline known as Giant's Causeway, in a town called Portballintrae. Sean struck up a friendship with the old man, a wise old bird who taught him valuable lessons about life.

"Anything else?"

Reilly took a long swig of his beer. "Nothing you can put your finger on. He's just distracted in general."

"I can think of something that's capable of causing such a distraction."

"Oh, you can, can you? And what would that be?"

"Sounds to me like he may have met someone."

Reilly nearly choked on his beer. "Would you listen to yourself? This is Stewart Gardener we're talking about. There's only been one woman for him, always will be."

"You listen to yourself, Sean Reilly! He's only human. He's been without close companionship for a year now. Maybe he feels it's time, and he's found someone. Which is why he's distracted."

"I think you've been drinking with the faeries back home. I'm telling you there's no woman in the boss man's life. He doesn't have the time. Dear God, he's not so much as looked at another woman since Sarah."

"Have it your way, but you'll see I'm right, so you will!"

Chapter Thirty-five

With the meal long since finished, Gardener and the minister had made themselves comfortable in the living room. Dimmed wall lights and the soft music had created a relaxed atmosphere. She'd talked about her job and he'd listened intently, but he still didn't know a lot about the real person behind the collar.

"What really influenced your decision to become a minister?" asked Gardener.

"My aunt," Jacqueline paused. "Well, I call her my aunt, but she's my great aunt really. She's my grandmother's sister, not my mother's.

"I'd like you to meet her, Stewart. She's been a tower of strength to me since my mother passed away. I think you'd like each other. She's lived her entire life according to the Bible. But one thing she doesn't do is force her opinions on you. On anyone, really.

"I was angry when my mother died. I blamed everyone, including myself. Sometimes I thought she'd died because of me, because of something I'd done. I couldn't work out what. It's funny the things you think when you're a child. If your parents argue and they mention your name, you think you've caused it. My aunt pulled me through."

Jacqueline sipped her wine. "She was only a baby when the family left Romania and came to England. They had no money, nowhere to live, but above all, they knew God would look after them. When I realized how much strength and conviction her faith had given her, I knew that it could work for me. She leads a very simple life, asks nothing of anyone, and she's so happy. When that finally sunk in, I knew it was what I wanted. To be just like her."

Jacqueline filled his empty wine glass without asking if he wanted more.

"You've never mentioned your father," said Gardener. "Is he still alive?"

"I haven't seen him for years. I've never forgiven him for the nasty things he said and did after my mother died. He was awful to me. I think he blamed me for her death. He used to shout at me, hit me, criticize me for the slightest thing. Which is how I ended up with a chipped tooth and a broken little finger." She held her left hand aloft for him to see. "I think he wanted me to take my mother's place, be everything she was. How could I? I was only ten years old. I could barely make toast, yet he expected his meals to be there."

"Didn't your aunt help?"

"I don't think she was aware of what was going on. He tried to keep a lid on everything. Kept us apart, instead of bringing us together so we could all help each other. He was selfish, manipulative. Sly. He never truly learned to love someone, not even my mother."

"When did you go and live with your aunt?"

"When I was thirteen. My mother had been dead three years. My father spent too much time at work to notice me. He had nothing but his precious newspaper."

"He was a journalist?"

"I think he started as a tea boy and worked his way up. The period of time I'm talking about, he was the owner. Don't ask me how. I've no idea where the money came from to buy the newspaper. He always said we were broke. I was never given pocket money. He didn't seem to trust me with the housekeeping. Can you imagine how embarrassed I was when I needed items of personal hygiene? I couldn't take any more."

Jacqueline sat in silence, perhaps composing herself. "He never came to see me. Do you know I never even had a birthday card from him?" Her eyes filled with tears. "So, you see, no mother, no father."

"It must have been hard."

"Which is why I looked towards my aunt. She was my mother, in every sense of the word."

Jacqueline smiled. "My aunt always claimed she had more children than any other woman alive. She's a walking encyclopaedia on plants. She has them all over the house and calls them her children."

Gardener laughed loudly. "She should meet my father. They'd get on like a house on fire."

He finished his wine. Jacqueline fetched another bottle from the kitchen. "Are you sure?" he asked.

"No. But I'm relaxed, I'm enjoying our evening together, and I'd like it to continue."

He didn't comment, so she poured another, before asking: "So, your father is a plant man?"

"Oh, you wouldn't believe it. He found something he wanted out of life and stuck with it. He inherited the business from his father. Apparently, my grandfather was a workaholic. Ran himself into an early grave. My grandmother took the business on and eventually passed it down to my father. He's retired now, but you still can't get him out of the greenhouse. Even in winter!"

"Your father and my aunt should definitely meet." Jacqueline paused, hesitated before continuing. "When we were laughing earlier, about your father and my aunt being a good match, maybe we are."

That one comment completely turned his mood. His stomach flipped. His legs weakened.

If he managed to keep his food down, it would be a bonus. It was the one thing he'd been terrified of hearing.

Jacqueline took his hand and stood up. She was obviously expecting him to do the same.

He did, but his emotions were all over the place. Any red-blooded man would have jumped at the chance the minister was offering. But he wasn't any man.

Her expression grew concerned. "What's wrong?"

A little over a year had passed since Sarah's death. He had never allowed his thoughts to stray from her memory. She had meant the world to him. Still did. The situation between him and Jacqueline wasn't right. She wanted more than he could give.

"Is it me?" she asked.

He had only ever made love to Sarah. She had been his only partner. He simply couldn't deal with what Jacqueline was asking for.

"No. I'm afraid it's me. I'm sorry."

He found his hat and made his exit, leaving Jacqueline alone.

Chapter Thirty-six

Gardener stood up and stretched his aching muscles, sighing loudly as he did so. Glancing at his watch, he saw it was still early, a little after seven o'clock. He'd spent the last three hours in the garage tending to the needs of the Bonneville.

He'd arrived home a little after one o'clock. The house was still warm. Everyone had retired for the night. He'd made some tea and sat near the fireplace, trying to figure out the mess he called his mind. As much as he liked the minister, he simply couldn't see himself being anything more than a friend. It was far too early to start a relationship with anyone. Maybe he never would again. Even if he hadn't been frightened of starting something physical, the timing was not right. His workload was too demanding.

Gardener had fallen asleep in the chair, empty mug in hand. He awoke two hours later when the room had chilled. Instead of going to bed, he made another drink, changed into his work gear, and slipped into the garage, confident that it would help him relax and think more clearly.

He'd really made some headway with the Bonneville. He'd managed to lift it into a specially made frame his father had put together years ago for his own bikes. From there he'd removed the wheels and the exhaust pipes, both of which were going to need extensive renovation. But he wasn't going anywhere. He had time on his side.

He'd read that the bike had a compression ratio of 8.5:1, was fitted with an alloy head, a half-race inlet camshaft, and Amal Monobloc carburettors fed by a remote float chamber. None of which he fully understood the function of, but all of which were now on the bench in front of him. He was happy with what he'd achieved.

The garage door that led into the house opened. His father walked in. "Here you are."

"Morning, Dad."

"I was getting a little concerned about you. Your bed's not been slept in. Kettle's boiled. Would you like something?"

"Please. Where's Chris?"

"In his room."

They headed into the kitchen. Malcolm put a cup of herbal tea on the table, sitting opposite Gardener. "You look as if you haven't slept all night."

"Well, not much of it anyway. I was home about one. Fell asleep in the chair. Woke up a couple of hours later and went into the garage."

"Looks like the Bonneville was a good investment."

Gardener thought about that. "I'm beginning to think so. I just wish Sarah was here to see it."

"I'm sure she's watching from somewhere."

"I sincerely hope so." He sipped more of his tea.

"How's Chris?"

"Disappointed. A little concerned. Maybe you should have let us know you were home."

"I know." Gardener took another sip. "About last night. It wasn't what you think. In fact, far from it."

Malcolm leaned forward. "You don't owe me any explanations, son. There are some things in our lives we should keep private. I should think my son's love life might be one of them."

"Chris might be looking for answers."

"It's a difficult time for him. Psychologically, he probably hasn't recovered from his mother's death yet. Give him time, he'll come round."

His father's response, although wise, did nothing to alleviate his guilt. "What did you end up doing yesterday?"

"I took him into town. Spent a bit of money. We had dinner, tea, and then went to the cinema as planned."

Although his father was seventy, he was fit for his age. He stood a little over six feet, with a full head of steel grey hair and a strong, angular face. Gardener envied his father's physique and his complexion, which – in his opinion – had been the result of a good standard of living and plenty of fresh air.

"Stop worrying about him." His father paused. "Hark at me. I worry about you. You work all the hours God sends. It's time you thought about yourself. Did something with your life other than work."

"I have to work hard," replied Gardener wearily. "These cases won't solve themselves."

"There are other policemen."

"But they all take their orders from me. It's not the type of job where you can switch off. There's always someone committing a crime somewhere. Almost every minute of every day. The problem I have at the moment is two murders on my patch at the wrong time of the year. Not that there's a good time, but Christmas fast approaching doesn't help."

"Certainly won't help Lesley Vickers," replied his father.

"I know how she feels. So do you, come to that. I know they're a big family, but I doubt it will help. There's just more of them to miss David."

"Have you any leads?" asked Malcolm, sipping his coffee.

"Not so far. You know what infuriates me? We've had three missing children. One now dead, and no one has seen anything."

"I don't think people pay any attention anymore, son. Life is lived at a pace that doesn't give you time to stop and think. They're all flying around in their own little world."

"Maybe you're right."

"Your job's no different, Stewart. All credit to you for being dedicated, but it's not healthy."

"I'm trying to secure a good life for us all, and it's getting harder. God knows what's happening to the economy. Nothing ever gets any cheaper. I sometimes think we'll all end up working every waking hour just to keep our heads above water.

"Listen, I want to thank you for all the help you've been. Especially with Chris. I'd hate to think what kind of a mess he or I'd be in now without you."

"You've no need to thank me, son. I love being around him, and I appreciate having a roof over my head. It means I can have quality time with you both."

"You've been a tonic for both of us. I think it's you that's kept us all together. I realize how much I'm taking you for granted. You're always there for Chris after school. You cook his meals, clean the house. You go out with him more than I do. Don't think I haven't noticed. I have, and I'm eternally grateful."

Gardener paused before changing the subject again. "You said I ought to get out more. What about you? The relationship with us must have its drawbacks. The only interest you seem to have is the gardening club once a week."

Gardener sensed his father's hesitation before answering. "Stewart, I'm happy with my life. When your mum died, I didn't know how I was going to cope. My whole world was just one big void. I was hollow on the inside. I felt as if someone had ripped my guts out and poured ice-cold water through my veins. Despite all that, you were there for me. Looking after you was the best therapy I could have had. And though it may not seem like it to you, it was what kept me going.

"After Sarah died, I knew it was going to be tough. I wanted to use my experience to help you. I appreciate everything I'm getting out of it. I'm spending time with my son, and my grandson. It doesn't feel like a chore. You certainly don't have to apologize for anything."

A lump formed in Gardener's throat. "I just want you to know I appreciate it, Dad."

"I know you do. We're a family, and families help each other."

A break in the conversation allowed Gardener to return to the subject of his father's club.

"So, about this club. You can't be learning much. After a lifetime in the business, you must know everything there is to know about plants."

"It isn't the plants so much as the company."

"Really?" Was that a glint in his father's eye he'd noticed? "Anyone in particular?"

"No, not at all."

Gardener was onto something. His father's reply was too quick and guarded. "Oh, come on. What do you take me for? I'm a detective. You think I haven't noticed a smarter appearance than usual of late? The new aftershaves? The fact that you've been coming home progressively later?"

Malcolm's wide grin led to a defensive chuckle. "You're too bloody sharp for your own good."

Gardener was about to speak when Chris came stomping down the stairs and into the kitchen, dressed in jeans, a sweatshirt, and trainers.

"You okay, Chris?" he asked, tentatively.

His son volunteered a cursory grunt while helping himself to some cereal.

Malcolm rose from the table. "I think I'll leave you two alone. I'll be in the potting shed if you want me."

Chris sat opposite Gardener and proceeded to destroy his Weetabix, banging the spoon into the dish, sighing heavily.

"Something bothering you, Chris?"

"What makes you think that?"

"I think we'll call it intuition. Whatever it is, don't bottle it up. Everything will seem twice as bad. You're angry with me."

"It's nothing to do with me, is it?"

"What's nothing to do with you?"

"What you get up to!"

"What did I get up to?" If Gardener wanted Chris to show his cards, using psychology was the only way to do it. In all honesty, though, now was not the best time.

"You stayed out all night!"

"Which I'm entitled to do. But as it happens, I didn't. I was here."

"You could have let Granddad know. He was worried."

"So, it's your granddad you're worried about?"

Chris was still prodding the Weetabix. "You're never here for me these days, Dad."

Gardener felt his anger building. "That's not true, and you know it."

"It is true. All you think about is your job. We were supposed to go out yesterday, but your job came first."

"There's nothing I can do about the hours I work. You know that. I always make sure your granddad is here to cover for me. He fills me in on what's going on. I try to be here when I can, but at the moment, the job is more demanding than usual. You know what happened to David Vickers. It's up to me to catch the person responsible, see it doesn't happen again."

"Whatever!" Chris shouted. He slammed his spoon down and left the table, storming out of the kitchen.

Gardener stood up, following Chris through the living room, up the stairs and into his bedroom. He wasn't leaving it. He'd been intending to apologize to his son and, as usual, the debate had escalated out of control very quickly.

"Don't walk out on me, Chris. We won't solve anything."

Gardener was appalled as he stopped suddenly and examined the state of the room.

"When was the last time you cleaned up? Look at it, it's a tip!"

Chris's bed was unmade. Drawers and wardrobe doors stood open, their contents spilling out onto the floor. The bin overflowed with crisp packets and chocolate wrappers. Endless piles of CDs were out of their cases.

"Oh, you've noticed something!"

"I couldn't fail but notice, could I?" shouted Gardener. "Before you go anywhere, I want your room spotless."

Chris made to push past him. Gardener halted him by placing a hand on his shoulder.

"I've told you once already, don't you walk away from me."

"What difference does it make if my room's clean or not? I doubt you'll see it for another year."

For a split second, Gardener saw Sarah in his son's face. During their frequent disagreements, Sarah displayed an infuriating, pouting-mouth expression that followed a line of sarcasm. Chris had inherited the trait.

"You don't care anymore."

"Stop saying that!" Gardener yelled.

"Okay, if you care, what happened to the new trainers I asked for?"

"Trainers? What trainers?" Gardener was momentarily stunned, unable to remember any conversation regarding trainers.

"If you'd been listening, I told you I needed a pair of new trainers for the five-a-side trials. I haven't got them, so I probably won't get picked." Chris edged past him and headed for the stairs. "It's always the same. You're never here. When you are, you never listen! It could have been me instead of David Vickers, but I doubt you'd have noticed."

"Don't you dare say that! You come back here now and apologize, you little…" Gardener chased after him but wasn't quick enough. Chris was out the back door, and riding his bike down the path.

"Chris? If you don't come back, you're gonna be in serious trouble, young man." Gardener was furious, running after his son, determined not to let him put too much distance between them.

Chris glanced back. Judging by the alarmed expression on his face, he wasn't staying around if he could help it. Malcolm emerged from the potting shed.

Gardener raised his hands in the air as Chris turned the corner and shot down the main street. Gardener turned to face his father, infuriated. It was more than the episode with Chris that had caused his mood. He felt he was beginning to lose control of everything.

Malcolm put a hand on his shoulder. "Calm down, son."

"You should have heard the way he spoke to me."

"Give it a rest. He'll come back when he's calmed down."

Gardener turned without saying anything. Back in the kitchen, the telephone was ringing.

He couldn't work out what was going wrong between him and Chris. Maybe it had something to do with the anniversary of Sarah's death preying on his mind. The phone continued to ring. Gardener couldn't for the life of him remember Chris saying anything about trainers. Did a memory loss constitute being a bad father?

Still the phone rang. He went back inside and lifted the receiver. "Stewart Gardener."

"Sir, it's Frank Thornton. Is your mobile switched off?"

Gardener checked and found it was. Couldn't remember when he'd done that.

"What can I do for you, Frank?"

"I have a couple of messages. They sound important. Derek Summers has made contact. He's free this afternoon if you want to see him."

"Good. Ring Sean and have him pick me up. What's the second?"

"Janet Soames, she has important information for you. Very urgent, so she says."

"Did she leave a number?"

Gardener wrote down the details, then dialled her after hanging up on Frank. "Mrs Soames? Detective Inspector Gardener here."

"Oh, Mr Gardener. I've been trying to contact you. It's about David Vickers. I spoke to one of my friends yesterday. She saw the boy who took David from school. Apparently, they were in the post office on the day in question. He had quite a bit of money. Bought David some computer games."

"Can you give me your friend's details? Would she recognize him again?"

"Oh, yes. It was his face, you see. She said she'd never forget the face. It was strange, misshapen. Covered in warts."

Gardener felt nauseous, allowing the phone to drop.

"Mr Gardener... are you still there?"

Chapter Thirty-seven

The car journey was spent in near silence. It was only after Reilly parked the car and killed the engine that he turned to face Gardener.

"Is something bothering you, boss?"

Gardener paused before he spoke. "You remember the night Sarah died? I had a run-in with a youth I nicknamed 'Warthead'." Gardener rubbed his forehead. "We may have found a witness who saw Warthead with David Vickers on the day he was abducted. Buying him presents."

The call to Mrs Soames had left Gardener enraged. During the year following Sarah's death, he had constantly been on his guard where Warthead was concerned. He'd watched every street corner, scanned faces in crowds. For a short period immediately after the incident, he'd questioned known thugs. No one claimed to have known the youth. As time had passed, he'd been convinced their paths would probably never cross again, particularly as the youth had a cockney accent. The chances were he'd disappeared back down south.

"Have you spoken to this witness yet?"

"Not yet. Janet Soames called to tell me."

"Okay," said Reilly. He pulled his mobile out. "I'll get Colin Sharp onto it. He can update the whiteboard."

Mushrooming grey clouds hovered menacingly overhead, typical of a December afternoon, as Gardener stepped out of the car and studied his surroundings. Derek Summers' huge house was Tudor, set in an enchanting forest with ornamental carvings and shaped bushes. A circular fountain stood proudly as the magnificent centrepiece on the gravel drive. The lawn was neatly trimmed. The building was well kept, with clean windows and freshly painted walls. The grounds, as far as Gardener could see, were litter free. There was obviously money to be made in the entertainment industry.

"I wouldn't mind a slice of this!" said Reilly.

"We are in the wrong business, Sean."

As they approached the steps leading to the house, the front door opened. An elderly butler emerged to greet them. "Good afternoon, gentlemen. Can I help you?"

Both detectives flashed their warrant cards before introducing themselves.

"Mr Summers will see you shortly. If you would like to follow me."

Gardener and Reilly exchanged glances but followed as requested. They were shown to a study, where they politely declined an offer of refreshments. The butler closed the door behind him as he left.

Gardener paced the parquet floor. The panelled walls were decorated with a variety of old-time music hall and film posters. Aside from the oversized writing desk and matching chairs, the only other decoration was a Persian rug.

Gardener turned to his partner. "Do you hear that?"

"What?"

"Exactly. Nothing. Absolutely nothing. When have you ever been in a house and felt so isolated, so cut off? You'd expect to hear something."

The study door opened. The host entered.

"Gentlemen."

Gardener's dislike of Summers was instant. He was small and balding except for a fringe of hair over his ears. He wore thin, wire-framed spectacles over a small snub nose. His moist lips were thick. He was dressed in a charcoal grey pinstripe suit with a white shirt and grey tie.

Summers chose to sit at his desk. Before speaking, he lit a cigar. "Now, what can I do for you?" he asked with a condescending air.

Gardener studied the agent's gold cufflinks with matching Rolex watch before answering.

"I'm DI Gardener. This is my partner, DS Reilly. We're investigating the death of a man we understand worked for you."

"And it was so urgent you couldn't wait till normal working hours?"

"I'm not fortunate enough to work normal hours, Mr Summers."

"Quite. So, who is it?"

Gardener was not impressed by Summers' brusque manner. He felt as if he was merely being tolerated. Reilly produced his pad and pen and started making notes as Gardener replied.

"Bernard Thornwell. He was found murdered yesterday. We have reason to believe he worked for you."

Summers inhaled deeply on the cigar, billowing smoke above his head. "He did, and he didn't."

Gardener could see he was going to have trouble with Summers. He'd had a gutful of that already today. "Which means what?"

"He did, but only on a part-time basis."

"What exactly do you do? I have a card here that says you're an entertainment agent."

"Yes." Summers puffed on the cigar. "Entertainment agent is only a part of it. I do employ people to work as clowns and Father Christmas for children, but I also run a casting agency for adults, and I'm actively involved with a film production company."

"What sort of films?"

"Travel documentaries. I have contacts abroad. My company promotes the travel industry in Britain."

"So, Bernard Thornwell, what can you tell me about him?"

"Nothing much. Worked for me as a Santa Claus in various department stores. On a number of occasions he attended children's parties as a clown."

"When did you last see him?"

"A couple of weeks ago, I think. I don't really remember, Mr Gardener. I'm a busy man." Summers started to inspect his nails, as though bored.

"Had he worked for you in the last two weeks?" asked Gardener.

Summers glanced at his watch impatiently. "Yes. I believe he was covering the Debenhams department store in the city."

"You believe? You either know or you don't."

Summers smirked, irritating Gardener further. "Mr Gardener, I can't mentally keep track of everyone. I would have records, however."

"In that case, go and get them." It was an order, not a request. Summers rose and left the study without a word.

"I don't like him," Gardener said to his partner.

"I'm none too keen on him myself."

The study door opened. Summers came back in with a number of books and ledgers.

"Here we are, gentlemen." He placed them on the desk and sat back in his chair.

"I'm taking these with me, Mr Summers. Is there anything else you'd like to tell me about Bernard Thornwell?"

"Not really. He was someone who worked for me on various occasions. We certainly didn't socialize. A pleasant enough chap, did a good job, punctual."

"Did you ever have any problems with him?"

"What sort of problems?"

"Anything. Did he ever turn up for work drunk? Did he have money problems?"

"Nothing I can recall."

Gardener put the books to one side and fixed him with a steely gaze. "It would appear that Bernard Thornwell had a colleague with whom he socialized. One Herbert Plum, who also died under mysterious circumstances. Did he work for you as well?"

The change in the agent's manner was only slight, but it was enough for Gardener. "Yes, Mr Gardener, he did."

"Did they use their own names when they worked for you?"

"Yes."

Summers had not taken a drag on his cigar but continued to hold it. The ash was growing in length.

"Did Plum also work on a part-time basis?"

"Yes. Where are you going with this, Mr Gardener?"

"For a man who's lost two of his employees recently, you don't seem overly concerned," commented Reilly.

"As you said, Mr Reilly, they were colleagues, not relatives."

"All the same, I'd be asking myself a number of questions. Like who's next? Have I done anything to upset anyone? Do you know what I mean?"

"I know exactly what you mean. If you're looking for me to do your job by providing you with suspects, then I'm afraid you're wasting your time, gentlemen. I pay my taxes, which pays your wages, so I suggest you look a little harder somewhere else." Summers stood up. "Now, if you've quite finished…"

"We haven't," Gardener said, sternly. On the outside, Summers was cool, but underneath, he was concerned. Gardener wanted to know why. "Two people who work for you are dead. And I'd like to know a damned sight more than you've given us. Who else do you employ in the same line of work?"

"Who is your superior, Mr Gardener?"

"Detective Chief Inspector Briggs, why do you ask?"

"Because I don't like your attitude."

"Feel free to complain any time you like, Mr Summers. However, I'm conducting a serious investigation, which I intend to solve. Everything I'm doing is within the law. Until I've finished, you will help with that investigation. Now, Bernard Thornwell and Herbert Plum. Are you aware of any of their associates? Do you have anyone else on your books in the same line of work?"

Summers sat back down, finally taking a drag on his cigar. "No."

"So, you run an entertainment agency which seems to specialize in providing amusement for the wee children, yet you only have two clowns who double up as Father Christmas. Sort of leaves you in a spot of trouble, wouldn't you say?" Reilly fixed his glare on Summers as he spoke.

"Not at all, Officer Reilly. If I were to rely solely on clowns and Christmas for my income, I'd hardly be living in such splendour, would I? Running the entertainment agency is only part of my business, and even then, I only used those two as a favour to them. Most of my business is concerned with acts on the cabaret circuit and theatres. I also provide look-alikes for a casting agency. Besides the travel films."

"Why were you doing favours for Plum and Thornwell?" asked Gardener.

"I've known the two gentlemen a number of years. They approached me for work and there was a time when I kept them both busy. But times change, Mr Gardener. Children no longer want parties with clowns. Nowadays it's off to McHerbert's and a computer game when you get home."

When Summers failed to elaborate, Gardener pushed. "You still haven't explained the favour."

Summers drew on the cigar, blowing smoke up toward the ceiling. "They were hardly what you'd call flush. Since I'd known and seen them both through the good times, I thought, as a favour, I could help them through the bad."

"Well, they've hit rock bottom now, have they not?" said Reilly. "So, you don't know any of their associates?"

"As I said, we didn't socialize."

Gardener stood and paced the room with his hands in his pockets. "Judging by what you've said, you'd have no idea why anyone would want to kill them?"

"None at all."

"You were never involved with either of them for any reason other than business?"

"I had no reason to be, Mr Gardener."

Gardener was beginning to sense the little man's smug attitude returning. "During what little time you did spend together, did either man seem worried about anything?"

"I've already told you, I didn't socialize with them. I hardly knew them."

"You said a few minutes ago you'd known them a number of years."

"Yes, but only as business associates."

Reilly leaned on his desk. "Tell me, aren't you the least bit curious why two people who work for you have both been killed within a week of each other?"

"I should think it obvious I don't travel in the same circles as my employees. Especially the part-time ones." Summers smirked.

"How do you know?" Gardener asked. "You said you don't socialize."

Summers shook his head before answering. "Look, gentlemen, I don't feel threatened. Now, or at any other time. I'm a simple man. I do my job, keep to myself, and I pay my way. Whatever those two were into, it's none of my business."

"Any experience with drugs?"

"Drugs?"

"Yes... drugs. The entertainment industry is notorious for drug taking. I wondered if you'd encountered any drug problems?"

"Occasionally. I am aware of the narcotic problems within the business. There were a couple of instances some time ago where I had to stop using a couple of artists. They nearly brought a theatre into disrepute. Nothing more than that. I certainly don't take them."

Gardener switched topics. "Does the name Craig Sutton mean anything to you?"

"I can't say it does."

Gardener sat back down. "We discovered a number of pornographic films and magazines in Herbert Plum's flat. You wouldn't know anything about that, would you?"

"Should I?"

"Doesn't it concern you that a man you employed to entertain children also indulges in pornography?"

Summers stubbed out his cigar and glanced at his watch. "We all have our dark side, Mr Gardener."

"You haven't answered my question."

"No, it doesn't concern me too much. What they chose to get up to in their own time is up to them. Did you find any porn involving children?"

"Not yet," replied Gardener.

"Was Herbert Plum a convicted paedophile?"

"Not a convicted one, to my knowledge."

"Then there's no reason for me to be concerned."

"As I said, not a convicted paedophile. He may have been one, for all we know."

"I'm sure you'll understand how difficult it is to extract everything from employees. My only interest was how well he did his job. I had no cause for complaint on that score."

"Would you have employed him had you known?" asked Reilly.

"What kind of a question is that?"

"A straightforward one."

"I didn't know, so it doesn't matter," Summers replied.

"Herbert Plum was recently involved in an incident in a public house," continued Gardener. "Apparently, he told someone he had contacts in the film world. He then went on to offer a woman the chance to star in a pornographic film. You wouldn't have any idea who the contact might be, would you?"

Summers seemed surprised. "Why should I?" He gazed at the ceiling. "What a bloody mess!"

"Forgive me," said Gardener, standing. "I'm putting two and two together. It crossed my mind. Films. Entertainers. Entertainment agency. Plum's implicated you by association, Mr Summers. Is it possible he used your name without your knowledge? Let's face it, you're there in the Yellow Pages. Legitimate. Plum could have been riding on the back of your business for his own private reasons, without you realizing. Then again, maybe you did."

Summers flew out of his chair. "How dare you?" His cheeks were red, and the corners of his mouth were flecked with spittle.

Gardener said nothing but casually wiped his collar and smiled.

"I'll have your badge for this, Gardener."

"I don't have a badge."

"You know what I mean," Summers shouted.

"No," replied Gardener. "Maybe you should explain."

"Your outrageous accusations." Summers danced around the desk before standing directly in front of the two detectives.

"I haven't made any."

Summers raised a hand. "You intimated I made pornography!"

"But I didn't accuse you. Look at the facts, Mr Summers. Two corpses connected with your company. One with an unsavoury interest in pornography. Both, until recently, regularly employed by you. What conclusions would you draw?" Gardener turned to Reilly. "Are you ready, Sean?"

The detectives made for the door. As Gardener opened it, he turned back toward Summers, who had not moved. "One more question. I'm not a handwriting expert, but from your books, I'd say you were left-handed. Am I right?"

The little man gave him a perplexed expression. "What does my being left-handed have to do with anything?"

"Answer the question!"

"Yes, I am. Now, will you please leave? I do have appointments to keep."

"I appreciate your time, Mr Summers," Gardener smiled, tipping his hat. "But I'm not happy. I think you're hiding something. I will be back."

On the way back to the car, Gardener said to Reilly, "I want a full investigation on that man. I want to know everything he's done since the day he was born."

Chapter Thirty-eight

"Have you seen the papers?"

Briggs slammed a copy of *The Yorkshire Post* down on his desk. The two detectives stared at the headline: "Police Violence!"

It was no less than Gardener expected. As he read through it, the article was filled with details of the murder, uncooperative detectives, and police brutality. The broadsheet had then decided to run an opinion poll, 'Did the public have a right to know?' One diligent reporter had also insinuated a link between the Rawston incident and the corpse found within the grounds of St John's Church.

Briggs glared at Reilly. "Slipped your mind, did it, Reilly? The fact that you'd assaulted a reporter?"

"I didn't."

"It's not what he says."

"He sells papers."

"You took his camera away from him," said Briggs, leaning back in his chair.

"Which isn't assault," argued Reilly.

Briggs turned over the front page. "I think the photograph taken here paints a different picture."

In the shot, Reilly had his hands around the photographer's throat as they tumbled. "It isn't how it looks."

"So you keep saying. How is it, then? 'cause from where I'm sitting, it's assault."

"I tried to stop him taking any more photos, and I fell down the steps."

"Oh, come on, Reilly, even you can do better than that. You're not exactly known for using kid gloves. Are you really trying to tell me it was an accident?"

"What's the point in me saying anything? You'll believe what you want, at the end of the day."

Briggs turned to Gardener. "What have you got to say about it?"

"I'm with him. You've seen the photo, and you've obviously made your mind up."

Briggs stood, knocking his chair over in the process. "There's a lot of point! I want your version of events. All I've had from you two so far is a boat load of trouble, and you're no nearer to catching the killer. You've no idea what's being used to kill the victims. I have a landlord putting in a claim against us because you wrecked his pub. Now, we have the newspapers claiming police brutality. The Chief Constable is furious. I've had him breathing down my neck all bloody morning. So now can you see why I want an explanation?"

Gardener didn't need the aggravation or the pressure the case was putting on them. He was well aware of how it appeared without Briggs listing his grievances. "I know how bad things look at the moment, but the case is not cut and dried. You've seen all the reports. Whichever line of inquiry we take, it's a dead end."

Briggs sighed, repositioning his chair before sitting down. "We can't afford bad publicity. The newspapers could cripple us. Have you any idea of the repercussions a picture like this will have?"

"Of course I have. I've been in the force long enough to realize what parasites reporters are, and how they manipulate the public. But I can't pull answers out of thin air."

"More's the pity! Because before long, we'll need to." The atmosphere in the room descended into an icy silence before Briggs spoke again. "How did you get on with Summers?"

Gardener was surprised by the question. He'd expected Summers to have placed a formal complaint. Perhaps Briggs was playing his cards close to his chest. "I don't like him."

"I didn't ask whether or not you liked him."

"I didn't mean it like that." Gardener told Briggs about the interview, how he felt about Summers, and the fact that it was what he didn't say as opposed to what he did that led Gardener to believe a further investigation of the entertainment agent was necessary.

"So, what now?" Briggs asked.

"It's time we arrested Sutton."

"For what?"

"Suspicion of murder. He withheld information from you," Gardener said matter-of-factly.

Briggs sighed. "Tell me what you know."

"The landlord of the pub in Rawston said he'd overheard Sutton threatening to kill Plum and Thornwell if he ever saw them in the pub again. Later, he was overheard swearing revenge."

Briggs held his hands up. "None of which makes him a killer."

"Maybe not, but he didn't tell you, did he?"

"Well, he was never going to tell me everything. It was off the record. He was trying to bargain his way out of trouble."

"That may be, but couple it with Fitz's information about the syringe, and he's definitely a suspect. Although Fitz doesn't know what's being used, he knows it's injected directly into the jugular vein.

"The only way you're going to be able to do that without a major struggle is if you drug the victim first. Or you're extremely powerful." Gardener sensed his superior officer's reluctance to bring in his informant.

Briggs sighed. "Okay. Bring him in. Talk to him."

Chapter Thirty-nine

Gardener studied Sutton, wondering what made him tick. Covered in tattoos, he weighed well over twenty stone, most of which was a huge beer belly. His face still bore the bruises from his last meeting with Reilly. He didn't work, he was unsociable, and his main source of income was drug money, according to gossip. Gardener hadn't seen Sutton's girlfriend, but the thought alone made him shudder.

"Let's make it clear," Gardener started. "You haven't been arrested. You're simply here to help with our inquiries. You're free to leave whenever you want. You've not requested the attendance of your own solicitor, nor the duty solicitor. And you're quite happy with DCI Briggs sitting in. Detective Sergeant Reilly and I are investigating the deaths of Herbert Plum and Bernard Thornwell. How well did you know those men?"

"I didn't know Thornwell. Seen him in the pub a few times."

"What about Plum?"

Sutton sighed. "I didn't really know either of 'em."

"When we spoke to you less than a week ago, you called Plum a pervert, which suggests to me that you did. Or at the very least, felt you knew enough to pass an opinion."

Sutton's temper flared. "He were trying to pull me bird for a porn film. Me there! In the same flaming pub..."

"What exactly did you say to him?"

"I said I'd punch his lights out if I caught him talking to her again."

"And that's all?"

"More or less."

"Are you telling me everything?" Gardener pushed.

"Why wouldn't I be?"

"Because I have a witness who said you threatened to kill them both."

Sutton laughed. "I didn't mean it. I were just talking, trying to frighten 'em."

"You shouldn't say things you don't mean. After an argument, you threatened to kill them both if you saw them again. Both men are now dead. Try looking at it from my point of view."

Sutton pointed a finger. "Now look here, I never killed 'em. I might have said it. I were annoyed, I'd had a drink, but I didn't kill 'em!"

"Where were you on the night of Friday, 4th of December between 6:30 and 11:00pm?"

Sutton exhaled a long breath, glancing upwards. "I'd rather not say."

"Why not?" Gardener knew Sutton's alibi could land him in trouble that he'd be reluctant to admit to. Gardener didn't care. He had an investigation to run.

"Look, I can't tell you."

"That's a pity. You see, in order to eliminate you as a suspect, we need to be able to verify your whereabouts."

"I didn't do it!" shouted Sutton, gripping the edge of the table.

Gardener increased the pressure. "Then, tell me where you were."

Sutton glanced around the room. His breathing became heavier. "On a job," he muttered, quietly.

"Pardon?"

Sutton spoke through clenched teeth. "On a job. Are you satisfied now?"

"What sort of a job?"

"You know I can't tell you."

"You know you have to."

Sutton's hands were clasped together on the table, his fingers locking together and releasing in quick, spasmic movements. "I think I need to talk to my brief."

"Are you sure you want to do that, Mr Sutton?" replied Gardener, a little annoyed. His intention had not been to question Sutton about stolen paint. More to use it as a lever if needed.

"If you bring your brief in, I'll think you're hiding something. It might slip out that you were doing a job for Brian Thatchett, otherwise known as 'Thatchett The Hatchet'. You know as well as I do where he got that nickname from."

"Are you threatening me?" asked Sutton.

Gardener laughed. "Not at all. I'm simply saying that even with the best will in the world, it's impossible to keep everything from men like The Hatchet. Word eventually gets round that you spilled your guts to save yourself. Next thing you know, The Hatchet and his sharp little friend come looking for you, and you're history." Gardener paused and stood up, pushing his chair back. "Still…"

"Okay," said Sutton. "You win. You obviously know all about the paint job."

"Of course, I do," said Gardener, sitting back down. "But I haven't dragged you in to talk about paint. Did you ever notice Plum with anyone else other than Thornwell?"

"In the pub, you mean?"

"Anywhere."

"I never saw him outside the pub. He were often in the pub with a woman, one as runs the boarding house."

"Olive Bradshaw?"

"Aye, that's her."

"Were they friendly?"

"Sometimes."

"Enough to suggest a relationship?"

Sutton nodded. "I'd say so. They weren't always together. Sometimes he were with Thornwell, sometimes her. Before her brother popped his clogs, they all used to come in. There were summat funny going on there."

"Something funny?" inquired Gardener, his curiosity piqued.

"Nowt I could put me finger on, just summat odd. Wouldn't surprise me if they were all in films. Granny Sex, or summat like it. I don't know. Ask anybody in the pub, they'll all tell you."

Gardener was about to ask another question when Sutton continued speaking. "And then there were that freak! Ugly bastard he were."

"Who are you talking about now?" Gardener's skin suddenly started to itch.

"Oh, Christ! What were his name? Felix; that's it. Felix – face full of warts."

Gardener froze. A whole year had passed without a sighting of Warthead and, suddenly, two references within two days. "Face full of warts? Can you tell me anything else about him?"

Sutton shrugged. "There's not much more to say. He's about five feet tall, maybe nineteen or twenty, funny shaped head. Face full of warts."

"You ever hear him talk?"

"Yeah."

"Cockney accent?" pressed Gardener.

"No. Yorkshire."

Gardener was momentarily knocked off balance. What had happened to the cockney accent? Perhaps it was a put on. Gardener's problem suddenly escalated. If Warthead was local, how had he managed to evade him? Especially with a face like his?

"How was he usually dressed?"

"A fancy jacket. Black leather, gold eagle on the back. Some American slogan. Can't really remember."

"Genuine article? You wouldn't buy it in England?"

"I doubt it."

"Do you know anything else about Felix? Where he lived?"

"No, all I know is what I've told you. I only ever saw him about three times, but him and Plum were as thick as thieves when I did see them."

"Have you seen him in the pub recently?"

"No, last time were before Plum were killed."

Gardener's skin crawled, his guts churned. "Did you ever see Felix with anyone else other than Plum?"

"No."

"Not Thornwell?"

Sutton paused. "No, never with Thornwell."

"Did you see him with Plum when he was with Olive Bradshaw?"

"No. He were only ever with Plum."

"And you've no idea what kind of relationship they had?"

"What?" Sutton's expression suggested he was horrified by the question. "You mean, like, Felix and Plum, a couple of puffs?"

"I didn't necessarily mean that. I meant, how close? Father and son close, for instance? Or friends?"

Sutton paused and thought. Then shook his head. "I'm sorry, Mr Gardener, I don't know."

Gardener realized he was going to have to terminate the interview. He'd suspected all along that Sutton was no killer. Although he was disappointed, he had picked up some useful information. He checked his watch before nodding to Briggs and Reilly. To Sutton, he said, "One more thing before you go."

Gardener produced a document. "Can you just sign this for me?"

"What is it?" asked Sutton.

"It's nothing. Just a release paper. Lets you know you haven't been arrested, and you understand that you're not being charged. You know what it's like, all that red tape."

Gardener observed Sutton pick up the pen and sign the papers. With his right hand.

Chapter Forty

As Gardener approached the lab, he could hear Fitz on the other side of the doors.

Judging by the shouting, the pathologist's mood was bordering diabolical. As he opened the door, Fitz stopped mid-fury, turning and lowering his arms. He sighed at the sight of Gardener. "How many hours do they think I have in my day? I suppose you want a piece of me now, too?"

A quick survey of the lab informed Gardener that Fitz was letting off steam. The only other occupant was a lanky, twenty-year-old assistant tucked away in the far corner, paying little heed to the senior man. Gardener cautiously approached the gurney that Fitz was working on.

"What… is… that?"

"A mummy."

The sight of the bandaged corpse piqued Gardener's curiosity. "Where did it come from?"

"Sheffield."

Gardener studied it. The mummified rags were mouldy, covered in dust and cobwebs. The exterior appeared parched. He imagined one touch would disintegrate the whole thing.

Fitz continued. "Police in Sheffield found it in a cupboard at the top of the stairs. Young couple had bought the house. They were in the process of moving in, deciding what to decorate, where to put things, when they found it."

"How long's it been there?"

"Quite a while, I should imagine. It's virtually a carbon copy of the one found in a house in Rhyl, North Wales, in 1960. Leslie Harvey, a taxi-driver, was redecorating his mother's house while she was in hospital. The cupboard at the top of the stairs had always been locked since he was a boy. When curiosity got the better of him one day, he forced it open and found a mummy. It was stuck solid to the floor. They had to use a spade to prise it loose."

Gardener was surprised by his morbid fascination.

"Apparently Leslie's mother once had a semi-invalid lodger boarding with her. One day she found the lodger on the floor, screaming in agony. Shortly afterwards, the lodger died. His mother didn't know what to do, so she locked the body in the cupboard."

Gardener sighed but declined to comment.

Fitz strode over to the sink to clean up. When he'd finished, he said, "Follow me."

Gardener anticipated bad news. The pathologist entered his office and sat behind his desk. He slid a sealed bag with the syringe from the church grounds across the desk to Gardener.

"I take it you've found out what was in it?" Gardener asked as he examined it.

"Curare!"

"Pardon?"

"Takes some believing, doesn't it? I'm certain it belongs to the killer. It confirms earlier thoughts of the victim being incapacitated by something. You see, most drugs take time to act, which means the victim is capable of resistance. An injection of curare would paralyze the victim almost instantly, making a struggle impossible."

"What exactly is curare?"

"A skeletal-muscle-relaxant drug of botanical origin. It's used in modern medicine primarily as an auxiliary in general anaesthesia. But it's more widely known as a very old and lethal poison. One of the earliest encounters appears to have been during the exploration of the Lake Maracaibo region in Colombia by Alonzo Perez de Tolosa in 1548. Scientific studies of the substance began in the latter part of the eighteenth century with the Akawai Indians of Surinam. They used it as a poison on their arrows."

"Any idea why it's being used now? Here?"

Gardener was struggling to accept Fitz's findings. Lethal poisons, body-destroying chemicals. The outlook was growing bleaker by the day.

"Almost certainly as a blocking agent. It produces flaccidity in striated muscle. Which means it prevents nerve impulses from activating skeletal, or voluntary muscles. It's pretty dangerous stuff. I think the person you're looking for knows exactly what he's doing with it. It first affects the muscles of the toes, ears, and eyes, then the neck and the limbs and, finally, respiration. In fatal doses, death is caused by respiratory paralysis."

"Is curare capable of destroying the body?"

Fitz sighed. "No."

Gardener cursed and glanced upwards. "Marvellous."

"I wouldn't give up just yet. At least we know how the killer is operating. My guess is, the victims know the killer. I imagine they're taken by surprise, immediately injected with the curare which renders them disabled. Then the killer has the time to perform the real task."

"Would the victim be aware of what was happening?" asked Gardener.

"Almost certainly. We've done tests with curare. In fact, I did one yesterday with Richard." Fitz chuckled. Richard was his lanky assistant ignoring him in the corner. "Gave him a small dose. Frightened him half to death. He was aware of everything, even heard me talking, but he couldn't move a muscle. It wore off after a few minutes. He was all right. He didn't want to do it again, though."

That meant Gardener could certainly rule out Craig Sutton. Apart from the fact that Sutton was right-handed, he suspected Sutton was too big to work with such precision. Not to mention he lacked the intelligence to handle such a deadly toxin. The field was open again.

Gardener thought about Summers. Although he was convinced the agent had withheld information, there still wasn't enough evidence to suggest his involvement. Where did Warthead fit in? The motive was clear – revenge.

Someone out there had a grievance, a score to settle. The biggest question, however, was what had Thornwell and Plum done to warrant such a terrible death? *Christ! What a can of worms.*

"What are you thinking, Stewart?"

"I'm trying to eliminate suspects. Maybe I need to study the medical sector more closely."

"Possibly. As I've said, use too much, and you'll kill the victim. Your man is using the exact amount to keep his victim alive. Maybe even sadistic enough to talk to them, tell them why he's doing this before administering something even more disturbing. It's someone who's extremely intelligent, highly efficient. I think the syringe was deliberately thrown into the bushes for you to find. Whoever it is, they're more than likely playing games with us now."

"And you've still no idea what's destroying the body?"

"I'm sorry. I wish I could help you, but there's a distinct lack of evidence in that department. Matthew Stapleton is still no further on than I am."

Gardener rose and picked up the bag containing the syringe.

"So, where the hell do I go from here?"

Chapter Forty-one

Gardener's team was in the incident room at eight o'clock sharp. The air of trepidation was palpable. The last person in was Briggs, who shut the door and sat in one corner with his arms folded.

"There've been some new developments, but I'd like to see what you've gathered first," said Gardener. He was standing next to the spider chart with a pen at the ready. Glancing at Sharp, he asked, "Colin, what have you found out about Thornwell?"

Sharp addressed the gathering with the help of his notebook. "In some respects, he was similar to Plum. Bernard Thornwell was a sixty-three-year-old single male who lived in a bedsit in Middleton. Seems he had few friends, but a neighbour has confirmed one of them as being Herbert Plum. Thornwell was last seen on Friday afternoon when he left for work dressed as Santa Claus."

"Dressed as a Santa?" Gardener asked.

"Apparently, he used to get changed before he went to work. He was often seen in the local pubs wearing his uniform."

"Did this neighbour say anything about a clown's outfit?"

"No, only a Santa suit."

"Did he have any female acquaintances? Has he ever been married?"

"According to the neighbour, he was at one time. He and his wife lived in the Holt Park area. When she died about seven years ago, he was left with a lot of debts. He sold the house to clear them, and ended up in Middleton."

"Okay," said Gardener, bullet-pointing the information Sharp had relayed on the chart. When he'd finished, he turned back to the group. "There's a task for someone. Find out from his previous address all you can about him. What his wife was like, how the debts accumulated. Speak to old colleagues, neighbours. Go as far back as it takes. Dig up everything you can."

"Do you want me to cover that?" Sharp asked.

"No, I have something else in mind for you. Anything else to add?"

Sharp returned to his notes. "Unlike Plum, he paid his tax, national insurance. Had bank accounts, credit cards, and from what I've found out, didn't owe anyone anything."

"Compared to Herbert Plum he seems like a saint. But someone wanted him dead. So, there has to be an incident in his past. I want to know what it was. Did you search the flat, Colin? Any pornography?"

"It was clean, everything in its place. Food in the cupboards, bed made. The room was pretty tidy, considering he was a widower. No porn, but then again, no computer, which might answer for a lack of porn."

Gardener had hoped for a different answer. There had to be something to tie Plum and Thornwell together, apart from the fact that they both worked for Summers and were killed in identical circumstances. "Anything else?"

"No," said Sharp, sitting back down.

"Okay, good work. Your next task is to investigate an entertainment agent by the name of Derek Summers."

"What do you want to know?"

"Everything from the day he was born. Find out everything you can. Sean will tell you what we know, but I want you to go and personally build a dossier on the man. Whatever progress you make, you report directly to me. No one else, do you understand?"

"Yes, sir."

"The rest of you, listen carefully. Fitz gave us some important information yesterday. The syringe we found in the churchyard contained a lethal poison called curare."

"It's Agatha Christie," shouted Frank Thornton, glancing round, laughing.

"Very droll, Frank." Gardener waited for the laughter to subside before continuing. "In almost all the cases that Agatha Christie used it in her novels, someone was killed with it. Our killer is not using the curare in fatal doses. Fitz thinks it's being used as a paralyzing drug. He believes the dose is precisely measured so the victim is aware of what is happening to them. To make them suffer.

"Whoever is using the poison knows exactly the right amount to keep their victim alive and for how long. It's whatever they use after the curare that's really doing the damage."

"Does Fitz know what that is?" asked Briggs.

"Not yet."

"Do we need to widen the net, include doctors?" suggested Thornton.

"It's possible," said Gardener. "It could also be a chemist. I want every hospital consulted on curare, see if any amounts of the poison have gone missing. I want a check of all the doctors' surgeries. Find out if any of them keep it, particularly Thornwell's doctor." Gardener turned to Sharp. "I presume he had one."

"Yes, sir."

"Good. We'll need his details, check him out. I want two of you to continue digging into Plum and Thornwell's past. Dig deep. Check the sex offenders list. Could only be one isolated incident binding these two. I want to know what it is. For the time being, we can leave the drug dealers alone. It's not their territory, it's too specialized.

"The manipulation of the poison suggests the killer knows what they're doing. They are cunning. The syringe was probably left on purpose. Which means they're playing some kind of game with us. We need to be on our guard. Sooner or later, they're going to make a mistake. I want no stone left unturned. I also want someone checking out the dangerous drugs register. It's a big operation, and it'll take nearly all of you."

Gardener allowed the information to digest before choosing his next topic. Hesitantly, he turned to Reilly. "Will you do the honours, Sean?"

Reilly passed an artist impression around the room, a composite sketch of Warthead.

"Does everyone have a copy?" Gardener held his aloft. He'd hesitated before presenting the picture because he knew what the reaction would be.

On cue, the whole room descended into silence as each of them stared on and digested.

"Isn't this…" Brigg asked.

"Where the hell has this scum been hiding?" asked Rawson.

Briggs finally finished his sentence. "Isn't this the bloke who pulled the trigger on your missus?"

Gardener nodded. "The information I have about the photo-fit is minimal. They call him Felix. He's about five foot three with a face full of warts and a misshapen head. He's usually dressed in jeans, and a black leather jacket with a golden eagle emblem on the back and an American slogan. He's perhaps nineteen or twenty."

"Is he involved in all of this?" asked Thornton.

Gardener nodded again. "To what extent I'm not sure, but I would like to speak to him in connection with the child abductions. He was seen with David Vickers on the day he went missing, buying him presents."

"I don't believe this," said Sharp. "We've had stuff out on this bloke for a year… because of what he did…"

"It's okay, Colin," said Gardener, "you can say it."

Sharp's expression said that he was still too embarrassed to bring it up. "Well, since he, you know…"

"I think what he's trying to say is," offered Briggs, "that we've been looking for him since he shot Sarah, and we haven't found a thing. Now, we're involved in one of the biggest child abduction cases we've ever had, and who should rear his ugly head but this scally?"

"Well put," said Dave Rawson. "Even ugly doesn't do it justice."

"How is he tied in with this lot?" asked Bob Anderson.

"From the information compiled, we know he was a colleague of Plum's. The two appear to have been quite close."

PC Benson put his hand up. "I think I might have seen him recently, sir."

"Where?"

"One of the nightclubs in Leeds. But it was late and I'd had a few."

"I appreciate that, *and* the fact that you haven't been with us long so you may not know the backdrop to what we're talking about. Have you noticed anything strange about his behaviour? Drug peddling, anything?"

Benson paused. "I'm sorry, sir. I never paid him a great deal of attention, other than to look at him."

A mixture of emotions warred within Gardener. Disappointment, due to the lack of information surrounding Warthead. Frustration, because his wife's killer was alive and elusive. Anger, because he desperately wanted the chance to avenge Sarah's pointless death.

"Never mind. From now on, you're all looking out for him. Frank, Bob, I'd like you two personally on his case. When you find him, bring him straight here. Whatever the time, day or night. When you find him, find me."

"It might not be that simple, Stewart," said Briggs.

"Meaning what?"

"Meaning that this might be personal."

"Not yet, it isn't," replied Reilly.

Sharp nodded, agreeing. "We want him for questioning, sir, in connection with the abductions. But he might not be involved."

"Bit of a coincidence, isn't it?" said Briggs. "But if he is, Stewart, then it *is* personal and I'll have to remove you from the case."

Another silence descended. As Gardener peered around the room, he realized it didn't take a genius to work out what they were thinking.

Anderson broke the tension. "Then you'll have to remove us all, sir."

"Pardon?" asked Briggs.

"I'm not being awkward, sir, and I'm not threatening anyone or anything," replied Anderson, standing to address the DCI.

You could have heard a pin drop. "But I think I speak for all of us when I say that the night that scroat put a bullet in Sarah he *made* it personal… for all of us. He might as well have shot us all."

The rest of the team nodded and stood in unison.

"So yes," continued Anderson. "It is personal, but not just for the boss."

Chapter Forty-two

Malcolm sat comfortably. He'd been wined and dined. He'd enjoyed the company. The surroundings of Anei Bâlcescu's conservatory would be more than adequate to while away the rest of the evening. Anei wheeled in a trolley containing coffees and an assortment of homemade cakes.

"You certainly know how to spoil a man."

"Some men are worth spoiling. We have a proverb in Romania. We don't eat to live. We live to eat. You are a man who enjoys your food."

"I've enjoyed myself tonight. That's the best meal I've ever eaten." Malcolm truly meant what he'd said. It had been his first traditional Romanian dish. Cabbage à la cluj hadn't sounded particularly appetizing, but when he'd tasted the chopped cabbage and mince served with sour cream, his taste buds had tingled.

"You flatter me." Anei smiled.

"I've always believed in credit where it's due. It was a wonderful meal, thank you."

"Binevenit." Anei cut and passed over a large piece of cozonac, a traditional pound cake usually baked in

Romania for religious holidays. The pair ate and drank in silence. It was the most comfortable feeling in the world.

Malcolm had known Anei for three months. They had met at the gardening club, but for the last month, they had secretly been meeting at her farmhouse. Their love of plants was not the only thing they had in common. They had the same taste in music, good food, and books. Since the death of his wife Wendy, Malcolm had not met anyone with whom he felt he could be close.

Anei was different. He wasn't after a physical relationship. Merely companionship. He was relaxed in her company, felt no pressure. Whenever they were together, he felt a sense of belonging. A feeling he found hard to explain, yet it seemed so natural.

Anei rose from her seat. "I would like to show you something."

She left the room, returning quickly. In her arms, she carried an old brown cardboard box, tied together with a gold ribbon. As Anei untied it, Malcolm noticed her hands. They were not the hands of an old person. The skin was youthful, no liver spots. Her nails were well manicured, despite the fact that she worked the farm herself.

Anei pulled out a number of photographs, spreading them out on the table before them.

"These are of my family. I miss them so much. In 1940, Germany helped Hungary take the North Western part of Transylvania. Our home. If we had stayed in Romania, we would probably have been killed. We left a prosperous farm, and arrived in England with nothing."

"It must have been hard for you."

"It was very bad. We escaped the clutches of the Nazis in 1943. My parents and my sister, Irina, Jacqueline's grandma, who was twelve at the time. It was a very hazardous journey.

"We had God to guide us. We arrived in Southampton and took work on a farm, living in one of the barns. When my family had proved our worth, the landowners converted the barn into a home for us. Eventually, they retired, sold up, and moved to Yorkshire. We went with them in the hope of finding work."

Anei paused. Malcolm saw the tears in her eyes. "Tragedy struck on the journey. My parents had hired a car and were putting fuel in at a petrol station. I was only three years old, but I will never forget. My sister, Irina, took me to the toilet. The petrol station was at the bottom of a big hill. A lorry lost control. I think the brakes failed. It was carrying petrol. There was an explosion. Killing our mother and father, and the truck driver. We were shielded because we were at the back of the station. In fact, we had gone into a field to pick some flowers. Irina panicked, and we ran. We didn't know what else to do. I think she thought we would both be sent back if we were caught.

"It was a long night, and I have no idea how far we kept running, but we finally ended up at a farm. We slept rough, in one of the barns again. For maybe three or four nights, evading the farmers. Irina was caught stealing food by the owner. Somehow she managed to persuade them to let us help on the farm. It was like arriving in England all over again. We stayed. Perhaps our parents would have been better off if they had stayed where they were. We'll never know."

Anei smiled. "That was where Irina eventually met her future husband. He didn't want to help with the farm. He was always playing football, hiding from work. But he made good." She found and passed over a newspaper clipping of her sister's husband Sid, proudly holding a trophy in the air, a football underneath a raised foot. The headline told of a local boy accepted by Leeds United.

"He looks so proud," said Malcolm. As he read the clipping, he sensed that tragedy had struck their lives again. "Something happened, didn't it?"

"Sidney was involved in a hit and run. He lost a leg. They never caught the driver."

"That must have been awful. How did you cope?"

"We were very lucky. Sidney's father had been in Germany at the start of the war. He was taken prisoner. He didn't return until many years after the war had ended. His wife, Sidney's mother, had died during that time. But when he came back, he brought with him stolen Nazi treasure. When he saw what happened to Sidney, and how we were all struggling, he sold some of it to help us. But his father never lived long enough to see what would become of his investment. He had been treated so badly by the Germans."

Anei's mood darkened. "Sidney's father killed himself one night. He had terrible dreams. When he woke up, he was convinced the Germans were coming back for him."

She grew silent. Malcolm noticed her haunted expression. She took his hand. "We all worked hard. The farm prospered. We sold our plants and vegetables. Sidney started working for a newspaper to earn some extra money. We put that into the farm. We were proud people, you see, and we wanted it to work. For Sidney's father." She glanced around the conservatory. "I am the only one left, the farm is all mine now."

Anei scooped up the photos, putting them back in the box. "Tell me about your family, Malcolm."

He didn't feel there was much to tell. Certainly nothing compared to Anei's journey. "My parents were very successful. My father had his own fruit and vegetable business in the heart of Sheffield. Which had been handed down to him from his father, who had started out with a small barrow in one of the markets. But my dad was a workaholic, which was his undoing. Back then, he'd have worked night and day if my mother had let him.

"He won a large contract to supply most of the market traders and some of the local shops. It meant moving premises, something bigger. That's when he worked all the hours God sent. My mother was not happy. She shouted at him, told him he was being stupid, that he shouldn't work so hard. She was right. The last time she saw him alive was when she had cooked his evening meal and taken it to his office. He said he was too busy to eat. They argued because he looked so stressed. She left in tears. My mother was beside herself because her last words to him were not good ones. She apparently said she hoped his meal choked him, because if it didn't, work would."

Malcolm finished his coffee. "When I finally accepted what had happened, I remember thinking that I'd have to help out my mum seeing as Dad was no longer around. I found a number of jobs. A paper round before school, the village store after school. She made me stop all that. She didn't want me ending up the same way as my dad. We didn't need the money. The business had provided us with a good living. My mother downsized and ran the business herself. She said my father would have wanted it."

Malcolm sighed.

Anei broke the silence that followed once Malcolm had finished. "Mai vrei o cafea?"

He paused, then laughed. She had been teaching Malcolm to speak Romanian. For practice, she often asked him a question in her native tongue, expecting the appropriate answer. He realized she'd asked him if he wanted another coffee.

"Da bine. I think."

"Very good! You are learning fast." She poured another. Without asking, she plied him with more cake.

"Do you get lonely out here?" he asked, glancing out the windows at her home.

"I lead a simple life, Malcolm. I ask for nothing. I rise early and bake, spend time with my animals, work the garden. I keep myself busy. The two most important values in my life are never far away. My plants and my niece."

"That's something I can admire. I must admit, I thought I knew a lot about plants. You've got me beaten, hands down."

"Please, do not underestimate yourself. You are a clever man with plants."

"Not as good as you. Take these, for instance." Malcolm pointed to the Venus flytraps.

"You've managed to cultivate those year-round."

"It is not as difficult as you might think. In its native country, the plant grows in bogs which lack nitrogen. The insects that land inside supply this. So, for me to grow the plant, I need a nitrogen supplement, good compost, and rainwater."

Malcolm finished his cake, placing his empty plate back on the trolley.

"More?"

"Oh, not for me, thank you. If I eat anything else tonight, I'll burst."

Anei smiled. "You're like Jacqueline. She does not have a large appetite."

"I can see that you're proud of your niece, the way you talk about her."

"Yes. And you are equally as proud of your son. It is time to put our plan into practice, no? Are you sure about my niece and your son seeing each other?"

"To be honest, I'm not." Malcolm thought back to his conversation with Gardener, who had claimed nothing had happened.

"From what Jacqueline has said, there is definitely something happening."

"Maybe. It can't hurt to give them a little help."

Malcolm left the conservatory and phoned Stewart to tell him he would be out for the night and wondered if he could collect him sometime the following day.

"All set?" asked Anei, as Malcolm returned.

"Yes. He was curious, though."

"He's a policeman. He'll be asking questions of himself all evening."

"I could tell he wanted to know what was going on, but he was very tactful." Malcolm settled back, relaxed. He'd enjoyed his evening, and it was made all the better for not having to rush home.

"I phoned Jacqueline earlier. She was visiting me tomorrow anyway. I made an excuse and asked her to do a little shopping for me. She suspects nothing." Anei sipped her coffee. "I'm pleased she has settled in the village and made new friends. Her life has not been easy."

"You've never talked about her parents."

It was a while before Anei answered. Malcolm wondered if he had upset her with his remark.

"Her mother died of breast cancer when she was ten years old. She came to live with me when she was thirteen." Anei sighed. "She no longer has a father, either."

"I'm sorry." He placed his hand on Anei's, offering what little comfort he could. There had been genuine hardship in her life. He admired not only Anei's spirit, but that of the whole family. Despite the difficulties, they supported each other, drew strength from their unity and God.

Anei broke the silence, tightening her grip on Malcolm's hand. "We should not be sad. It is nearly Christmas, a time for celebration. In Romania, all families come together at Christmas."

She suddenly fell silent again, staring at their clasped hands.

"Is something wrong?"

She turned to gaze into Malcolm's eyes. "I have to go away for a little while. Don't worry. I have to make a journey, to my patrie, my Romania. I left when I was so young, and I have never been back. I am old now. I want to go back and visit while I am strong enough to do so. I want to show Jacqueline where I was born, what it was like to be with people you could trust. I need to feel it once more before anything happens to prevent it."

Malcolm smiled, relieved that it wasn't a problem. "Is that all? I'm happy for you, Anei. I think you should go. You and Jacqueline will have a wonderful time."

"Thank you." Anei smiled, not only with her lips, but with her eyes as well.

"And I'll be waiting for you when you return, you can tell me all about it." He kissed her lightly on the cheek.

"You are a kind man, Malcolm Gardener. I'm going to miss you."

Malcolm laughed. He didn't know what to say.

"But tonight, we will celebrate. Where's the wine?"

Chapter Forty-three

Olive Bradshaw's hardened expression reminded Gardener of a gargoyle. Her features then softened as she entered the denial stage. "Pornography? No. I'm sorry, Inspector, but I think you have the wrong man."

Since Gardener's last visit, the landlady's living accommodation had been stripped bare. He'd been surprised to learn that contracts had been exchanged, and she and her sister had packed everything into boxes ready for moving. Gardener stood with his back to the window, amused by her indignant repudiation. "I have not got the wrong man. I've done my homework. I believe that Herbert Plum was a paedophile."

"Well, I'm sorry, Inspector, but you've obviously made a mistake. Hasn't he, Mabel?" She glanced at her sister. Mabel nodded, seemingly unsure what to say.

"No mistake. During the search of his flat, we discovered pornographic material."

"How do you know it was his?" retorted the landlady, her arms folded defensively.

"Was it yours?" asked Reilly.

The landlady scowled. "It most certainly was not."

"Then it must be his," said Gardener. "We also found a sex drug called Papaverine, which could suggest he led a very active sex life. That would contradict your story of him having very little contact with the outside world. Have you any further comment to make?"

"Why should I? I'm not his keeper," she retorted.

Gardener stepped over to the table and leaned in close. He'd given her every chance. "No, you were a little closer than that, weren't you? You were his lover, isn't that right, Olive?"

She almost jumped out of her chair. "Who told you that?"

"You're not denying it, then?"

"I... I..."

"Everything we found in his room, and the information we've since gathered, point to him being involved with someone. I'd rather it was you than two missing schoolgirls."

Olive Bradshaw dropped her hands in resignation, her eyes watering. She fished her handkerchief out from the sleeve of her cardigan and blew her nose. "I'm sorry, Mabel." Her voice was barely audible. "Please, don't be angry with me."

Mabel stood up, wrapped her arms around her sister. "Don't upset yourself, Olive. I'm not angry, but I am disappointed that you couldn't have told me."

"I didn't want to hurt your feelings. We've always been close."

Gardener was confused. Today she appeared concerned for the deceased. The night of his murder she was only worried about the cleaning bill. "So, you were having a relationship?" he asked.

Olive Bradshaw merely nodded. Although she had helped to solve one mystery, a number still remained. Plum's connection with Warthead for one. Gardener withdrew the artist impression from his inside pocket.

"Do you recognize the man in the photo-fit?"

She made an effort to study it before replying, "No." She passed it over to her sister.

"Oh, the poor man, I'd know if I'd seen him before."

"What do you want him for, Inspector?" asked Olive Bradshaw.

"We think he may have abducted the missing schoolchildren. But he was also seen with Herbert Plum on a number of occasions in the pub."

"Oh, surely not." She covered her mouth with her hand. "I can't believe Herbert would have anything to do with the missing children." Once again, she hid her face in her handkerchief.

"You're positive you've never seen the man? He's never been to the house?"

The landlady composed herself. "I'm sorry, Inspector. I'd remember if I'd seen him."

Gardener believed her. "It's important. Anything you do remember, no matter how trivial, let me know."

"Inspector, Herbert was a good man. A kind man. I can't believe he would have anything to do with children."

Mabel offered to make tea. Gardener suspected it was a good excuse for her to leave the room. Both detectives declined her offer. He turned back to Olive. "How would you describe your relationship with him?"

"I was lonely. Mabel hasn't always been here, and even when she was, she had her own circle of friends. Herbert and I often shared an evening in front of the telly, a night in the pub. Sometimes I'd visit his room and we'd have a cup of tea..." She let the sentence fade, sniffing and sobbing.

"You were good friends. It was a casual relationship."

"Yes."

Gardener sighed, disappointed. He sensed he was going to glean little more information. He was pleased at having cleared up the relationship angle, but he had hoped for more. Plum was as much a mystery to her as he had been to everyone else. "I'll leave you my card, Miss Bradshaw. But please, think about what I've said."

Olive Bradshaw nodded. Mabel returned with the tea.

Gardener changed the subject. "Christmas is going to be quite hectic for you both, what with the move. When are you expecting to go?"

"Next week, Inspector. Quite frankly, I'll be glad to see the back of this place. There's no good memories here."

"You will remember to let me have your new address, won't you?"

The two detectives made for the door. The landlady followed them. Gardener turned.

"One more thing. On the night of the murder, you said you heard the commotion. What exactly do you mean by that?"

She paused, as if in thought. "The noise."

"What kind of a noise? Did you hear any raised voices?"

"No. Furniture banging around. A crash. Mable and I were outside the Carter woman's door. We'd had an argument."

"About what?"

"The flat next door to her. She was complaining about us moving boxes in and out, as usual." Olive quickly turned to Mabel. "But she's not bothered about the noise when she's entertaining, is she, Mabel? No. She's quick to complain when it suits her, that one. I'll be glad to see the back of her, and no mistake."

"What happened after you heard the banging?"

"I went up the stairs, and shouted to Herbert," replied Olive Bradshaw. "Asked him if he was all right. He didn't reply."

For the first time, Gardener noticed an expression of guilt on the landlady's face. He had never come across anyone who changed their moods so quickly. She was impossible to read.

"You heard a crash but no raised voices. He gave no reply to your inquiry. Did you shout again? Or try his door?"

"I tried the door, but it was locked."

Gardener struggled to believe she would let such an incident go by uninvestigated. Especially with someone she was sleeping with. "That's it? You weren't concerned? A sixty-year-old man on his own? He could have had an accident, may have needed your assistance. We're talking about a man you had a relationship with. You must have felt the impulse to do something, surely?"

She grew defensive. "As I've already said, Inspector, I wasn't his keeper. He liked a drink. I thought he might have been drinking, knocked something over. We were late for bingo."

"I see." Gardener paused. "So, you just left? You were late for bingo, so you didn't hang around to see if he eventually opened his door?"

"No."

Gardener locked eyes with Olive. "Or, in fact, if someone else opened his door?"

Chapter Forty-four

Nicki Carter was hesitant with her answer. "I've seen him. Don't know him, but I've seen him."

"Where?" Gardener studied the girl. The bruise under her left eye had disappeared. Her clothes were cleaner than the last time they'd met. She was wearing a white T-shirt with blue denim jeans. The flat was cleaner. The fresh smell of lavender polish hung in the air. The baby was once again with Nicki's mother. Gardener wondered what the reason was. "Come on, Nicki, I have to know."

"Outside school."

"Which one?" Gardener's patience was wearing thin. Everywhere he went, people had half-stories to tell him. They only seemed to tell him what they wanted. No one took anything seriously. As if they were all playing games. "Was he with anyone?"

"Middle school, near Old Lane." She didn't answer his second question. It was obvious she was holding something back. Nicki Carter nervously lit a cigarette.

"Who was he with?"

After a pause, she replied. "The pervert, Plum."

Frustrated, Gardener sighed. "Why the hell didn't you tell me that before?"

The girl was anxious, rubbing her hands together in circles. "You never asked."

Gardener fumed. "The last time we spoke, you said Plum was a pervert. The man in the photo-fit is wanted for questioning in connection with the missing schoolchildren. We know these two had an allegiance. You knew about it, but never mentioned it. Why?"

"He were dead, for God's sake. I didn't think it mattered. The bastard got what were coming to him anyway."

"That's not the point! You withheld important information from me. If you'd told me two weeks ago, we might have got to the bottom of this and had people charged. You're damned lucky I don't charge you with obstructing the course of justice." Gardener was so pissed off, he felt like arresting all of them. Nicki Carter, Olive Bradshaw and her sister, and Summers. The whole fucking lot.

"I'm sorry." Nicki Carter took a drag on her cigarette.

He didn't really think she was.

"Why were you at the school?"

"Collecting me sister. Me mother were busy."

"So," said Gardener, trying to calm down. "You saw Plum and Felix together. Doing what?"

"Nothing. Just hanging round the gates. When Plum saw me, he said summat to the other bloke, and they both left."

Gardener changed the subject. "We've been speaking to Olive Bradshaw."

"What's wrong with that old bag, now?"

"She said you'd had a disagreement the night Herbert Plum was killed. You never told us that either. What was it about?"

"Same as always. Odd noises coming from next door. All sodding hours. She's another one who doesn't care how much bloody noise she makes."

Gardener hunched his shoulders as he felt a cold draft skate across the back of his neck. He turned, noticed an open window. "Did you hear anything on the landing above? Voices? Crashing furniture?"

"No. Can't say I did."

"So, you heard nothing. Olive Bradshaw indicated it happened around 6:30pm. Did you hear anything afterwards? Like his door closing? Someone running down the stairs?"

"No. I've said, the bairn were upset most of the night. So, I were seeing to him."

Gardener was ready to scream. Couldn't someone give him something to go on?

Chapter Forty-five

Back down the stairs, Gardener knocked on Olive Bradshaw's door. No answer came. He glanced at his watch. "I don't believe it. Where the hell are they now?" The whole scenario was really starting to infuriate him. "Come on," he said to Reilly. "Let's go."

Gardener strode down the path, determined to find answers to his questions. He unlocked the car and was about to open the door when a familiar throbbing sound to his left diverted his attention. A man riding a motorbike pulled up opposite them, killed the engine, and rested the Bonneville on its side stand.

"Look at that!" said Gardener to his partner.

"Is that the same as yours?"

"Give or take a few years."

Gardener strolled over. The rider removed his helmet and nodded. Gardener envied the bike, wondering if his would ever match the one in front of him. The Triumph was in pristine condition, shined like a pin, with new wheels and new tires. All the chrome was highly polished, and the paint job was unlike anything he'd ever seen before. "Nice machine. How long have you had it?"

The man smiled. He was in his mid-fifties with a small amount of grey hair at the sides of his head, a grey moustache and beard, and small lens spectacles. He was a little overweight, but he handled the bike well. "About seven years, now, mate. Mind you, spent the first three doing it up. Why? Are you interested?"

Gardener detected a Liverpool accent. "I'm restoring one at the moment." He passed the man a business card. "Maybe you can let me know where to get the parts."

The rider smiled, passing over his own business card bearing the name Jeff Harrison. "Do one better than that, mate. I own the business. Give us a ring when you're ready, and I'll sort you out a good deal."

Gardener smiled. "Much appreciated."

"No problem. I'm sorry, but I'm going to have to dash." He pointed to the house behind him. "Mother's not too well. Hasn't been right for a couple of weeks, not since that nasty business over the road. The one you're probably investigating, given what your card says."

"Sorry to hear it." Gardener tipped his hat. "Hope she goes on okay. I'll give you a ring."

The man gave him a thumbs-up sign and walked down the path to his mother's. Back in the car, Gardener glanced at Olive Bradshaw's house before turning to Reilly. "I don't know who to believe anymore. What to believe!"

"I don't think you can put much store in what the Bradshaw woman says. She is a strange one."

"Isn't she just? When I met her on Friday night, she was going mental about the mess, complaining about the commotion. We interviewed her on Monday, and she was totally different. Today, she had us believe she had feelings for Herbert Plum, but she wasn't prepared to investigate the disturbance because it would have made her late for bingo. I can't understand the people around here. What the hell's wrong with them, for God's sake?"

"They're either very stupid or very frightened. Could be that someone's controlling it all very carefully," offered Reilly.

"I can't believe anyone would have that much power."

Reilly's eyes met Gardener's. "I've a feeling that before this is over, it's going to get very nasty. We've opened up a big can of worms. What worries me is who we're going to find wriggling in it before we've finished."

A knock at the car window on Reilly's side startled him. The Irishman pushed a button.

The window descended.

"Excuse me, gentleman, but aren't you the two detectives who were caught up in the churchyard murder?"

"Who the hell are you?" asked Reilly.

"Dave Bennett. I'm with The Yorkshire Press."

Gardener studied the man. He was in his late forties with salt-and-pepper-coloured hair, a tanned but wrinkled face, dark brown eyes, and a false smile. He was tall and gangly, and wore a suit from the 1960s which had not stood the test of time. He had to stoop to peer into the car. Even from where he was sitting, Gardener could smell his bad breath. "I'm sorry, Mr Bennett, but we have no comment to make."

"Mr Gardener, isn't it?"

"Go away," said Reilly.

"The public has a right to know what's going on. Are you visiting these premises in connection with the church murder? I know a body was found here last week."

"We are here on police business, but I'm not prepared to comment any further."

"Well, can you tell me, is there a connection between the missing schoolchildren and the murders?"

"I'm not in a position to comment at the moment."

Dave Bennett put his head completely inside the car, forcing Reilly to hold his breath. "A colleague of mine informs me you arrested a local drug dealer only this week. Was it about the murders or the schoolchildren?"

"A local person did help us with our inquiries, but we didn't arrest him," replied Gardener. "Perhaps your colleague isn't as good as he thinks he is. Now, if you don't mind, we have other business to attend to."

Bennett was persistent. "Is it true you're pursuing your wife's killer in connection with the case?"

Gardener's temper hit boiling point. Fucking journalists. How the hell had Bennett come by that piece of information? How was it that the people he loathed most in the world seemed to have the habit of asking the most personal questions? Was he in the middle of some huge conspiracy? "Roll your window up, Sean."

Reilly did, suddenly amused by the fact that Dave Bennett had been quick enough to remove his head, but not his tie.

"Well, look what we have here, boss."

Bennett banged on the window, sudden apprehension carved into his features. "Mr Gardener, you'll have to answer these questions eventually," he shouted.

Reilly started the car and waved, smiling as he did so.

"My tie. You've got my tie!" The expression on the reporter's face was priceless as Reilly inched the car forward.

Chapter Forty-six

"Stewart?"

"Jacqueline?" He stepped backward, glancing at her uncomfortably. "What are you doing here?"

"I was about to ask you the same question. My aunt lives here."

Jacqueline was the last person he'd expected to see. The situation was bizarre. "I'm here to collect my father."

"You'd better come in."

Gardener did as he was asked. Jacqueline closed the door. She was traditionally dressed for ministerial duties in a long black gown with a white scarf. She smelled fresh. *White Linen*, if he wasn't mistaken. Sarah's favourite. From the kitchen, he detected the unmistakable aroma of fresh bread.

"This is awkward," she said.

He knew what she meant and felt it as much as she obviously did. "It doesn't need to be. About the other night…"

"Please." She held up a hand. "You don't have to explain. I understand. Believe me, I'm a minister."

He simply nodded, appreciating that she really had figured out what he was feeling.

"Another time, another place."

"Yes, I know," she smiled. "You'd have jumped at the chance."

Gardener laughed. "I wouldn't have put it quite like that."

Jacqueline smiled as well. "Forgive me for changing the subject, but do you mean to tell me that the elderly, well-mannered gentleman in my aunt's kitchen is your father?"

"Sounds like him."

"I can't believe it. Did you know anything about it? He's been here since I have, and they're getting on very well together."

"He's been here all night."

"Never!" Jacqueline's eyes went wide, mouth agape with schoolgirl naiveté.

"They're playing games with us. They're obviously up to something."

"Sounds like it. Especially as my aunt let me answer the door and hasn't come through."

Her expression softened. "It's lovely to see you."

"You, too. But right now, I'm curious. I'd like to know everything about their little liaison."

"So would I."

As they entered the kitchen, the atmosphere was charged with anticipation. Anei warmed to Gardener immediately, and the two of them fell into a leisurely conversation. Future plans were made for another, more organized meeting.

Chapter Forty-seven

Frank Myers gripped the sides of his aged armchair and heaved himself upwards, narrowly missing the TV when his arthritic knees gave way under his enormous bulk. On the screen, a naked teenage girl performed oral sex on a partially clothed Father Christmas. In the background, another teenager waited her turn. Myers groaned as he raised himself to his feet, and shuffled over to the window. His knee cracked again. He doubled over, pausing while the pain subsided.

He was aware the problem was self-inflicted – a mixture of old age and excess weight. Sixty-one years old and twenty-four stones wasn't a good basis for a healthy life. He'd been told to lose weight more than once. Who cares? It was his life. He would do as he pleased. He wasn't having any pompous, self-opinionated, overpaid doctor telling him what he was and wasn't going to do.

Myers gingerly straightened up. He continued over to the window, carefully nudged the filthy net curtain to one side in case any sudden movement caused it to disintegrate. Washing and cleaning was women's work. It didn't matter to him whether the place was clean or not. There were better things to do in life. Outside, the snow had started to settle. Large white flakes hit the window before dissolving into tiny beads of water.

Myers stared down from his second floor flat, evaluating the wasteland. Two local hooligans strolled past, unaware they were being watched. The row of terraced houses opposite him stood hidden in the darkened recesses of the few working sodium-coloured streetlights. Most of the homes were derelict, some of them boarded up. The rest resembled the aftermath of a war: broken windows, missing roof tiles, piles of bricks, rubble piled in heaps in the small front gardens.

The scene was a gloomy reminder to Myers that his life and the neighbourhood had much in common. They were both bombed out, with no one left to care. Anyone who had any sense didn't live here. They had long since moved, been driven out or had died. That left the remainder, the degenerates with whom he had to live.

Myers had lived here long enough to realize that if the yobs didn't flush him out tonight, they would eventually. What a screwed-up neighbourhood Beechtown is. Pimps, whores, muggers, thieves. An endless list of low-life dregs, all competing to gain the coveted title, King of the Shit Pile.

Myers glanced at his watch, irritated. "Where the fucking hell is that Chinese?" He'd give them another five minutes, then phone and put a rocket up their arses. He'd ordered it over an hour ago. "A man could starve to death."

Myers suddenly heard a screeching of brakes followed by the blaring of a car horn.

Peeking through the net, he saw the local joyriders at it again. Some poor bastard'll receive an early Christmas present in the morning when he goes searching for his car. Engine revving, exhaust smoking and wheels screeching, the joyriders cleared out.

Myers turned away from the window. The disc had moved on. The teenage girls were now sitting astride the Santa, one on his waist, the other on his face. Myers snatched up the phone, dialled a number.

It was answered on the second ring. "Golden Lotus!"

"Where's me fucking supper?"

"I'm sorry," replied the female voice.

"You fucking will be! I ordered it over an hour ago."

"What name?"

"Myers! I'm bleeding starving."

"Very sorry, Mr Myers. Weather bad, not be long now."

"I should bloody well think so. I dare say you'll be knocking summat off for being late?"

"Very sorry, Mr Myers, be there soon."

Myers replaced the receiver, irritated by their pathetic excuses. "It wasn't snowing when I ordered it." Back at the window, a peaceful solitude had presided over the street.

Myers returned to the middle of the room, slumped into the chair. A layer of dust sprayed outwards like a cloud of blowflies.

God, could it be any worse? It was all Summers' fault. The sly bastard. If the man paid half decent money, I wouldn't be in the mess I'm in.

Living in Beechtown was not Myers' ideal position in life. No money, no car, no wife. The job he had wasn't worth writing home about. Playing Santa Claus to a bunch of snotty nosed kids for a pittance.

Who the fuck did Summers think he was, anyway? What right does he have to dictate to me what I can and can't do? Or how much I'll work for?

But Myers knew exactly what right. He'd known for some time. He knew the hold Summers had over all of them. Thornwell and Plum had finally paid the price. He wondered if Summers had been responsible for their deaths.

Well, if he thinks he's calling the shots anymore, he's got another think coming. Fuck Summers! I'm not waiting around in this dump any longer for him to come and sort me out.

Myers had tried phoning Harry Clayton, but he hadn't returned from his holiday.

You never know with Clayton. He's as sly as the rest of the bastards. Maybe it's him. Maybe Summers is using Clayton to sort out the rest of us. Come tomorrow morning, I'm out of here. Fuck the landlord, he can whistle for his rent. Fuck Summers, he knows what he can do with his underpaid jobs. From now on, it's Frank Myers that counts. To hell with the rest of the world.

The sound of a car engine outside startled him from his thoughts. Once again, Myers heaved himself out of the chair, puffing and panting, grimacing from the pains in his knees as he hobbled toward the window. With a quick glance, he noticed the car had been parked half on the pavement.

"About fucking time." Myers watched, impatiently. "Well, come on then, what are you doing?"

He noticed Jenny Price walk past the car. *Bleeding whore! Aye, it were your bastard mate as done for me.* Myers paused his thoughts, irritated by his hunger. "For fuck's sake, will you hurry up?"

Jenny Price disappeared from view. Myers' thoughts turned to her mate. *Carol summat-or-other. What did it matter now? The bitch had died last year. AIDS.*

Too much whoring around, I shouldn't wonder. Before she'd died, she'd turned tricks for Myers. She was dirty, and it had cost him, but he had loved it at the time. Wasn't so happy now.

Despite the low volume from the TV, he could hear the orgasmic groans, reminding him the tape was still playing. As he turned from the window, he noticed the driver's door opening. He walked over and stopped the DVD, then returned to the window. The street was deserted. It was still snowing. A trail of footprints led to the front door of the flats.

Downstairs, Myers could hear the deliveryman taking the stairs, one at a time, slowly and deliberately. *Chinky bastard! I'll teach you to take your time.* Myers reached the door as the knock came. He unlocked it, opening quickly, hoping to surprise his visitor with a mouthful of abuse before refusing to pay.

It all happened in the time it took him to blink.

Myers staggered backward, caught off-balance by the speed of the assault. "What the fuck have you done?" His eyes roamed down across his body to the source of the pain. It wasn't really hurting, more of an irritation. Then he saw it. "A needle… fucking stabbed me!"

Something was wrong. He was slowing down. He tried to direct his right arm to remove the syringe, but it wouldn't co-operate. Myers was suddenly aware that his body was traveling in a different direction. Backward. He was falling. His eyes finally came to rest on the ceiling.

His attacker came into view, staring down at him.

Myers lay on the floor, trying to rationalize what was happening to his body. His breathing was erratic. He could see. He could hear. But he couldn't feel anything. His whole body was paralyzed. He couldn't move a muscle.

He heard movements around his flat. Then the door closed. Realization dawned on him.

He was trapped! Unable to talk, move, or defend himself. Whoever had stabbed him with the syringe – filled him full of whatever – he was now at their mercy. His attacker appeared suddenly, dressed in black jeans, a jacket, and a balaclava with eyeholes.

"Hello, Frank."

Myers didn't recognize the voice. It certainly wasn't Harry Clayton. The build was too small. From what he could see and hear, it was no one familiar. But it had to be someone who knew him. Otherwise, how did they know his name? It had to be someone they all knew. And if it wasn't Clayton, there could only be one other suspect. Summers.

"I expect you're wondering who I am. What I'm doing here, what this is all about. All will be revealed, Frank."

Myers was frustrated. Why the hell couldn't it have been tomorrow? He'd have been out of here by then.

"The stage you're at now, you're probably wondering what was in the syringe." His attacker paused. "Well, even if you're not, I'll tell you. It's called curare, Frank. I won't bore you with detail. It's a muscle relaxant, which is why you're paralyzed. Exactly the correct amount, of course. Too much and I'd have killed you. I don't want you to die too quickly. Or pain-free. Not after what you did to me.

"I do believe you're thinking about it, now, Frank. You're wondering who I am, what you've done to me. Perhaps you should also be thinking... when?"

He was surprised when his assailant's next move was to straddle his body and sit on his fat belly. "Cosy this, isn't it, Frank? Are you as comfortable as I am? I do hope so. Not hurting you, am I? Oh, silly me. You can't talk, can you? Bet you'd like to."

Myers' temper flared.

When it wears off, you'd better be fucking quick, or you're dead. No one fucks with me and gets away with it! Apart from Carol whatshername, of course!

"I bet there's a few things you'd like to say to me. It's the perfect opportunity, really, now we're on our own. Not like that night all those years ago. The last time we met."

Myers wondered where his Chinese takeaway was, realizing that the longer the situation went on, the more chance they had of being disturbed. He saw his attacker checking the time.

"I've almost outstayed my welcome, Frank, so let's get down to business."

Myers saw another syringe appear. It was held aloft, and a small amount of clear liquid was pumped out. He became aware of an obnoxious, vile odour.

"Awful smell, isn't it, Frank? I think it rather suits you, myself. You, disgusting piece of filth. Have you any idea how long I've waited for this day?"

Myers wanted to scream with frustration. Whatever it was, he wanted to beg forgiveness, say he was sorry, even though he couldn't remember what his attacker was talking about.

"You all thought you were so superior, didn't you, Frank? You took advantage and played the numbers game. Four of you, one of me. Remember that night, do you? I was like you are now. Trapped. I couldn't go anywhere. Couldn't fight back." His attacker paused. "So, how does it feel, Frank? Alone? Isolated? Frightened? I know them all well. I've lived them all so many times since. Well, here's a small thought to hang on to. How you're feeling now is far better than you're going to feel in a few minutes."

His assailant gazed at the syringe with emotionless eyes, giving nothing away.

Myers realized he wasn't ready to die. He'd always considered himself hardened to the world and the people in it. That he could face up to anything. If truth be known, he'd never really suspected that AIDS would kill him. He'd blocked it out. But now, in the final stages, he was frightened. He'd bargain anything he had.

"Okay. Here's what's going to happen. I'm going to inject your jugular vein with the contents of this syringe. You should just about be coming out of the paralysis now. As you come round, you'll feel a sudden surge of adrenaline and your heart will pump much faster, which is perfect for this stuff. The faster it gets round, the quicker it can do the damage. It's going to hurt, Frank. In fact, it'll kill you!"

Myers felt the difference almost immediately as his attacker injected him with the second syringe. The paralysis subsided, only to be replaced by something new. The temperature of the room changed. Maybe it was only him. He wasn't sure. He could feel his pulse racing. He was almost having palpitations. Myers was on fire. His whole body racked with pain.

"We're nearly there, aren't we, Frank? I think it's time you knew."

His assailant pulled off the hood. Myers finally came face to face with his killer. Plum's killer. Thornwell's. His eyes widened with disbelief.

"Quite a shock, isn't it? Bet you thought you'd never see me again."

Myers forced out an agonizing scream. He started to gulp air, struggling to inhale as much as possible. His throat was blocked. He was choking. As he started to convulse, his breathing problems were soon outweighed by further pain. Searing red-hot needles pricked his skin from the inside. His whole body was under an immense amount of pressure, reaching the point where he thought it was likely to burst. Although Myers could see, his vision was fast becoming impaired by a series of coloured lights.

He screamed and continued screaming until he could no longer hear himself, as the engulfing pain destroyed all his senses.

Chapter Forty-eight

Pete Nash climbed the stairs two at a time. The manager at The Lotus had freaked out on the phone, saying the cost of the meal would come out of his wages, and so would that of any other meals he was late with tonight. At the time he hadn't cared. He had been stretched out across the back seat, engine running, heaters on, receiving a blowjob from Katie Crawford. She was nothing to look at, had no personality, and didn't care how she earned her money. His wife didn't like oral sex, or any sex for that matter, which meant he had to pay for most of what he wanted.

At the top of the second landing, Pete Nash stopped, knocking loudly. Then he heard the screaming. It sounded like someone was being tortured. He'd heard about the gangs in Leeds, the drug barons. They were mean bastards.

The screams on the other side of the door continued. Nash was frightened but decided to knock again. He shouted as well. And fidgeted, wondering whether or not to leave the takeaway on the step. He didn't need the agro. He was late enough. If the guy on the other side of the door was being tortured, he probably deserved it.

Then the door opened. A black blur leapt out, crashing into him. He was aware of the Chinese takeaway hitting the wall to his right, the black blur jumping down the stairs to his left.

The force of the assault unbalanced Nash. He crashed into the banister rail, going over in slow motion.

On his way down, Nash passed the person dressed in black. His own screams equalled those he'd heard upstairs. As he plummeted, his outstretched right arm hit the first-floor banister and snapped. He continued to bounce into obstacles, but it wasn't enough to stop him altogether.

As he hit the concrete floor at the bottom, his neck snapped.

In his dying moments, he was aware of someone walking past him.

He remembered he'd left the car engine running. The Chinese family wouldn't be pleased.

Chapter Forty-nine

Gardener carefully negotiated the path leading to the front door. The overnight snowfall had transformed into a dirty grey slush. On either side of the walkway, the small garden had the finest display of weeds he had ever seen, overpopulated by fast-food cartons, carrier bags, and used condoms. Reilly followed close behind, with Briggs in tow, his hands clasped to his mouth, mumbling about the cold.

Before Gardener entered the house, he turned, scanning the neighbourhood. He saw squad cars, ambulances, police officers, and a near-derelict house with scenes of crime tape. The one noticeable point over and above everything else was the fact that no one cared enough to even pry.

A young mum with a baby in a buggy scurried past the gate. She never even turned.

Further down the street, three young boys played football, shouting at each other, paying little attention to the authorities. Life continued as though he and his team were invisible. An everyday occurrence.

"Are we going in, then?" said Briggs, irritably.

A body lay where it had fallen, engorged blue lips on ashen skin, lifeless eyes staring vacantly into space. Two constables shielded the body. One was PC Benson.

"What have you found out?" asked Gardener, peering up the staircase.

"According to his wallet, his name's Pete Nash. I can't tell you anything else about him at the moment, sir. We're running him through the system. We've had a call from a Chinese takeaway, The Golden Lotus. It seems he's a delivery driver for them. Went missing last night. The car's not in the lot outside."

"Surprise, surprise."

Reilly ascended the first three stairs. "Any witnesses?" asked the Irishman.

"No, sir."

Gardener glanced at the ceiling, disappointed. "Who found the bodies?"

"The landlord. He came to collect the rent arrears from Frank Myers. After finding Nash, he went upstairs and found the door to Myers' flat was open. He's still up there." Benson paused. "Looks like Nash fell from the top floor."

"Okay." Gardener pulled out his mobile and phoned Fitz, requesting his presence, and the undertaker. The procession of officers climbed the staircase to Myers' flat. For Gardener, it was simply a repeat of the two weeks previous, but with a different address. The house was equally as run down as the Rawston place, but Myers appeared to have been the building's sole tenant. He sidestepped the remains of the Chinese takeaway, intermingled with what he took to be the landlord's vomit. Combined with the smell from inside the flat, it was enough to upset the most cast-iron of constitutions.

The door was open. Gardener noticed that the Crime Scene Manager, Steve Fenton, had laid out the stepping plates. He was standing on one, simply staring around the room. He wore a scene suit, but not a mask. His eyes were watering. Fenton nodded to them as they approached.

He stepped out of the room using the plates. "I was here first, sir. I thought I might as well put the plates out for you."

Gardener suspected the repugnant smell would stay with him long after the case had been closed.

Fenton introduced Mr Singh, the landlord, who had remained outside the door.

Gardener ignored him, glancing around. The room was dirty, with a threadbare carpet. The windows were covered with old nets and tattered curtains that had never been washed, in his opinion. Apart from a small table and chairs, Myers had a bed, and an armchair placed in front of a DVD player. The television was on but the screen was blue. Gardener noticed the DVD player was switched on but not playing. He could see a tiny bathroom leading off from the room they were in.

"Jesus Christ!" said Briggs.

What was left of Myers was in the exact same condition as Plum and Thornwell when they'd been found. Stripped of innards with a layer of wet skin stretched over the skeletal frame.

Gardener glanced at Singh. The senior officer estimated he was around fifty, balding, with a face full of grey curls like a ball of wire wool cascading down over his bloating belly. He was dressed in a variety of ill-fitting grey robes, which were overdue for a wash. Or perhaps they weren't dirty. Maybe it was only their colour. His shifty eyes focused on Gardener as he started to rant and gesticulate.

"Myers, not a very nice man, oh no. He owed me money. This man did not pay rent for one month. And look at the place. How am I to rent it again?"

Gardener couldn't figure how he'd been able to rent it at all. "How long has he been your tenant, Mr Singh? Any problems?"

"Two years. Plenty. Mostly rent. Always late."

Gardener noticed Reilly had joined the CSM. Briggs appeared stunned. It was the first time Gardener could recall seeing him speechless. Gardener continued with a series of questions, all of which led him to the conclusion that Myers was no different than Plum. He was a loner, no friends, behind with his rent, always paid cash. It was a carbon copy. With one exception. Where there had been a difference of opinion on Plum's popularity, there didn't seem to be for Myers.

Gardener glanced around, thinking. Was it a business deal that had gone wrong? It seemed unlikely. None of the dead men appeared to have had a brass farthing. He was convinced they were linked by an isolated incident – but what? And were there any more involved? Would it all come back to the smarmy entertainment agent?

Gardener turned to Singh. "Any idea what he did for a living, how he earned his money?"

Singh shook his head, indicating he didn't.

"Sir?" Fenton interrupted his train of thought. "You might like this." Fenton held a syringe. He'd been searching through the remnants of the Chinese takeaway.

"Found it down there." Fenton pointed to a dark corner.

Gardener observed the dilapidated structural condition of the building. A damp stain shaped like Ireland ascended the wall. Cobwebs hung in all corners. Grimy, once-white paint blistered on the skirting boards and doorjambs. He studied the banister rail. Surprisingly, it remained solid, with no signs of impact damage. The spindles were coated with Chinese gravy. He glanced over, noting the position of the body two floors below.

"What do you think, Sean?" His sergeant was standing behind him.

Reilly peeked over, thoughtfully, his arms folded across his chest. "He obviously disturbed the killer. And paid the price."

"I wonder if he saw who it was. He was delivering the Chinese, walked in on them. Had to be disposed of. What do you reckon?"

"He definitely interrupted whatever was happening. From the position of the body, I'd say he fell all the way down. Over the edge, not down the stairs. Whoever the killer is, I think they shot straight out of here, barged into him. The rest is history."

Gardener heard Fitz's arrival two floors below. He used the stepping plates to stride back into the room. The locations and the conditions in which the victims lived were beginning to piss him off. Dirty people in dirty surroundings. How anyone could live in such squalor was beyond him. Pete Nash, however, was not part of the equation. He had been an accident. Singh suddenly reared up at Briggs. "The man was a liar, a thief, and a cheat." He then turned to Gardener. "You go look in the bathroom. Two suitcases."

"Sean, take a look, please. What are you suggesting, Mr Singh?"

"He was leaving. Look at the apartment, it's bare!"

Gardener couldn't tell. He'd naturally assumed that Singh was one of those landlords who charged the Earth for their accommodation, showed up once a week for the rent, and then conveniently disappeared when faced with complaints or repairs. "What's missing?"

"Everything!" said Singh, waving his hands around once more. "Bathroom empty of towels, toilet rolls, shaving equipment. His clothes are in suitcases. Everything! People always take advantage of me."

Gardener wondered why Myers had planned to leave. He stood with his hands in his pockets, scrutinizing every inch of the room. Myers was not taking a holiday. His living arrangement was his choice. There were no personal ornaments, no paintings, no magazines, no newspapers, no photo-frames containing pictures of immediate family. On the walls, lighter patches indicated there had been paintings. There was nothing at all to tell them about the man who'd been killed.

Was Myers an associate of Plum and Thornwell? Perhaps he was. Maybe he'd found out who was responsible for their deaths. Maybe it was Summers. Had Myers also worked for Summers? If he had, why hadn't Summers told them? He must have known it would trace back to him. With Myers dead, would they find Summers had vanished?

Reilly appeared at the door. "I've found something you might want to see, amongst his personal documents." Reilly handed Gardener an old invoice, a bill for commission, from Derek Summers. From behind his back, he produced a Santa hat. At least one of his questions had been answered.

Gardener passed the invoice to Briggs.

He scanned it, glancing at the senior officer. "Summers didn't tell you about Myers, did he?"

Gardener shook his head as he stepped over to the window and opened it. He needed fresh air. Outside, amidst the desolation, still no one had gathered to see what was going down.

He turned back to Briggs, his finger pointing accusingly, his anger evident in his voice.

"Summers knows about all of these deaths, and I'll lay odds he knows why."

"Maybe he does. Bring me hard evidence."

"Haven't we got enough evidence here? Why is he withholding information? What is he hiding?"

Briggs glanced at the landlord. "Mr Singh, would you go downstairs now, please? I'd like a private word with my officers. We'll sort it out from here."

Singh left, complaining about the mess and the rent arrears and how he was going back to Asia.

Briggs turned to Gardener, who was now in conference with his sergeant. "Reilly, what are your thoughts on Summers?"

"I agree with the boss. It wasn't what he told us, it was what he left out. I got the impression he was too careful with his answers."

Briggs eyed Gardener. "Did he make any reference to Myers? Or anyone else that worked for him, apart from the two dead ones?"

"No. But he's hiding something. I don't know what, but so help me God, I'm going to find out. Look at the evidence. Three elderly men, all dead, all living alone in slums. All working for Summers. Maybe it's a grudge. Maybe they have something on him."

"So, what else do you know about him?"

"Nothing," answered Gardener. "You had to be there to know what I'm talking about. He's sly. He's creepy, and he's lying. I asked Colin Sharp to look into his background."

"I think the boss is right," Reilly added. "That man makes your spine tingle. He didn't show an ounce of concern that his employees had been killed."

"What do you want to do?" Briggs asked.

"We're going back this afternoon. I want a Section 8 search warrant for his property and anything else I want. Even if Summers isn't the killer, I'm pretty sure he's involved. There's a link, and I'm going to find it."

Briggs was about to respond when Fitz walked into the room. "Nothing new here, then," said the pathologist.

"Steve Fenton has another syringe, Fitz."

Fenton passed it over.

"Anything else I need to know?"

"No," said Gardener, "I think we're about finished. Steve, you and your team carry on searching."

Gardener turned to the pathologist. "Fitz, the body downstairs, anything to tell me?"

"I'd estimate time of death around ten o'clock last night. I can't say for certain, but I think the fall killed him. I'll know more when I've examined him."

Gardener walked out of the room and called PC Benson up the stairs. "Benson, the team is on their way. Take a couple of constables with you and comb the area. I doubt you'll find anything, but try all the same."

Gardener pointed at the syringe Fitz held. "Fitz, I need the analysis as quickly as possible."

Fitz nodded.

Gardener turned back into the room and stood silent for a moment. He strode over to the DVD player, bent down, ejected the disc. He put it back in and waited for it to load before pressing the play button.

When the action started, Briggs' jaw dropped. "Oh, Jesus Christ!"

They watched, horrified, as the two missing teenage girls, whom they'd all struggled to find, were degraded in front of their eyes. The perverted recipient of their attentions was none other than Herbert Plum. In a Santa suit.

Chapter Fifty

Neither detective waited for an invitation before pushing past the elderly butler as he opened the door.

"Is Summers at home?" inquired Gardener.

"He is, sir, but he's with a client."

"Tell the client to leave," Gardener called over his shoulder as he headed towards Summers' study.

The elderly butler tried to keep up. "He gave me explicit instructions not to be disturbed."

Gardener was tiring of the old butler. He gave Reilly a nod. The butler was thin and wiry and at a guess, seventy years old, with white hair and a complexion similar to stiffened grey cardboard. Reilly placed a hand on the butler's shoulder. "Listen, Jeeves, I'm sure it'll look a lot better if you disturb him. You get my drift?"

The butler nodded. "I'll see to it, sir."

When they were finally allowed to see Summers, he was sitting at a cluttered desk enshrouded by smoke. Gardener reached the middle of the room and smelled perfume. He wondered who had visited and how they had left. As he glanced around, his eyes came to rest on a door in the corner, which he had somehow failed to notice on his previous visit.

"I find this intrusion highly irregular, Mr Gardener. You'd better have good reason."

"There'd be little point being here if I hadn't." Gardener sat down, removed his hat, and waved away the smoke around his head. Reilly remained standing. "There have been further developments. I have more questions for you."

"I've told you everything I know."

"I doubt that very much," replied Gardener, silently seething. "Which is why I have a search and seize warrant for your premises and your books."

The expression on the agent's face could have frozen an active volcano. His pupils dilated. Gardener felt as though he was staring down a double-barrel shotgun. The cigar on which Summers had been about to take a drag remained motionless in mid-air. "I beg your pardon?"

"You heard me. I have two officers in a squad car outside, with two men from forensics. I also have a search warrant for your premises." Gardener handed it to Summers for inspection.

"This is outrageous! I don't know what you think you'll find."

"For your sake, I should hope nothing."

"I will, of course, seek legal advice, Mr Gardener."

"Feel free," Gardener smiled. "Now, if you don't mind, I'd like the team to make a start, and I'd like you to answer my questions."

"Am I under arrest?"

"Not at all, you're helping with enquiries," Gardener said as he left the room. He went out to the squad cars and motioned for the forensics team to begin. He then rejoined Reilly and Summers in the study, continuing on as if he never left. "Last night, Mr Summers, where were you?"

Summers re-lit his cigar. "Attending a Christmas dinner hosted by the Entertainment Agents Association."

"Where? What time did it start and finish?" Gardener asked.

"The Queens Hotel in Leeds. Started about six-thirty. Finished around midnight."

"Were you with anyone?" asked Reilly.

"No, I went alone."

"How convenient," Reilly sneered.

"Did you stay all evening? Where did you go once you left?" asked Gardener.

"As a matter of fact, I didn't. I left at eight. I didn't feel too well. I came straight home."

"And your butler can verify your return?"

Summers hesitated. "No, I gave him the night off."

Gardener wondered why he paused. "So, you went out for the evening, alone. You took ill, came home alone to an empty house. Spent the rest of the evening how? By yourself?"

"I don't like your implications, Mr Gardener."

"And I don't like your answers, Mr Summers. Were you by yourself for the rest of the evening?"

"Yes, but before I went to bed, I had a phone call from the chairman of the association. Checking on my health, you understand. I'm sure the phone company'll have a record of the call."

"We've no doubt they will," retorted Reilly. "But what would it prove? It doesn't prove you were here. All it tells us is that a call came to your house. We want to know your movements for last night. And you've told us, but you have no way of proving where you were."

Summers smirked. "But surely you have enough brains to realize, Mister, er..."

"Reilly!"

"Quite. Surely you realize there are people who can verify I was at The Queens between six-thirty and eight in the evening?"

"Maybe they can, and you're going to give us a list of names so we can check it out. But we're more interested in your movements after you left. The ones you seem to have difficulty proving, do you not?"

Summers grew defensive. "I think it's time you told me why you're here."

"Does the name Frank Myers mean anything?" asked Gardener.

For the second time in as many minutes, Summers bore an expression of displeasure.

"What about him?"

"He was killed last night, at his home."

"And you think I had something to do with it?"

"You tell me. What concerns me is why you lied to me the last time we met. I asked if you had anyone else working for you in the same capacity as Plum and Thornwell. You said you hadn't."

"Which was true."

"Then can you explain why he was in possession of a bill for commission from you?"

"He owed me money."

"How could he if he didn't work for you?"

"When you came to see me, his employment had already been terminated."

"Do you really expect us to believe that?" snorted Reilly.

"You can believe what you want," said Summers, resting back in his chair, sucking on the cigar.

Reilly leaned in closer to Summers. "We're beginning to. And from where I'm standing, it doesn't look so good for you."

"When and why did you terminate his employment?" inquired Gardener.

"He was arrogant. Turned up for work when he felt like it, had a drink problem. He was rude to customers. I finished him at the beginning of December."

Gardener didn't feel as though he was progressing. Summers had an answer for everything. Except, of course, the missing two hours. "Something else you never told us about was his association with Plum and Thornwell."

"I didn't know there was one."

"Come on, Mr Summers. You run an entertainment agency. They all worked as Santas for you. Are you telling me they didn't know each other?"

"I told you last time, Mr Gardener. I didn't socialize with them. I have no idea what they got up to in their private lives. I do have more important things to think about."

"Like your film production company?" Gardener sensed Summers' discomfort. "Tell me a little more about it."

"There's not much to tell."

"You like that line, don't you?" said Reilly. "If only we could believe it."

Summers sighed loudly as if he'd said all there was to say on the matter. "It's a film production company. We specialize in travel documentaries. Teams of people drive all over the country, filming resorts, hotels, places of interest. We use it to promote holidays in Britain."

"What's your involvement?" asked Gardener.

"I put up the money."

"And that's it?"

"Yes, Mr Gardener, that's it."

"Where is it based?"

"Buckinghamshire, inside Pinewood Studios."

"Rather a long way. How did you become involved?"

"I think you're straying from the point. I thought the reason for your visit was to establish my movements last night."

Gardener stood up fast, banging his fist on the desk. "Don't tell me my job. I'm investigating a series of murders. I'll ask whatever questions I please. Do you understand me?"

Summers didn't answer, but his expression said they had him worried.

Reilly spoke up. "Seeing as we have a warrant, you'll have no objection to me having a nosey round, will you, Mr Summers?"

"So long as you have no objection to my butler joining you."

"None at all. In fact, I'd appreciate the company." The butler was summoned, and the pair of them left the study, leaving Gardener alone with Summers.

"So, where was I?" Gardener feigned losing his train of thought. "Oh, yes. Plum, Thornwell, and Myers all worked as Santas for you. They sometimes doubled as clowns. They never appeared in the films you make, did they?"

"Not at all, Mr Gardener. The film side of my business is strictly separate."

"And the only films you're involved with are travel documentaries?"

"I've told you."

Gardener left the desk, studying the movie posters. He scrutinized each one. The frames, the edges, everything he could take in, down to the most infinitesimal detail. He was certain the man was involved, and if he was going to avoid being dragged over hot coals for the warrant he had acquired, he needed evidence. Maybe he also needed a change of tactics. "Are you a big movie buff, Mr Summers?"

"Yes. I've always loved the cinema, particularly the old-time musicals. They don't make them like that anymore."

"No. And have you always wanted to be involved with films?" Gardener had moved over to the door in the corner. The aroma of perfume was stronger. He turned to face Summers, leaning back against the door.

"No. Not really, Mr Gardener." Summers stood up. "Look, if you're here to establish where I was last night, I've told you. All this talk of films is leading nowhere. I run a film production company that has nothing to do with my theatrical business. Now, I appreciate you have an investigation to carry out, but I suspect you'd be better employed elsewhere. The only common link for the three Santas is that they worked for me. I had nothing to do with their deaths and, if necessary, I can provide alibis for the nights they were murdered."

"I'm pleased to hear it. But what really gets me, apart from the fact they all worked for you, is their common interest in pornography. I find it hard to accept they all had such an obsession with it, that they should end up starring in the films themselves."

"Pardon?" said Summers, clearly disturbed.

"You heard me. I have in my possession a pornographic film in which Herbert Plum was having sex with underaged girls. And not just any underaged girls."

Gardener walked slowly across the room, to within an inch of the entertainment agent. His disgust of the man was beginning to increase. He could smell guilt, but he needed more. "Teenagers that are currently on the missing persons list. So, that makes more than one common link, Mr Summers."

Even through the cigar smoke, Gardener could see that the colour in his face had drained.

When he finally spoke, his once calm reserve had disappeared. "Are you saying that the people I employed to work with children are part of a paedophile ring?"

"I seem to remember hinting at it last time, only you weren't so concerned then."

Gardener sat back down.

Summers opened a cupboard door in the desk, grasping a bottle of whiskey and a tumbler. After pouring, he downed the fiery liquid in one. He poured another.

Gardener could see he was shaking. He felt he needed to be sympathetic, make the man think he was apologizing to him. Perhaps that would knock him off balance.

"Mr Summers, I'm only trying to do my job. If it looks like I'm persecuting you, it's only because I'm trying to get to the bottom of things and, at the same time, help you prove your innocence."

It was some time before Summers spoke. When he did, his mood had changed yet again.

He stood up, closed all his diaries, placed them at the end of the desk. "You said you wanted my books. They're all here. I think it's only fair to tell you, there is a fourth person employed within the group. His name's Harry Clayton. You'll find all his details in the red diary on top. But you won't find him until Monday. He's on holiday in Spain. On Monday morning, you'll find him at the

Debenhams department store in the city." Summers sat down.

Gardener wasn't sure how to read his mood. In the short time he'd been there, he'd seen so many changes. Self-confidence, surprise, fear. "Why didn't you tell me before? It would have made my job easier. It may have led us to the killer. We may have prevented Myers being killed, which could have led to information about what's going on. Have you any idea why someone would want to kill these men?"

"No, Mr Gardener, I haven't." Summers sipped his whiskey. "I should have thought the fact that they were child molesters and killers would be reason enough."

A knock on the door disturbed them. It was Steve Fenton. "Sir, have you got a minute?"

Gardener glanced at Summers. "Stay there. I'll be back."

Outside the study, the rest of the squad assembled with Fenton and Reilly. Fenton held out a pack of syringes.

Gardener's stomach turned. "Where did you find them?"

"Bathroom, in the en-suite bedroom."

Gardener took them from Fenton.

The butler broke the suffocating silence, as though he'd read Gardener's mind.

"They're for Mr Summers, sir. His condition, you know."

"What condition?" Reilly asked.

"He's a diabetic, sir. I sometimes have to help him."

Reilly shook his head, raised his arms in the air. "He has an answer for everything."

Gardener grew irritated by the fact everyone had an alibi. "In that case, I want you to get a sample of the insulin, and give it to one of my officers for testing."

The butler turned, but Gardener stopped him. "The room in the corner of the study. Where does it lead to?"

"It's the library, sir."

He turned to Fenton. "Well done, Steve. Have you found anything else?"

"No. Clean as a whistle."

"In that case, follow him and get the insulin sample." Gardener was disappointed he hadn't found more, but the syringe was a start. He and Reilly returned to the study. Reilly strode past Summers and into the library. Gardener watched Summers, wishing he had the ability to read minds. Reilly came back out of the library, nodding. "It's clean."

Gardener gazed at Summers. "Write down the name and address of your doctor."

"Pardon?" asked Summers.

"Just do it," said Gardener.

The agent did so, passing over the paper.

Gardener took his hat from the desk and placed it on his head. Both policemen headed for the door, but Gardener turned back. "There is one more thing, Mr Summers."

The agent glanced up. "Yes?"

Gardener hesitated. "No, maybe it doesn't matter." He turned to leave.

Summers stopped him. "What is it?"

"It's a long shot. I really don't think you can help me."

"Try me."

Gardener pulled the photo-fit of Warthead from his inside pocket, unfolded it, and held it aloft for Summers to examine. "You wouldn't happen to know him, would you?"

The hesitation was so minimal, that unless you had an obsession with catching the person who had killed your wife, you would never have noticed it.

"No, I'm sorry, Mr Gardener, I don't."

"I didn't think you would."

Gardener and Reilly left the mansion and headed out to the car. "Did you find anything, Sean, anything at all?"

"No. The butler was like a shadow." Reilly sighed. "Look, I'm sorry, boss. I want to wrap this case up as much as you do, but I couldn't find anything to tie Summers in. I feel the same as you. He's a creepy little bastard. He has an answer for everything, but there's no evidence to suggest he's your man. You know, as much as I hate him, if he has killed three paedophiles, who cares?"

"Don't think I haven't thought of that already. But at the end of the day, we have a job to do, whatever we think."

"More's the pity." Reilly started the car and drove off. "More's the fucking pity."

Chapter Fifty-one

It was a little after six-thirty when Gardener arrived home. Back at the station, he'd had another run in with Briggs about the lack of evidence to support his theories. More annoyingly, the incident in Beechtown with the press had reached his ears. All he really wanted was to take a shower, go to bed, pull the covers over his head, and stay there forever.

As he entered the kitchen, the various aromas of a full Christmas dinner made his mouth water. Malcolm was by the cooker, wearing an apron and oven gloves. Chris was next to him, also wearing an apron, and a chef hat. The heat was welcoming.

"Come on, Dad." Chris offered his father a glass of wine, taking him by the hand.

In the living room, the table had been set for five. The place had been transformed with decorations, balloons, spray snow, and a huge tree with dangly toys and presents in one corner. A log fire roared heartily. Spook jumped down from Gardener's armchair, curling around his legs, meowing.

A lump formed in his throat. It was exactly the same sort of greeting Sarah would have given him. She'd always believed Christmas should be special, no matter what was happening in their lives. Particularly with his job. He could see her clearly in his mind. The pitch of her voice rising the more excited she became. How her eyes glistened with emotion, especially on Christmas morning when they were all unwrapping presents.

Gardener hadn't realized, but his father was standing behind him. He glanced at Chris.

The pair of them must have worked so hard. In the time it had taken to walk from the kitchen to the living room, he had all but forgotten about serial killers, paedophiles, drug dealers, and smarmy entertainment agents. It was nearly Christmas. Tonight was about his family.

"Don't you like it, Dad?"

Gardener placed his arm around his son's shoulder. "I love it, son." He turned to his father. "You must have been at it all day. You look tired, Dad. Come and sit down."

"I'm fine, but I'll have a few minutes. Everything is almost done."

Gardener sat down and put his slippers on. Spook curled up on the mat in front of the fire. His father sat next to him.

"I've invited Anei and Jacqueline. I wanted us all to have Christmas dinner together. No doubt you'll think I'm a sentimental old fool, but Anei has made me feel special, and I wanted to do something for her."

"Why tonight? Why not Christmas Day?" asked Gardener, a little taken aback, unsure of how he really felt about it.

"Jacqueline and Anei are spending Christmas in Romania. Anei wants to go. She's not been back to her homeland since she left. Chris, you go and run your poor old dad a hot bath, and I'll finish off in the kitchen," said Malcolm, glancing at his watch. "They'll be here by seven-thirty, and I want everything just so."

Chapter Fifty-two

Gardener found himself running through the park. Up above, grey storm clouds were brewing. Brown leaves crunched underfoot due to a mild ground frost. The park was empty of people and animals, creating a feeling of isolation.

He was running while he was staring at the sky. The shapes of the clouds were frightening him. He knew something nasty was going to happen, but he couldn't figure out what. Only that it would involve him. He tried to remember why he was there. Was he searching for someone? Meeting somebody?

He halted at the bridge that crossed the small stream. As he walked over, he could see dead fish in the water. Fishermen were sitting on boxes at the side of the bank, their rods cast. Why? Couldn't they see the fish were dead? He was about to start running again when he noticed his mother and father. They were not walking but gliding. His mother was constantly admonishing his father for the forgotten TV license.

Gardener panicked. He had to tell her. He reached into his jacket for his mobile phone, but neither the jacket nor the phone were there. Glancing down, he noticed all he had on was a pair of shorts.

As he stared ahead, his parents disappeared. He could see Sarah in the distance, sitting on a bench, staring vacantly ahead as mothers pushed their children on swings. That was why he was here. He was here to meet Sarah. She had something to tell him. He started running towards her, somehow aware that if he didn't, she would be in danger. Leaving the bridge, he turned right, following the path. Gardener froze in his tracks as he saw the vagrant called Bob Crisp.

Crisp was staring at him, waving his arm. He was talking as well, but Gardener couldn't hear anything. He was reluctant to move any nearer. But he had to if he wanted to reach Sarah.

She was in some kind of trouble. He closed his eyes, ran as fast as he could. As he passed the vagrant, he heard something about a new life and that he must save Sarah.

What the fuck was he going on about? He already knew he had to save his wife. He simply didn't know why.

Gardener opened his eyes and found he was only yards away from her. Sarah's golden blonde hair was swinging carefree in the wind. She was dressed in a white cotton dress, his favourite. The one he had bought her for their anniversary.

Running towards her, he opened his arms, aware that a shadow was approaching from his right.

The cockney accent startled him. "I told you. Stop meddling in my affairs!"

Gardener glanced at Warthead, saw the gun aimed at Sarah.

"No. Don't shoot!" But Warthead didn't listen. Gardener stared at his wife as the gun went off. The white dress turned a deep shade of red. Sarah disappeared.

Gardener shouted. He was losing her all over again…

The next time he bellowed, he woke up and fell to the floor. The landing was a bad one. He hit the bedside cabinet with the corner of his eye and rolled into the wall.

"Fucking hell!" he shouted, reaching out for the bedside lamp. He only succeeded in dragging that to the floor. Gardener lost his temper, threw it across the room. Why did he always dream about Sarah? More to the point, why her death?

He stood up, pulling his dressing gown from the bed. The clock read 02:05.

It was going to be a long night.

Chapter Fifty-three

Twenty minutes later, he was sitting at the kitchen table with a cup of herbal tea in one hand and a photograph of Sarah in the other. In front of him was his hat, her parting gift. The one that meant so much to him.

He placed the tea and the photograph on the table and picked up the hat. Even now, he still couldn't work out why she had bought it. He'd never told her he wanted one, and she'd never shown any interest in hats all the time he'd known her. But she had bought it for him, and he loved it. He wouldn't part with it.

He poked his finger through the bullet hole, thinking how lucky he'd been on that night.

The bullet could so easily have blown his head apart. Maybe Sarah would still have been alive.

Gardener thought about that possibility for some time. He wouldn't have liked that. Not because he would have been dead and she would have lived, but because he couldn't stand the thought of her having to suffer like he had.

Gardener grew extremely angry. One careless moment was all it had taken. One stupid instant when he couldn't forget the fact that he was a policeman. He put the hat on the table and placed his head in his hands, trying desperately to think through the night in question, and everything that had happened since.

Where had Warthead been? Why the cockney accent, if he really was from Yorkshire? How had he managed to evade Gardener all along?

He tried to clear his mind, to think rationally. He would have to delve into the police records. As far as he could remember, they didn't even have a name for Warthead. Unless of course, Craig Sutton had been right, and he was called Felix. Gardener stood up, put his cup in the sink. He would have to find out the name of the man who had been killed. If he'd been married, then maybe Gardener could go and see his widow. See if she knew anything of any value. It's possible that it was not an isolated incident, but a deliberate one.

There had to be a connection with his current case. He could leave no stone unturned. It needed resolving. And although it was personal, it was possible that he could avenge Sarah's death in the bargain. Only then did he feel he could have the hat repaired.

Gardener crossed the kitchen, slipping into the garage. He removed the cover from the bike, popped in his favourite CD, and listened to Cher's *Love And Understanding* while he started work.

There wasn't too much left to do before the machine was completely stripped down. He would then have to examine everything carefully. Some parts would need replacing, while others could be repaired. He would need an estimate of how much it would cost. He also needed to set a timescale for completing the restoration. The biggest decision would be the frame. It would need taking back to bare metal and being treated before priming and painting it. He wondered whether or not he should do it, or farm it out.

The question of what to do with the bike when he'd finished was a major one. Would he sell it?

Or would he keep it and ride it?

Chapter Fifty-four

Gardener checked the clock on the wall. It read 2:30. He'd been in the police station for three hours, chasing down all the archive material he could find relating to the death of the man involved in the fracas with Warthead. It was warm, and he was tired because he'd had little or no sleep in the last thirty hours. He picked up the bottle of water in front of him, unscrewed the cap, draining half the contents in one go.

He reflected on the meal last night with his family and the minister's. His father had cooked perhaps one of the best traditional roasts he had ever tasted. Maybe he thought that because he had had little chance to grab any decent food in quite some time. Police diets left a lot to be desired. Most of the lads survived on McDonald's because that was usually the only thing open at four o'clock in the morning. He'd always remained adamant that he would not eat junk food, preferring to go without rather than subject his system to that rubbish.

Although the conversation was pleasant, it felt stilted at first. He couldn't help but shake the feeling that Malcolm and Anei were hoping something would develop further between him and Jacqueline. They knew it wouldn't.

He returned to the task at hand. In total, there had been forty-eight witness statements on the night Sarah died. No one knew Warthead by name, though some had seen him in and around the city before. Reports confirm he made his escape that night by running down Bond Street, disappearing through the dark arches.

The name of the man Warthead killed was Tony Parsons. He'd owned his own IT business in Skipton, close to where he lived. He'd been married with a daughter. Tony had been on a night out with some of his employees, a mild stag night of sorts. He'd left them to catch the last bus home. One witness statement, however, stood out above all the others. One of Tony's colleagues, a man called Glen Cooper, said that Tony had suffered the year from hell because his son had died of a drug overdose back in January. Gardener wrote down the address in Skipton.

The weather was pleasant but cold – blue skies, plenty of sunshine, no heat – as he headed out to investigate. He arrived in the market town forty minutes later. It took him another ten minutes to find the house he wanted. It was a detached mock-Tudor with a double garage and well-kept lawns. There were gas mantles on either side of the front door set back in an alcove. He knocked loudly and rang the bell.

The door opened. The girl who answered was no more than sixteen. She had short dark hair and was neatly groomed. Clear skin and white teeth. She wore the tightest blue jeans he had ever seen, with a cream-coloured sweater hanging off one shoulder so you could see the black bra strap. "Where's the fire?"

Gardener smiled, flashed his warrant card. "DI Gardener, Major Incident Team. I'm sorry, it was a bit loud."

The girl glanced at his hat. She blinked several times, staring more intensely, lifting herself up a little. "You the sheriff, then?"

"You could say that."

"God, that was quick. I didn't mean to jump that red light. It can't have been more than half an hour back."

Gardener held up his hand, shocked that she was actually old enough to drive. "Stop right there. I'm not bothered about the red light. I'm here to speak to a Mrs Stella Parsons."

"How did you get that hole in your hat?"

"It wasn't easy." He thought the girl was lovely, probably meant no harm to anyone, but she was a typical airhead. He suspected it would be hard work to glean the information he wanted.

"Who did you say you wanted to talk to?" Behind her he could hear loud rock music coming from another room. He also noticed an iPod lead over her shoulder.

"Can I ask your name?"

"Lyndsey Branningham." Stella Parsons had obviously moved on. He couldn't blame her.

"How long have you lived here, Lyndsey?"

"My parents bought the place about six months ago."

"Are they in?"

"Do you think I'd be playing music this loud if they were?" She bellowed over her shoulder to someone to turn it down. Another teenager appeared from the room in question, dressed only in his boxer shorts.

"Oh, fuck," he shouted, and flew back into the other room.

"He's not with me," she said.

Eager to move things along, Gardener continued with his questions. "Do you know the people who lived here before?"

"Not really," replied Lyndsey. "But from what I've heard, they had an awful time. The husband was killed in Leeds about a year ago. I think he was shot. The year before that, they had lost their son to drugs, and the wife finished up in a psychiatric ward. I don't know where, though."

Gardener's heart sank. Right place. Wrong time. That left no one to verify the story for him.

"It was a right night from what I've heard, a copper's wife was…" Lyndsey Branningham stopped mid-sentence as if she'd worked out whose wife it had been and what the hole in the hat was all about.

He thanked the girl for her time, then went about trying another dozen houses down the same road. Most of them confirmed the story, adding little more. One neighbour, however, gave him gold when she recognized the profile of Warthead. She figured Warthead was the reason the son had died of a drug overdose, and that the father had made it his mission to seek out revenge because he figured the police had done nothing to help.

By the time Gardener headed for home, it was dark and he was really tired. He was bloody hungry, but his appetite was diminishing pretty quickly.

Chapter Fifty-five

"Where the hell have you been? I expected you at nine o'clock! I've got a store full of people out there! Most of them children expecting to see Father Christmas."

Harry Clayton had finished changing into his suit. He was sitting down tying his bootlaces. "For God's sake, give us a break. I'm only a few minutes late."

Harry struggled with his laces as he tried to listen to his boss. Before leaving the Spanish mainland, he'd had an all-day bender with some of the locals. It had continued late into the night, almost until the departure of his early morning flight. The flight had been his only chance to sleep. If he were being honest with himself, he shouldn't be here. Still, plenty of coffee should put him on the right track.

"You're more than a few minutes late, Clayton. You're an hour, to be precise, and I'm not happy about it. I've had mothers on my case since the store opened. No one's given me a break. I've even had the kids nagging me as well. Sort yourself out."

Harry Clayton studied the store manager. He was tall and gangly and bespectacled, with a complexion like a piece of ciabatta bread. His hair was lank and greasy. The texture of his voice was so rough, if you closed your eyes, you'd have thought you were having a conversation with Marge Simpson. He was permanently grumpy, something else Harry couldn't stand.

The store manager gave a final warning as he headed out of the changing room. "I'll be talking to Summers about you."

"Fuck you!" said Harry, after the manager had left. Harry didn't care. He only had till the end of the week before the Christmas holidays started. He could spend the break having another big drinking session with Myers, set up the next venture.

Harry's business trip to Spain had been successful. The contacts had been impressed with the new pornographic material he'd supplied. Harry had returned with some good stuff as well.

He wasn't sure about the new snuff-and-sex films. They were a little too gross for his tastes, but from what the Europeans had said, the market for it was increasing. It wasn't his forte. He'd stick to teenagers.

Another sharp rap on the door distracted him. The manager was still on the warpath.

"Clayton, move yourself."

"I'm coming, I'm coming!"

Harry shuffled out, finally dressed. Satisfied, the manager accompanied Harry to the grotto. The store was fit to bursting, full of Christmas cheer. Most of the staff wore Santa hats, although a few of them dressed in full costume. Bells were ringing, carols were playing, children were shouting and screaming, and the building was engulfed by a dazzling display of colours. The aromas of pine and fruit and brandy permeated Harry's nostrils.

The approach to the grotto made Harry feel like a superstar taking the stage of a pop concert. It was set inside a huge, open front marquee. Harry climbed on his sleigh. *Here Comes Santa Claus* invigorated the crowd. Children cheered noisily. Harry waved constantly as the reindeer pulled him along his journey to the grotto.

His home for the day was another sleigh set amidst an array of snow-covered pines. Grey painted boulders were strategically placed around the grotto for his elves to sit on. Carefully concealed fog machines enhanced his arrival. A resplendent light show and a ringing of bells hidden inside the pines all added to the spectacle of his arrival.

Harry jumped off the moving sleigh and stepped into the grotto, still waving. He felt that his entrance was over the top, but he had a job to do and played along with it. He boarded the second sleigh, positioned a few inches in front of a curtain that backed onto a corridor with toilets.

Harry sighed as the music subsided. He was hot and tired and already had no desire to be there. He hadn't even started yet.

Chapter Fifty-six

Three coffees and two hours later, Harry had entertained at least a dozen kids. Although the caffeine had boosted his energy, he was in need of food and a toilet break. Harry had one more little girl to see. She was six years old and suffered Down Syndrome. The elf took the girl by the hand. Her mother held her other hand, and together they strolled towards Santa Harry.

"Hello," said Harry, as he took the girl's hand. "What's your name?"

"Christina," replied her mother.

"Hello, Christina." He lifted the girl onto his knee. "How old are you?" The little girl wrapped her arms around Harry's neck and smiled at him dolefully, her big, sad eyes staring into his.

"She's very shy," said her mother, an attractive brunette. "She's six."

"Well, Christina, who's six, let me see if I can find you a present. Would you like that?"

Christina laughed. She had a gap in her front teeth where one had fallen out. Harry reached into the sack on his left and pulled out a small box. He passed it to Christina before delving back into it. The second box he had was much larger than the first. "Now then, Christina! What do you think of these?"

The little girl lunged forward, excitedly. The girl tightened her grip. The force of her charge pushed him backward. She was stronger than he'd imagined. Christina screeched loudly into his ear, and Harry detected an odour of Coco Pops on her breath. He tried to remove her arms, but she seemed to be caught on something. Christina jumped around on his thighs, narrowly missing his genitals. The little girl let go, and Harry felt a sharp pain on the left side of his neck.

"My, my, she is excited."

"I'm so sorry," replied her mother, smiling, lifting Christina off Harry's knee. "I've never seen her like that before."

"Don't worry about it," scoffed Harry, wiping his neck with a handkerchief. As he inspected the piece of cloth, he noticed a speck of blood. The girl must have scratched him.

Harry stood up to straighten out his robe. He was sweating. With the heat and the lights and Christina jumping around, he'd grown weary.

Christina's mother strolled away, the girl holding her hand, gazing up at her. She clutched both of her presents tightly to her chest with her other arm. Christina's mother was talking to her, smiling. They glanced back at Harry. He watched, continuing to wipe sweat from his forehead and the back of his neck.

Harry started to shake. He felt hot and cold at the same time. Checking his watch, he realized it had been sixteen hours since he'd last eaten. It was high time he paid the canteen a visit. As Harry was about to move, his pulse raced. His heart was pounding, as though it was too big for his body. He also noticed his breathing had changed. He had to sit down. He'd gone longer without food in the past. It must have been all the alcohol.

Harry sat on his sleigh. His breathing quickened, making his vision blurred around the edges. The pressure inside his head was slowly building, as though his skull was shrinking. Then the pins and needles started. His toes, his fingers, his arms; even inside his head. Within seconds, the pain grew more severe, red-hot needles on the inside of his skin.

Harry managed to stand up. One of the elves approached and asked if he was all right.

Harry's breathing was so erratic he couldn't calm himself down enough to reply. He opened his mouth, but the sound that came out was a restricted gurgle. He heard the elf shout for assistance.

Another two quickly appeared. They all fussed around Harry, asking stupid questions he couldn't answer. Concerned customers had now gathered at the entrance to the marquee, their curiosity mounting.

Harry staggered blindly around the grotto-like Frankenstein's monster, clutching his chest. His entire body felt as if it was on fire. Searing pain raced through every muscle. His nerve endings tingled. He slumped to his knees, his hands gripping the sides of his head, his eyes screwed tightly shut.

Harry suddenly bellowed. His deep, guttural roar startled curious shoppers. Women and children screamed hysterically. Mothers pulled at their offspring, covering their eyes. The elves scattered in all directions. "Oh, Jesus! For Christ's sake, help me!"

Harry raised himself to his feet. He opened his eyes and saw the pizza-faced manager pushing his way through the crowd. Harry thought he was going to explode. Blood charged around his body like an express train. He trembled violently and lost the use of his legs again. He was aware of Pizza-face talking to him, shaking his hands and pointing his finger. He then tried to shield Harry from the shoppers with the flaps of his jacket.

Harry had passed the caring stage. The tremors in his body were now so savage he could neither see nor hear the manager.

Chapter Fifty-seven

Gardener heard the near hysteria as he entered the store. What should have been a happy throng of Christmas shoppers was more like a mob of extras in a disaster film. Two mothers ran past him, clutching their crying children, their faces a mask of confusion. A well-dressed woman smashed into a nearby display of crockery in a frenzied attempt to escape.

As Gardener quickened his pace, he could see a man dressed as Father Christmas on his knees in the middle of the grotto. He'd covered his face with his hands, and he was screaming. At his side, a man dressed in a suit glanced round anxiously. Gardener climbed the steps into the grotto, flashed his warrant card. "Stewart Gardener, Major Crime Team. What's happening? Who are you? Who's he?"

He stared down at the man in the Santa suit, hoping, praying it wasn't Harry Clayton.

"I'm Andy Farlow, store manager. This is Harry Clayton. I've no idea what's wrong him."

Gardener leaned down to help the man. The Santa's screaming reached a pitch of uncontrollable terror.

He gripped Clayton's arms and tried to talk to him. His words were drowned out by Clayton's hysterical shrieks.

Clayton's hands flew outwards suddenly and seized Gardener's jacket. As Clayton screamed, Gardener almost gagged. He'd smelled it before, but never in the early stages. He twisted his face away from Clayton, staring at Farlow, his expression complete bewilderment.

"How long has he been like this?" shouted Gardener. Farlow didn't reply.

A sound emanated from Clayton's throat, a cross between a burp and a gurgle. Unable to contain the mounting pressure, Clayton's body started to disintegrate. His eyes went first, forced out of their sockets. A dirty brown liquid gushed outward, down Clayton's face, into his mouth.

Horrified, Gardener let go, but he wasn't quick enough. Clayton vomited, splashing Gardener's jeans, and a little of his shirt. Gardener fell backward and scrambled to his feet, unable to do anything but watch helplessly as every orifice of Clayton's body leaked the black and brown sludge.

Clayton eventually fell to the floor of the grotto, twitching, screaming, gurgling – totally debilitated.

Gardener turned. Andy Farlow stood behind the nearest pine. Helpless, he examined the crowd, hoping to spot someone he recognized from their investigation, someone he suspected. He flipped open his mobile, called the station, requesting every available officer, SOCOs, the Home Office pathologist, and an ambulance.

When he was finished, Gardener dragged Andy Farlow from behind the pine. "I appreciate you're not well, but this is a crime scene. I want every member of your staff to help maintain the crowd and keep them as far away from this grotto as possible. Lock all the doors and don't let anyone leave, or let anyone in except my officers. Do you have a first aider on site?"

The manager nodded weakly. Gardener was about to ask whom when a man appeared. He was short, fat, and bald, and carried the first aid box with him. Gardener doubted that would help in the slightest. He pointed to Clayton, and the man immediately responded.

At the back of the grotto, Gardener noticed an opening in the curtain behind the sleigh. Beyond the curtain, a corridor led to the toilets. He found them empty. Other than a cleaning closet, there was nothing else. Despite the panic in the store, his footsteps echoed in the empty, silent passage. As he approached the rear of the grotto, a syringe dangling in the curtain caught his eye. A wave of cold fear passed through him. His throat dried almost instantly.

Gardener took a handkerchief out of his pocket, clasping the syringe with it before stepping back into the grotto.

Clayton lay motionless, slowly dissolving. Gardener heard popping and bubbling sounds as the compound within tore him apart. The first aid man had given up. His expression was a mixture of panic and sorrow. Andy Farlow stood by the entrance, talking to an assistant, who was trying his best not to stare.

"Stewart?"

He turned. "Jacqueline?" He guided her towards the middle of the store. "I wouldn't go in there if I were you."

"Too late. I've already seen it. The poor man. What happened?" Jacqueline's eyes were as wide as saucers. "What's happened to you?"

"A long story, as always." He showed her the syringe. "I was too late again. What are you doing here?"

"I've brought my aunt for a little shopping spree, but I seem to have lost her." The minister stared wildly around the store. Gardener noticed the medical team running down the centre aisle, followed closely by Reilly and a couple of constables.

"Don't worry, we'll find her. I need you to go over to the front doors of the store. Eventually we'll get round to taking a statement from you both."

"Of course." She touched his arm and smiled.

Chapter Fifty-eight

Gardener relived the horror of the episode as Reilly drove. They were on their way to Gardener's home before going to see Fitz. He needed to change his clothes. "I've never seen anything like it, Sean." He stared straight ahead, unable to focus on anything but the incident.

"He disintegrated in front of me."

The vivid recreation of Clayton's dissolving body refused to leave his memory. Gardener recalled his frozen expression, the terror in the man's eyes moments before they left their sockets. As if he knew what was coming, yet still searched for a way to prevent it. His white-knuckle grip on Gardener's jacket. The scream that had set Gardener's nerves jangling. The smell.

"Any news on the syringe from Myers' flat?" Reilly asked.

Gardener gazed at the syringe. In the car, the vile, cloying odour felt stronger. "Not yet. But that one may have been filled with curare. This one can't be."

"Why the change of method?" Reilly asked as he negotiated a busy city centre roundabout, choosing the exit that would eventually lead to Churchaven.

"Whoever's responsible, they have some nerve. It's one thing to kill a person in the comfort of his own home when you know you're not going to be disturbed. Or on the grounds of a church late at night. But to do it in a store full of shoppers, mid-morning..."

"Seems obvious to me Summers is our man. He's the only one we know connected to all four murders. He's the only one who knew where Harry was going to be. He has an answer for everything we throw at him."

"Apart from the porn." Gardener's brow creased. "I'd say he is too defensive when you mention porn and his film company in the same breath."

"I've noticed."

"Having said that, he surprised me on Saturday. When I mentioned the DVD of the Santas, he immediately resigned his books and told us about Clayton. If you were involved, surely you wouldn't be so cooperative."

Reilly stopped for a traffic light. "Unless he'd engineered the whole thing. Let's face it, he knew all four of them. He doesn't much care about their deaths. He keeps packets of syringes, supposedly for medical reasons. Perhaps the reason he told us was because it wouldn't make a blind bit of difference. Whatever Clayton knew, he would take it to his grave. Summers would get to him before we could."

Gardener thought it was good enough, but he had not actually seen him in the store. Although he had not read all the witness statements before leaving, he did ask for a list of names and addresses they had collected until that point. Summers was not on that list. Which, admittedly, didn't mean much.

"Have you seen Colin Sharp?" Gardener asked Reilly.

"Not since you gave him his project."

"I need to pin him down. If we're going to learn anything about Summers, we need to find out what Sharp has. What does bother me is that although there's no one else in the frame, I'm not entirely convinced it is Summers."

"The curare?"

"And whatever's in here." Gardener lifted the syringe.

"There might be more than one. Summers may not have the knowledge, but what about his butler?"

Gardener rolled his eyes and shook his head. "It's possible. The real brains behind it could be Jeeves, or whatever his name is. Summers would have the ability and the strength, the butler supplies the knowledge."

Reilly drove the car through the double gates to Gardener's house, onto the red brick drive. He parked the car and switched off the engine before jumping out.

Gardener glanced at his partner. "You're a deep thinker for an Irishman."

"I'll be taking that as a compliment, shall I?"

"Naturally," said Gardener.

"You're all heart, Yorkshireman." Reilly slapped Gardener on the back. "To be sure, I don't know what I'd do without you."

"You need me to keep your feet on the ground. By now you'd have killed Summers and moved on to the next case."

Reilly erupted with laughter. "I think it's time I moved on to the next partner."

Gardener checked around the house. No one was home. "I need a change of clothes, then we'll go and see

Fitz. Help yourself to coffee. And can you do me a favour? Ring and find out where Summers is."

Chapter Fifty-nine

Gardener showered and donned fresh clothing within twenty minutes. He selected a new pale blue shirt he'd bought at the sales at the weekend, with a pair of black corduroy trousers. Back in the kitchen, he hung his leather jacket over a chair. His hat was on the table where he'd left it.

"Any luck with Summers?" Gardener asked, filling a glass of water from the tap. He put his glass down and picked up Spook, who was circling round his legs. "Hello, Spooky, what are you doing inside?" He put the cat back on the floor and poured a saucer of milk.

"No," said Reilly. "At least if he'd been in all morning, he would have had an alibi."

"We'd only have the butler's word for it."

"He'll be down in the cellar, concocting more of his potions. You know, while I've been sitting here on my own, I've been thinking..."

"I thought I could smell burning."

Reilly grinned. "I hope that transfer request comes through. No, seriously. It's an awfully big house for one person and a butler, don't you think? I had the impression yesterday that I didn't see all of it."

"False panels and secret rooms?"

"It wouldn't surprise me."

"It's strange you should say that. On Saturday, in the study, I could smell perfume. And it was stronger by the door in the corner. The library. Is there any way out through there?"

Reilly shrugged his shoulders. "None that I could see."

Gardener sipped his water, thinking about it. He flipped his mobile, called the station. Colin Sharp wasn't there. Briggs had requested that Gardener be put through to him if he called. Gardener hung up before the conversation went any further. He tried Sharp's mobile but gained no answer. "Try Summers again."

Reilly did, but there was still no answer.

Gardener finished his drink, placed his empty glass in the sink. "Let me show you something before we go."

Gardener took Reilly into the garage. He switched on the lights. Reilly whistled through his teeth when he saw the Bonneville. Although not fully dismantled, there was little left to strip from the chassis. Gardener caught the smell of oil, and the paraffin he'd been using to clean the smaller parts with.

"So, this is what Sarah bought you?"

Gardener nodded. "Nice, isn't it?"

"She's a beauty. I never took you for a biker."

"I was, in my younger days. Could never afford one of these. Then when I could, Sarah and Chris came along, and it seemed more practical to get a car. Couldn't afford both, so the dream had to go."

"What are you going to do with it?"

"I'm not sure."

"What would Sarah have wanted you to do?"

Gardener thought for a few moments. "She would have told me to ride it at least once. See if it was everything I thought it would be."

Reilly slapped him on the shoulder. "There's your answer, then, son. Just promise me one thing."

"What's that?"

"You get two crash helmets. I'd like a wee go on this beauty."

Gardener smiled. "You're on."

"Mind you, we'll not be getting far on this." Reilly had what was left of the seat in his hands. "How much is a new one?"

"I've no idea."

"Maybe you should ring your man. You know, the one we met in Rawston."

Gardener paused, glancing at his watch "That's a good idea. Can't see them being cheap, but when we've seen Fitz, I'll take you up on that. You haven't seen my Dad pottering around, have you?"

Reilly shook his head. Although the back door was locked, Gardener still paid a visit to the potting shed and the greenhouse. At the door to the shed, he turned to Reilly. "He's found himself a girlfriend, you know."

"You're kidding me!"

"No. Apparently they've been seeing each other for a few weeks. Meeting secretly at her house when they're supposed to be at the gardening club."

Reilly chuckled. "Well, the randy old fox. And you didn't know? You, a detective!"

"I know. Takes some believing."

"Mind you. I don't reckon he's the only one."

Gardener opened the door, stepped inside. "What do you mean?"

"Come on, son, you don't have to act the innocent with me. My wee wife's a good judge of character. Laura thinks there's something going on in your life as well." He saw Gardener hesitate. "Listen, the expression on your face has just told me everything. Well, come on, who is she?"

"I think you and Laura have been sniffing too many shamrock seeds." Gardener smiled, leaned back against the doorframe. "It's not what you think."

"Try me."

Gardener fidgeted with his hands. "There is someone, but it's one-way traffic. She's Jacqueline Bâlcescu, she's a minister. I've seen quite a bit of her over the last few months when I've been tending Sarah's grave." The memory of his late wife came to mind. Even though nothing had happened, he still felt like he was cheating on her somehow. "We've talked a lot. She invited me for a meal one night. She wanted me to stay." Gardener didn't say anything else.

"And you couldn't?"

After a pause, Gardener answered. "No, I couldn't. It was too soon, Sean. I just couldn't commit. What does that make me?"

"Sensible?" replied his partner.

"That's not how I saw it. I was frightened. Of what, I'm not sure. I was with Sarah for twenty years. She was my wife, the mother of my child. She was everything to me. I'll never find that again. I was terrified. The thought of staying over and going to another woman's bed, touching her in a way I've only ever touched one woman, genuinely terrified me. I couldn't do it."

"Look, son, if that's how you felt, then good on you. I think it's too soon anyway. I admire you for it. It's not every man who can show the control you did. I said sensible because you have that wee son of yours to think about. And to be sure, a relationship with a minister wouldn't be an easy one."

"Do you really admire me for it?" asked Gardener.

"I wouldn't say it if I didn't. And you know that."

He did, which was why he loved Reilly like a brother. "Thanks, mate, that means a lot to me."

Reilly nodded. "Take it steady, you'll know when the time's right. Now, maybe we should get going before that psychopath of a pathologist starts to hunt us down."

Gardener laughed. He was about to close the door when he froze. The hairs on his neck bristled, and his legs wobbled.

Reilly saw his eyes go wide. "What's wrong?" He pushed past Gardener, barrelling into the shed. He turned to face his partner. "What is it?"

Gardener turned, glancing everywhere. He felt as if his veins had frozen. "Can't you smell it?"

Reilly's expression darkened. "Smell what?"

Gardener moved around Reilly, lifting boxes, pushing inanimate objects out of the way.

"For God's sake, what are you looking for?" Reilly asked incredulously.

Gardener turned, about to speak. Instead, he reached past Reilly to a shelf, pulling down a plant housed in a shallow pan. He held it close, almost dropped it.

They both stared at it for a moment, then leaned into the plant and sniffed. Reilly drew back. "Jesus Christ!"

Gardener grabbed the Venus flytrap again, leaned in close, and inhaled once more. The same vile odour of rotting garbage and excrement the corpses had smelled of penetrated his nostrils.

He put the plant on the nearby work surface, then stepped out of the shed and turned slowly to his partner.

Reilly had obviously read his thoughts. "Bit of a long shot, isn't it, boss? It's too much of a coincidence for my liking. Let's go and see Fitz, see what he has to say."

Gardener agreed, but it didn't make him feel any better. His partner was right. It was too much of a coincidence to ignore. After all, what were the chances his father, and possibly his father's older girlfriend, had access to what could be the murder weapon in his investigation?

There had to be a logical answer. So why couldn't he see it?

Chapter Sixty

By the time the two detectives arrived at Fitz's lab, the corpse of Harry Clayton had been laid out on a gurney. Fitz was working by himself, humming along to music from an opera by Verdi. The pathologist glanced up as they entered. Gardener noticed Clayton's body was still decomposing.

"Have you got a minute?" he asked the doctor.

"Of course," replied Fitz. He led them into his office and sat at his desk. Gardener closed the door behind him.

"We've come across something we'd like you to take a look at," Gardener said, nodding to Reilly.

Reilly removed the plant from a carrier bag. He passed over the syringe at the same time.

"Smell the plant."

Fitz inspected them both. "I've no need to."

"We need to know if it's possible this plant was used to melt those men," said Reilly.

Fitz drew a sharp intake of breath. "Could the enzymes from the plant cause the destruction we've seen in the four bodies? I'm not a botanist, but it might be possible."

After searching around his desk, the pathologist found what he wanted.

"The results of the syringe analysis from Frank Myers came back from the lab this morning."

"And?" asked Gardener.

"The problem when you start from scratch is that you don't know what you're looking for. Let me see. Characteristics of known chemical groups. The content of the syringe doesn't fit into any. Opiates and amphetamines also drew a blank. The only thing we know for certain was the compound destroyed the proteins in the body. To answer your first question, gentlemen, yes, the plant enzymes from the Venus flytrap are probably powerful enough to do it."

It was not what Gardener wanted to hear. The fact he'd found the plant in his father's shed stuck in his mind. Too much of a coincidence. "You'd need a good botanical knowledge to be able to carry out using this enzyme, right?"

"Definitely. You'd have to know what you were doing in order to extract it."

"What about the curare? Surely you'd need to be a chemist?"

"Not necessarily. Curare is also extracted from a plant. Before we get carried away, I think we need to test the plant and the contents of the syringe as a proteolytic acid. We need the confirmation. Let me have the plant and the syringe tested. In fact, I'll take them over to the university myself. While I'm there, I'll go along to the botanical department and find out what I can about the Venus flytrap."

Gardener checked his watch. "When are you going?"

Fitz hesitated. "I suppose I could go now."

"We'll come with you."

Chapter Sixty-one

After leaving the plant and the syringe for testing, the three men sought out Vanessa Chambers. They found the botanist in her office. She was approximately thirty; blonde and bubbly. Although she gave the impression of a scatterbrain, Gardener liked what he saw. She spoke with a confident upper-class accent.

"Doctor Fitzgerald! What a lovely surprise. What brings you here?"

It was the first time Gardener could recall Fitz being called by his full title.

"Business. I'd like to introduce a couple of colleagues of mine who have an intriguing problem, to say the least."

Vanessa glanced at Gardener. "Where have you been hiding him?"

Reilly smiled when Gardener blushed as Fitz made the introductions.

"Take a seat, if you can find one," Vanessa said as she rushed around the office clearing books and magazines.

Gardener found a seat and briefly went through what he knew, disclosing a little about the case and his possible theories.

"Oh, this is interesting," she squealed. "What can I tell you about the Venus flytrap? It was described by Darwin as 'one of the most wonderful plants in the world.' Insects are attracted by red pigment and secretions of nectar on the inner surface of the trap lobes where the sensitive trigger hairs are. A single touch has no effect. But a second touch within a few seconds will induce sudden closure of the jaws.

"Specialized glandular hairs on the upper surface of the leaf secrete a fluid that helps digest the prey. It's thought that the movement of hydrogen ions, giving changes of acidity, occurs in the walls of some of the cells. What is now well established is that the secretion of the glandular hairs contains a mixture of enzymes, the most important being proteolytic."

"Which is what, in English?" Gardener was growing impatient. Fitz had a habit of doing exactly the same thing to him, talking gibberish.

"Breaking proteins into smaller fragments. The fluid kills and digests the prey. When the trap reopens, it reveals a skeleton."

A series of images of the dead men swept through Gardener's mind.

Vanessa continued. "The digestive enzymes include proteinases, peptidases, and phosphatases, all of which break down the body of the insect."

Gardener leaned back in his chair. "So, if the fluid secreted by the flytrap was injected directly into the jugular vein, would it have the same effect on the human body?"

"Very probably." Vanessa giggled – an excited, childish laugh. "How ghastly. What an awful way to die. Would be terribly painful. As it travelled around the body, it would literally dissolve everything, reduce it to a liquid mush, leaving only the skeleton."

Fitz interrupted. "Vanessa, would the enzymes disappear?"

"Oh, yes. Leave no trace of themselves, only amino acids."

Gardener noted an expression of confirmation from Fitz. "I'd say we've found our answer, gentlemen."

Gardener turned to Vanessa. "Be honest with me. Would it be possible to extract the fluid from the plant?"

Vanessa placed her hands around the back of her head. Her face changed expression a number of times, and she muttered to herself while thinking. "Yes. It's very possible. Particularly if you know what you're doing. Unique as well. I've never come across it before."

Gardener was disappointed. Not with the botanist's knowledge. She'd answered each question confidently. None of her responses were what he wanted to hear, however. Vanessa Chambers had given Gardener everything he needed, but little of what he wanted.

"One last question. What's the best way to cultivate the plant?"

"Ideally, wet sphagnum bogs, rainforest leaf litter, seasonally wet sandy soils, and moist mountain soils are the best environments. You can cultivate the plant in a greenhouse, however. The compost would have to be acidic, and of low fertility. Only rainwater should be used when feeding. Plastic pots are suitable, but as many carnivorous plants have sparse root systems, shallow pans are often preferable to standard pots. Full sun is best, but artificial light from fluorescent tubes will do."

Vanessa clapped her hands excitedly. "Oh, I must say, you gentlemen have marvellous imaginations. Fancy coming up with something like this. It would make a wonderful book."

Gardener rose from his chair. "Wouldn't it just."

Chapter Sixty-two

It was a little after six o'clock when Gardener drove through the school gates. He locked the car and jogged towards the building. Once he'd collected Chris and dropped him back home, he would have to go straight back to work. Gardener flipped his mobile and called Jeff Harrison to ask about the price and availability of a seat for the Bonneville.

The reply was a shock. "That much?"

"Depends what you're looking for, but the King & Queen seat really is the business," replied Jeff. "Tell you what I'll do, I'll drop the brochure off at the station for you. Have a look and get back to me."

Gardener put the mobile in his pocket. Two hundred and fifty pounds was a bit steep. Still, he could always dream. He rubbed his hands together, blowing into them as a cold wind encircled him. The huge glass building enlightened a darkened sky, reviving memories of his own schooldays.

As he entered the reception, he noticed the hushed atmosphere. He passed two teachers in the corridors leading to the sports area. The nearer his approach to the gym, the more he could hear voices. As he reached the changing rooms, Chris's friend Tommo came charging out, kit bag slung over his shoulder, his hair still wet from the shower.

"Tommo! How are you?"

The boy's expression was one of surprise. "Mister Gardener!"

Gardener detected something odd about the youth. He was normally bright and cheerful.

Today, he seemed defensive. Alarm bells started to ring in Gardener's head. "Tommo, where's Chris?"

"I don't know."

"Do you mean you don't know where he is at the moment? Or you don't know where he is at all?"

"At all, Mister Gardener."

Ice water surged around Gardener's veins. He knew Tommo well enough to know the lad appreciated a joke, but he was sensible enough to realize where to draw the line. Tommo's expression had transformed into genuine concern.

"When did you last see him?"

"Dinnertime. He said he was going to get some chips."

"And you haven't seen him since?"

"No. But we were in different parts of the school this afternoon. I said I'd see him at football."

Gardener felt nauseous. There was probably a logical explanation. Maybe Chris had changed his mind, gone straight home. His son should be here, though. Chris loved football. He wanted to play today. Images of Warthead burned into his brain, unbidden.

"Where's the sports master?"

"In the gym." Tommo nodded his head toward it.

"I'll catch you later, Tommo." Gardener ran down the hall. He found Raglan and a couple of pupils cleaning up. Raglan was short but broad, with a ruddy complexion. He had powerful arms and legs, and retained a military posture. Gardener had always felt that the man couldn't accept the fact he was no longer in the Army and refused to allow his authority to be flouted. He'd often heard reports of Raglan barking at the boys for little or no reason.

Raglan spotted Gardener on his determined approach. "Gardener! What brings you here?" That was another thing Gardener didn't like. Raglan never used a title, only a surname.

"My son," he replied.

"Haven't seen him."

"When did you last see him?"

"Can't remember. Saw him around the school this morning. Reminded him about the football. If he can't be bothered to show up for the game, I don't see why I should waste my time chasing him. Good spell in the army wouldn't do that lad any harm."

Gardener flipped, and moved so fast he frightened even himself. Using his forearm, he pinned Raglan against the gym wall. "Don't you read the newspapers, you pompous prick?" he growled.

Raglan was flustered, surprised by the attack. "Take your bloody hands off me, Gardener!" Although Raglan had been military trained, he struggled to break the policeman's grip.

The two pupils assisting Raglan quickly ran off.

"There are children going missing all the time. One of them from this school, now dead!"

Gardener released Raglan, but his anger remained. "Didn't you think it was strange that Chris didn't show up?"

Raglan straightened his clothes. "You know what kids are like. Always changing their minds."

"In some cases. Not Chris. He's been going on about football for weeks."

"It's not my job to look after your son, Gardener."

"It is when he's in school!"

"But he isn't, is he? And I didn't know that. I've got more important things to do than run around after adolescent youths who are unreliable at the best of times."

Gardener was aware that the two youths had returned with another teacher. Once again, he grabbed Raglan by his collar, shoving him against the wall.

"Hey, come on, calm down!" shouted the teacher.

Gardener didn't know his name. Didn't care.

"You're not fit to be a teacher." Gardener's voice was threateningly calm. "When I find my son, you'd better hope he's okay. If he isn't, and if anything's happened to him, I'll hold you responsible. Then I'll come back."

"Look! I don't know who you are, but I think you'd better leave before I call the police."

The other teacher tried to break Gardener's hold.

He let go of Raglan, pushing past the other teacher.

"I am the police!"

Gardener stalked off, leaving both men open-mouthed.

Chapter Sixty-three

Reilly found Gardener in the park, sitting on the same bench where Sarah had told him she was pregnant. Gardener stared straight ahead, oblivious to his partner's presence. An early morning frost glistened underneath a pale blue sky graced with few white clouds. In the distance, a white cat stalked a bunch of sparrows. An old couple strolled by hand in hand, casting a wary eye at the tired man with a five o'clock shadow.

At last, Gardener turned to Reilly. "How did you find me?"

"It's our job to find people. Your dad's worried sick."

"I imagine he is."

"Of course he is. He hasn't seen you since yesterday, which is bad enough. But his grandson is also missing. How do you think he feels?"

"I know how he feels. He's worried about his son. And I'm worried about mine. There's a difference, though, Sean. At least I can take care of myself. My son is only thirteen."

Gardener's thoughts drifted back to the early part of the previous evening. After leaving the school, he'd spent some time sitting in the car, trying to put his mind in order. Feeling like an ogre. He'd found himself constantly asking the same question. Why did he keep losing the people he loved? His mother; then Sarah, a year ago. Now Chris.

As time had passed, he'd eventually forced himself to think logically. Gardener had left the school car park and checked all of Chris's friends. Each had told a similar story. Chris had left the school at dinnertime for a bag of chips. No one had seen anyone with him. More importantly, no one could recall seeing him return. The task had taken Gardener most of the night.

Two bottles of water later and a phone call home, which remained unanswered, fired his enthusiasm to continue searching. He had toured the places he knew Chris liked to go. The parks, the cinemas, the amusement arcades. Patrolling like a vigilante in search of his prey. The longer the hunt went on, the more fruitless the task became.

His thinking had eventually altered. He'd gone from a distressed father seeking his son, to a wanton man hell-bent on revenge. His mind had become a bubbling cauldron of animosity and hatred. His quarry, Warthead. The freak with the misshapen head had been imprinted in his mind like a Polaroid snapshot.

Gardener studied the Irishman's well-defined features. In the three years that they had been partners, Gardener realized how reliable he had been. After Sarah had died, Sean Reilly had been the man behind his return to work. He had proved to Gardener that he had the courage and the conviction to continue. He'd taught him to believe in himself. Life went on. Gardener had to persevere, if only for his son's sake. "How did my dad find out?"

"He had a call from the school about the incident. He called me soon afterwards. I told Briggs. We set the wheels in motion. And believe me, we're on the case with Chris. Briggs pulled out all the stops. Every officer we have is out searching for that wee boy. And I'm telling you, not one of them went home last night. I'm surprised you haven't seen the posters all over the city."

Reilly returned to the subject of his father. "You should have called your dad. He's disappointed. He hasn't said as much, but I can tell. You need each other, especially now."

Gardener sighed, resting his head in his hands. "I did call, but there was no answer. I know I should have continued calling. With everything that happened yesterday, I didn't know where the hell I was."

Gardener stared at his feet. He was tired. He'd had no sleep. His body ached all over because it was cold. His mouth felt like he'd been chewing a carpet. He glanced across the park. The sparrows had flown but the white cat remained, reminding him of Spook.

Gardener finally spoke again. He stood up, staring down at Reilly. "I'm confused. I'm tired. I'm angry. Most of all, I'm hurting. My son is out there. I don't know where he is. For all I know, he could be dead. If he's still alive, he'll be hurting as well. He'll be frightened. I can't stop thinking about it. I'm just going over it and over it in my mind. It's tearing me apart, Sean. I'm a policeman and I can't even find my own fucking son! How do you think it makes me feel?"

Reilly stood up. "I know exactly how you feel."

Gardener continued. "Do you realize what I'm saying? I don't want to think about serial killers and who's doing what to whom. I want my son back! To hell with the investigation. My son is the only thing that matters."

Gardener leaned back against a nearby tree. He was dizzy. When the feeling passed, he spoke again. "I don't know where my son is, but I've a bloody good idea who has him. Warthead's been following me. He must have been. He wasn't content to kill my wife. Now he wants my son."

"You don't know that for certain."

Gardener glanced upwards. A plane passed overhead. His mind was suddenly propelled into the past as he thought of himself, Sarah, Chris, and his father all jetting off for a tour of America. They had spent the first week in Disney World, and the second on the California coast. He had never seen Chris so happy. They had all been happy. Times were good.

Gardener continued. "No. You're right, I don't know for certain. But one thing I do know is that standing around here won't find him."

Gardener made to move. His right knee gave way, and he stumbled back onto the bench.

Reilly caught him, sitting down with him. "When did you last eat? How long do you think you can keep going like this?"

"Till I find him."

"And how long will that be?"

"I don't know," replied Gardener, unsure where Reilly was heading.

"Precisely. It could be days. You can't go without food all that time. You're no good to your son if you're dead."

"Maybe not. But while I'm wasting time eating, I could be searching." Gardener stood up again. So did Reilly, grasping his partner's shoulders.

"Listen to me. You're not on your own. You've got the resources of the whole team. Together, we'll sort it out.

Give me a few minutes, boss. I have something important to tell you. Spare me the time. Let's get some food inside you, and you can listen to what I have to say."

Gardener reluctantly agreed.

Chapter Sixty-four

The walk to the park gates and the mobile caravan felt like a marathon. Neither man spoke. The weather was improving, growing milder. When they reached the van, Gardener chose to sit at one of the tables. Reilly ordered.

Eventually, the Irishman returned and passed over a sandwich and a hot drink. To Gardener it smelled good, and though he expected it to taste like cardboard, it didn't. Even the tea wasn't too hot. But neither did anything to appease him.

"What did you want to tell me, Sean?"

Reilly finished his sandwich, took a long mouthful of tea. "I grew up in Ireland, as you well know. I had to learn the hard way, and I matured into an adult bloody fast, I can tell you. You had to be hard to survive. Me and my brothers were always caught up in street battles that started small and escalated into fucking wars before you knew it. It was always political.

"We moved to Portballintrae when I was seven, just off the coast, near the Giant's Causeway. I met up with an old-timer there, Laura's grandfather Seamus. He fascinated me. He was very wise, and he knew how to survive. Not just from the land, but almost every way you could think of. He used to take me fishing and we'd sit on the rocks for hours, listening to the water, staring out to sea. It was relaxing.

"Another thing he shared with me were the legends surrounding the Celtic people, and how they often helped him overcome his problems. Now, I'm not going to spend all morning boring you with those. So, I'm going to tell you about something that happened to Laura and myself. Something I've never told anyone else."

Reilly finished his tea. "It happened a few summers back. Our daughter, Linda, had taken a train to Belfast to see a concert. An hour before it started, there was an explosion at a church on the opposite side of the street. Fair rocked the place, so it did."

"Your daughter?"

Reilly nodded.

"I didn't realize you had a daughter. You've never mentioned her."

"Like I said, I've never told anyone."

Gardener noticed, for possibly the first time since he'd known his partner, a concerned expression. Behind the stone-enhanced exterior, Sean Reilly really was capable of showing emotion. It was a rare experience. He was perhaps the only person whom Gardener knew that seemed able to keep his emotions in check.

"The building had to be evacuated," he continued. "Hordes of people spilled out onto the street. Then another series of mini-explosions shook the place. A lot of people were killed and a lot more were hurt, I can tell you. You see, that's the sheer senselessness of it all. Bombs are not the answer."

"Where were you when it happened?" asked Gardener.

"I forget where I was now, but that's not important. A political organization called Black Velvet claimed responsibility. Now Linda, God love her, she was a wee chip off the old block. When Black Velvet grabbed one of her friends as hostage, our Linda waded in and tried to save the girl."

Reilly paused but Gardener said nothing.

Reilly's eyes had dampened when he glanced at his partner. "She took a shotgun blast to the face at point-blank range. The coroner said afterwards it would have been instant, she wouldn't have known anything. But we did. Laura was devastated. Couldn't eat, couldn't sleep, crying all the time. I was given leave from the RUC. Me being who I am, I decided no one was going to get away with doing this to me.

"I went underground with the sole ambition of carrying out a one-man vendetta. Through various contacts, I found the headquarters and persuaded a couple of dogshites to give me the information I wanted."

Reilly paused, leaving his partner with the impression that he didn't want to go any further.

"Suffice to say, before I left, I thanked them for their cooperation. The group responsible for the bombing took a number of hostages – Linda's friend being one of them. They were keeping them in a derelict warehouse on the outskirts of the city. I rounded up a couple of friends and paid a visit. There were only three people supervising: one of them was the man who pulled the trigger, and he was mine – all mine. We freed the hostages, and I delivered the three personally. In bags. As you can imagine, my reward was my passport to the top man. The man who'd pulled the trigger was his brother. We had a meeting, ironed a few things out, and he let me go. Nothing more was said."

Gardener shuddered when he thought of what his friend was capable of, despite having always suspected as much.

He made light of it. "Sounds like the Sean Reilly we've all come to know and love. Didn't the RUC find out what you'd done?"

"They might have suspected something, but they couldn't prove it. My point is this, my friend: you're going to have to follow my example."

"I'd gladly kill the bastard if I could find him."

"No, for God's sake." Reilly waved his hands in the air. "I don't want you to kill someone. I want you to go underground. Think back to the Thornwell killing. Who was sitting on a bench, waiting patiently to speak to us?"

"You mean Bob Crisp."

"Exactly. I told you at the time he was worth listening to. I think he knows a lot more. There's something in his past. And it wouldn't surprise me if Summers is connected. And what's more, I'll bet he knows about that bastard Warthead."

"But why not tell us at the time? If he had information which could have led to an arrest, why not tell us?"

"Who knows? Maybe he's frightened. Perhaps Summers has a hold on him. It goes a hell of a lot deeper than what we think."

Gardener considered the Irishman's words. "If I go underground, what's Briggs going to say?"

"He doesn't need to know. You know as well as I do he'll take you off the case anyway. Go home. Get some rest. Tonight, find your oldest clothes and go into the city and search out the vagrants. You have to find Bob Crisp. Find him, and I think you'll find your adversary."

Gardener stood up and made as if to leave. "I can't do that. Sean, we're three days from Christmas, and my son has been abducted. I want him home with me, where he belongs."

Reilly also stood up. "And you will! I've told you, we're all looking for him. Trust me, boss. I think I have a wee bit more experience in these matters. Keep your mobile with you and keep in touch. Most of all, do what I'm asking you to."

In the end, it sounded logical to Gardener. Perhaps Reilly was right. Maybe Bob Crisp would have the answers. No one else had.

Chapter Sixty-five

"He's my grandson. I had a right to know what was going on!" Malcolm banged his fist on the table, causing his tea to slop over the cup. He was sitting opposite his son.

Gardener stared at the clock. Late afternoon had slowly turned into early evening. It had grown dark. He'd returned home around midday after a meeting with Briggs. The DCI had told him the same as Reilly, go home and rest. The police were already searching for Chris. Gardener had agreed only because he knew it wouldn't affect his plans.

Once home, he'd gone to bed after reading a note left on the kitchen table from his father, who had resumed his own search. Although Gardener had slept, it wasn't continuous. He was unable to rest, and at one point, had a nightmare in which Chris was being chased down a series of dark tunnels that finally led him to a dead end. In the dream, Gardener was unable to reach his son. The vision terminated with Chris crying for help, as Warthead approached him with a syringe. Gardener joined in the shouting and woke himself up.

"I'm sorry, Stewart, but I don't agree with your tactics. I was worried sick after the school called and told me you'd assaulted two teachers."

"Assault's a bit strong. But they deserved everything they got." Gardener and his father had been discussing the situation for almost an hour since he'd risen. Each had listed their search areas, whom they had spoken to, and the possibility that Chris may not have been abducted but lay hurt somewhere, unable to contact them.

Gardener was disappointed with himself. Chris had been complaining about his mobile phone recently. It needed a new battery. After trying to identify the cell masts at the station, a cell dump on each had revealed nothing. Which must have meant either his mobile was switched off, or the battery had failed. Either way, he needed a new one.

"Well, whatever you did, they weren't pleased."

"They should pay more attention to what's going on around them, then," shouted Gardener.

"Yes, yes, I agree. Look, sitting here bickering isn't helping Chris. What are you doing tonight?"

"Same as last night. I'm going to look for him."

"I'll come with you."

Gardener thought about where he would need to go, and realized his father couldn't cope. "Dad, I'd prefer you to stay here. It's pointless both of us going out. If Chris is hurt and he does manage to limp home, he'll need a friendly face."

"Okay. Point taken. But take your mobile, and for God's sake, keep in touch," Malcolm said.

"Before I do go, there is something I need to ask. What do you know about Anei?"

His father held his gaze and hesitated. "What do you mean?"

"I'd just like to know."

"What, at a time like this? Your son has gone missing and you're interested in your father's girlfriend? I know you better than that, son. There's a reason. What is it?"

"It may be something, or it may be nothing. I'm just curious, is all."

Malcolm's jaw dropped. "You seriously don't think Anei has him, do you? Or that she has anything to do with it?"

Gardener raised his hand to ease his father's agitation. "No, of course I don't. But please, just satisfy me, and tell me what you know."

His father eyed him suspiciously, but gave in. "What can I say? She was born in Romania. Came to England during the war with her family. They eventually moved to Yorkshire, but a terrible tragedy befell them, leaving only Anei and her sister Irina. Irina managed to look after her.

They got work on a farm. Irina met someone there and married him. They had a son. After a lot of hardship, they managed to keep the farm. The reason I admire her so much is not the hardship she or her family faced, it was the decision to move."

"You mentioned a son. Have you met him?"

"I haven't, no. The son was her sister Irina's, not hers, which would make him Jacqueline's father."

"He's dead?"

Malcolm shrugged. "I assume so. I can't remember her exact words, but she implied he was no longer around."

"Which doesn't mean to say he's dead." Gardener had spoken more to himself than his father.

"Why do you ask?"

"I'm curious. Jacqueline once said her father wasn't very nice. Other than that, she didn't say much. But she didn't say he was dead, either. All she said was, she hadn't seen him for years. She went to live with her aunt when she was thirteen. Now, if her father isn't dead, then something must have happened." Gardener paused, sipping cold dregs of tea.

"Why don't you ask Jacqueline about it?"

"We're not as close as you'd like to think. Look, there's something else I'd like to know. Where did you get the Venus flytrap from?"

"You've been in my potting shed?" His father was appalled.

"I was looking for you yesterday afternoon. Where did you get it?"

"Anei."

"Where did she get it?"

"She cultivates them in her conservatory. Has quite a few of them."

He'd suspected as much. The hole was deepening. The questions piling up. Was it Anei? An even more disturbing thought was, 'how would Jacqueline feel?' She'd admired her aunt in much the same manner he had his father. But it could very well be one of them. What then?

Gardener's mobile rang.

"Boss?"

"Found anything?"

"Information. Get yourself ready, I'll pick you up in ten minutes. I'm taking you into the city centre, to the Dark Arches. You're looking for a man they call 'The Bear'. From what I've gathered, you can't get to Bob Crisp without him."

"Is that where he is? The Dark Arches?"

"I doubt it. But it's as good a place as any to start. Get the grubbiest clothes you can find, and I'll see you soon." Reilly broke the connection.

Gardener thought back to the day they'd met Bob Crisp, near the kiosk on the grounds of the church. If the vagrant had been shadowed by The Bear, neither he nor Reilly had noticed. He abhorred filth, vagrants, and anything else connected to them. Tonight, he was not only going to have to imitate one, but mix with them as well. He then thought of Chris, and why he had to do it.

Gardener left the kitchen and entered the garage through the connecting door. His work clothes were where he had left them after working on the bike, in a heap near the discarded dustsheet.

Back in the kitchen, he threw them in the tumble dryer to warm.

Reilly arrived quicker than he said he would. Gardener changed clothes, surprised that a mixture of odours, paraffin, oil, and sweat still remained despite a tumble dryer sheet.

"How's the search going?"

"Usual stuff. Briggs had officers at the school, he's spoken to everyone he can think of. In fact, he's set up a special unit to work twenty-four hours on the case. He's using the press for an appeal."

Gardener was touched by his superior officer's actions. "It won't get that far. Come hell or high water, I'll find my son before Christmas."

"I like your spirit, my friend. And you're not on your own. We'll find your son," Reilly said.

"Dad, I'm going," Gardener said to Malcolm as he entered the kitchen.

"Dressed like that?"

"It's a long story." Gardener paused. "Look, I'm sorry about what I said. Thanks for what you're doing."

"You're welcome, son. Whatever you're doing, I don't think I'm going to like the idea, so I won't ask. For God's sake, be careful!"

"I will."

As Gardener and Reilly were about to leave, Malcolm interrupted them. "I almost forgot."

He walked into the living room, returning with a small parcel. "It came earlier."

Gardener recognized Colin Sharp's writing. He stared at it for several moments, weighing the choices he faced. Could he afford to be distracted right now?

"Do me a favour. Keep it safe. I haven't time to read it."

Chapter Sixty-six

"What are you doing here, Reilly? It's late."

Reilly glanced up and saw Briggs in the doorway. He hadn't heard him approach.

"I could ask you the same question."

Briggs stepped into the incident room and dropped into one of the chairs. He sighed, removed his glasses, and rubbed his fingers across his eyelids. To Reilly, he appeared done-in: a crumpled suit, his tie hung low across an open collar, glasses that probably hadn't been cleaned for a week.

"I'm knackered," said Briggs. "But I can't settle. I keep thinking about Chris. Where he might be, wondering what I'd be like in Stewart's shoes. Everything's going round in my head. It's all a bloody jumble."

Reilly sighed. "I know what you mean. Have you never had kids? I didn't mean to pry, but the comment..."

Reilly noted the softer expression on Briggs' normally case-hardened features. "No. My wife couldn't have them. She was involved in an accident when she was about fourteen. Car crash; did a lot of internal damage. I suppose she was lucky to live." Briggs paused. "Drunken driver. I knew before we were married, but I loved her. Still do, after thirty years."

"I admire you. It can't have been easy."

Briggs smiled. "No, it wasn't easy. But it's like anything, you learn to accept. You fill your life with other things, like holidays, cars, big houses. Anything to hide the real pain. We both wanted children. She came from a big family."

"Did you not think of adoption?"

"A couple of times. It's not the same, though, is it? No matter what you say, you can't love the child the same as you'd love your own. Julie always said she wanted to feel the child inside her. There's no stronger bond than that."

"There is another way of looking at it. At least by adopting, you could provide a child with a better life."

"Don't get me wrong. We thought about it long and hard. But no matter how many times you discuss it, you have to feel it in here." Briggs pointed to his heart. "And we didn't. So, it wouldn't be fair on the child. At the end of the day, it doesn't stop your emotions from running over when you're chasing perverts and paedophiles."

Briggs threw his arms in the air. "I mean, what's the fucking use?"

Reilly had been surprised by Briggs' emotional outburst. There was, after all, a humane side to the man. "That's why I'm in here. I want to have another look at the DVDs we seized from Myers' flat. The boss reckons Summers is far too defensive when we try to link the porn to his film company."

"You think Summers is making the films? You think Summers is abducting children and running his own little empire of porn; head of his own paedophile ring?"

"That's about the size of it. Maybe we're wrong. I don't know. It's a hunch. If there's no connection on the disc, then we've lost nothing. But I don't trust the man. He's a parasite. When we searched the house, I had the feeling we didn't see all of it. There's a life at stake here. I can't stand by and do nothing. I owe it to the boss to pull my guts out on this. And if I'm right, we might know where Chris is."

Briggs remained silent for so long, Reilly thought he was never going to speak again.

"You don't have to watch it," he said to Briggs. "I'm not watching because I want to. If it means getting Chris back, though, I'll watch them continuously until I find what I'm looking for. There's only one more anyway."

"Okay," replied Briggs. "Fair comment. I'll get us a coffee and I'll join you."

When Briggs returned, Reilly set the disc playing. He was sick to the stomach at having to endure watching the teenage girls and the torture they were being subjected to.

Reilly paid attention to every minute detail in the background. By the end of the film, though, he had learned nothing.

He checked his watch, disappointed. It was a little after one in the morning. Reilly glanced at Briggs. "Look, I'm sorry I put you through it. I just thought…"

"I know." Briggs finished the sentence. "You're a good man, Reilly. I may not like your tactics, but I can't knock your dedication, either to the job or your friend."

"More compliments?"

Briggs laughed. "I think we'd better call it a night. Your missus won't be pleased."

Reilly sighed in defeat. "No. I don't suppose she will."

They were about to leave the room when a noise from the TV attracted their attention.

Reilly had forgotten to switch off the machine. On the screen, the disc loaded the final untitled chapter.

As Reilly watched on, his blood curdled, and his heart missed a beat.

Chapter Sixty-seven

Gardener studied his watch. Six hours he'd been in the city centre. It felt like six years. At two o'clock in the morning, the bustling metropolis was an alien environment to him – a collection of unfamiliar landscapes in a world where he no longer felt socially adept. Late night revellers spilled out of clubs singing Christmas carols, filling their faces, or groping each other while waiting in taxi ranks.

In the early hours, the city streets smelled of fuel and vomit and urine as drunks fought to gain access to doorways or telephone booths or anywhere they could find to perform bodily functions. The noise was phenomenal, more akin to rush hour on a Friday night. Unlike peak time, however, the noise and the crowds died quickly, leaving Gardener alone.

He was sitting on a park bench on the grounds of St John's Church, next to the kiosk where he'd first met Bob Crisp. Despite not knowing where to start, the obvious answer had been the city's down-and-outs. Surprisingly, there were very few around. Those he had come across were either intoxicated or refused to speak to him, possibly realizing that no matter how he dressed, he was not one of them. The few who were prepared to give him the time of day were rendered mentally incapacitated at the mere mention of Bob Crisp, or The Bear.

Gardener felt totally inadequate. More than once he'd questioned his motives and his actions. Shouldn't he be out searching for Chris, rather than some vagrant that may or may not have the answer? Gardener was confident his son had been lured away by Warthead. Like the other teenagers. Shouldn't he be searching for Felix, or whatever he called himself?

His spine crawled. He felt sick to the stomach as the words of Lesley Vickers returned to haunt him. A vivid mental picture of the day they stood by her son's grave entered his head. It might be your son next time. He couldn't let that happen. Anger was building within Gardener like a volcano. If he so much as caught sight of Warthead, he'd kill him on the spot with his bare hands. After he'd found out where Chris was.

He stood up and sighed. It was late. He was tired, hungry, and cold. He smelled. His mood was totally despondent. The only person in the world that mattered to him was missing – God knows where, being subjected to God knows what. He didn't have a clue where to start his search. Nor could he find the one person his partner suspected may provide him with answers.

Could life be any worse?

As if on cue, a voice behind him spoke up and said, "Well, look what we have here, boys."

Chapter Sixty-eight

Chris heard the rattle of crockery beyond the door at the far side of the room. The door unlocked, and in stepped the small man and the elderly butler he'd seen yesterday. At least, Chris thought he was a butler.

"Ah, Christopher. And how are you this morning?"

Chris didn't reply. He didn't want to. He was struggling to remember exactly what had happened. He could recall leaving school to go to the chip shop, but he'd never made it there. The next thing he remembered was waking up in the room in which he was now being held prisoner.

"I've brought your breakfast, young man. Of course, not knowing your preference, I've chosen cereal and toast. I hope you like it."

Chris was frightened. No one had done anything to him since he'd woken, but he was still unsettled. He had no idea where he was, how long he'd been here, or why. Or what these two wanted of him. As he glanced around the room, it reminded him a little of his dad's bedroom. It had a big bed, a sink in the corner, a separate shower room. It was clean and warm, but not to his taste.

"I do wish you'd talk to me, Christopher." The small, bespectacled man turned to the butler. "Don't you, Alfred?" He turned his attention back to Chris. "It'll make things easier for you in the long run."

Chris realized the advice was probably good. It may be better for him if he played along. He found himself thinking about David Vickers, wondering if he'd been in the same situation. He didn't want to end up like his friend. His guts swelled, his fear mounting. "Where am I?" he asked.

"I see you've found your voice at last. Such a sweet little sound, don't you think, Alfred? You don't need to know just yet. Not that it would make much difference. You couldn't do anything about it."

Chris wrinkled his nose. He could smell stale cigar smoke on the little man's clothes, and on his breath. He turned his head away from them. "You can't keep me here forever."

"I have no wish to."

"Then why am I here?"

"Because I want you here. For now."

Chris turned on his captors. "Why? When my dad finds out, you're in for it. He'll sort you out, both of you. He's a cop."

The thought of his father brought a tear to his eye and a lump to his throat. He remembered their recent argument and the things that had been said. He'd made his point, but he didn't feel any better about it now. He couldn't understand why he'd done it.

"It's taken you a while to mention your dad, hasn't it? I must admit, I wondered when you would. It may come as a shock to you, but I know your father."

It did come as a shock to Chris. If the little man knew his dad, then why hadn't they met before? That meant he had a record. It was a thought that terrified Chris. One that regurgitated the memory of his friend David. He felt pressure on his bladder.

"Well, if you do know my dad like you say, then you'll know what a mistake it is trying to keep me here." Chris's bravado made him feel a little better.

"You're sure about that, are you?"

"Too right, I am. When he finds out I'm here, you've had it!"

The little man laughed. "Oh, I doubt it."

Adrenaline replaced Chris's fear. "And if the Irishman gets you, you'll wish you were dead."

The little man addressed the butler. "Quite the little dreamer, isn't he, Alfred? If only his father were as good as Christopher thinks he is."

When the little man turned back to Chris, he noticed the immediate change of expression. The little man's eyes were like black marbles, and his smile was more a leer, not friendly as it had been so far.

Chris panicked. He'd overstepped the mark. Him and his big mouth. He wished he hadn't spoken. His bladder reached the bursting point. He didn't want to soil himself, but at the same time, he didn't think he'd be allowed to run to the bathroom without it appearing like he was trying to run away.

"Now you listen to me, young man. Your father isn't going to find you. He hasn't found the others, has he? Or who's responsible. Nor has he found their killer."

Chris's eyes opened so wide, he thought they were going to pop out and roll down his cheeks. He couldn't believe how cold eyes became when the eyelids were at their widest aperture.

What did he mean by 'the others'?

"As a policeman, your father has had his day. He's finished."

Chris's bottom lip trembled. He could feel the awful tightening of his throat, like when he was going to be sick. He hoped he wouldn't be. He knew the little man wouldn't be pleased.

He approached Chris and leaned down into his face. "If your father had been any good, he'd have saved your mother."

"Don't you dare talk about him like that!" Chris sprang up at such a pace, he launched the breakfast tray into the air. The crockery crashed against the wall, leaving a trail of soggy Weetabix slithering down to the skirting. The butler had taken a step back, nearly losing his balance. The little man was far more agile.

When Chris was on his feet, he had no idea what to do with his short-lived advantage. He saw a raised arm, felt the stinging blow to his cheek. He spun round and hit the bed, holding his face, sobbing. The little man gave him no time to recover, twisting Chris onto his back, and grabbing him by the throat to pin him to the bed.

"You're going to be sorry, young man. By God, you're going to be sorry. You see, I've now decided that your father is going to come here, because it's exactly where I want him. I'm going to make him sorry for meddling in my affairs. The pair of you have made me very angry. I'm going to see you pay."

Hot, steaming urine flooded Chris's pants.

"He'll be forced to watch what I do to you. Can you imagine how humiliating that's going to be? It'll probably kill him. Which will save me the job."

The little man turned and left the room. The butler followed, locking the door behind him.

Chris buried his face in his hands, crying, and silently pleading for his dad to help.

Chapter Sixty-nine

"Derek Summers, I'm arresting you under the Obscene Publications Act of 1964." Briggs glared at Summers with contempt. "You do not have to say anything, but it may harm your defence if you do not mention, when questioned, something you later rely on in court. Anything you do say may be given in evidence."

Briggs glanced at Reilly. "Take him away."

Summers stood up from behind his desk, staring at his butler. "Alfred, phone Frederick. Tell him to meet me at the station."

He turned to Briggs. "When my solicitor's finished, you'll realize you're making a big mistake."

Briggs ignored Summers as Reilly marched him out to the car. He turned to the other officers present in the room. "Search this place from top to bottom."

Chapter Seventy

"Gentlemen, I feel it's time to intervene on my client's behalf."

Reilly shot a disapproving glance at Frederick Dawson. It wasn't the interruption, but the fact that he disliked the obese lawyer as much as his client. Weighing in at around twenty-five stone, Dawson had thinning grey hair with an annoying squint in one eye, which happened to be slightly lower than the other. He was equally as condescending as Summers.

Dawson mopped his brow before he continued, which, as Reilly had counted, was at least the tenth time in as many minutes.

"You've had us both here for over an hour. Your questions, I feel, have led us nowhere. You arrested my client in connection with the Obscene Publication Act of 1964. Yet, you've presented us with no evidence and asked only a relatively small number of questions concerning the alleged crime. Which my client has strongly denied. Gentlemen, I suggest if you can't do any better, you'll have to bail my client pending further inquiries, of course."

"Of course," mocked Reilly. "My apologies, Mr Dawson. It's just that I want to get it straight in my head that your client…" – Reilly pronounced the word with the odium he felt it deserved – "…has no connection whatsoever with the pornographic film industry."

"My client has said so, more than once."

"You're sure about that, Mr Summers? You have never made a pornographic film?"

"No, I've told you!" said Summers. "How many times do I have to repeat myself?"

"And the men that worked for you, who are all now dead, their interest in pornography has nothing to do with you?"

"Not at all."

"Well now, we have evidence that one had sexual relations with teenage girls. You still deny any involvement?"

"I'm beginning to tire of this, gentlemen. You really have nothing on which to hold my client," said the corpulent Dawson.

"Now hold your horses, Mr Dawson. I'd like to show both you and your client a DVD which came into our possession recently."

Reilly noticed Summers had tensed a little.

Frederick Dawson stared at them, confused.

Reilly crossed the room of the interview cell and started the DVD player. Instead of watching the action he'd already seen, he chose instead to monitor the expressions of his captive audience. The film featured Warthead in a panelled library. He was standing in front of a desk. A teenage girl with a frightened expression was stretched across it, performing oral sex on him. After a few minutes, Reilly switched it off.

"What do you make of that, Mr Summers?"

"It's filth! I really have no idea why you wanted to show it to me."

"No?" Reilly feigned surprise. "Have you not seen it before?"

"I most certainly haven't." Summers glanced at his solicitor.

The solicitor was clearly taken aback, judging by his astonished expression.

"So, it's not your library?" said Reilly.

"Pardon?"

"I asked whether or not that sex film was made in your library?"

"Of course it wasn't. I keep telling you, I don't make pornography."

"Gentlemen," Dawson cut in, holding his hands up in supplication. "You have no proof that the library in question is the one in my client's home. It could have been anyone's library."

"Oh, but we have, Mr Dawson." Reilly rewound the tape and played it once more, pausing the film at a specific spot. "Take a closer look, both of you. You'll notice in the background, just on that wall there." Reilly pointed to the screen. "See the coat of arms, do you not?"

"Which proves what?" said Dawson.

"It proves it's your client's library."

"Nonsense! The coat of arms you're talking about is not clear enough to make a positive identification. It could be anyone's."

Dawson blew out a puff of air and mopped his brow, again.

Briggs intervened, picking up an A4 manila envelope, which had been on the floor near his chair. "We thought you'd say that. So, we took the liberty of asking our experts to enlarge the image of the coat of arms. It's amazing what they can do these days, isn't it?"

Briggs passed over the photos. Despite being a little grainy, the design, shape and insignias were all clear enough.

Summers grew flustered.

Briggs pointed at the photo. "If you look at the bottom of the coat of arms, you'll notice the name 'Summers'. You see, the Detective Sergeant is extremely observant, not to mention intelligent. Only this morning he drove to Sheffield. There's a shopping centre called Meadowhall. And down 'The Lanes' there's a shop specializing in name searches. They also have the most comprehensive range of coats of arms we've ever seen. And guess what? Here's yours!" Briggs passed over a computer-generated image.

After allowing the new information to sink in, Reilly asked, "Now, do you still deny it's your library?"

Summers glared at Reilly. As did Frederick Dawson, his brow furrowed, his concern evident.

"Mr Reilly! Mr Briggs!" Summers said, his attitude no longer condescending. "I had no idea my library was being used for immoral purposes."

"Did you not? You've no idea who's having sex across your desk?"

"None at all. Believe me, I shall get to the bottom of this."

"So will we."

"I have to tell you gentlemen that I do spend a lot of time out of town attending conferences," said Summers.

His condescending grin was really beginning to irritate Reilly.

"You're saying that all of the illegal material has been filmed in your absence?"

"Most certainly. I can tell you, as I have done on many occasions, I am not connected to any paedophile ring, nor have I any interest in the type of filth you've shown me."

Reilly noted a return of confidence in the agent's manner.

"Yes, I appreciate that. But you see, we have a wee bit more incriminating evidence. If you look at the bottom left-hand corner of the screen, you'll notice the time and date. It tells me, as it should you, that the production – despite being reasonable quality – is an amateur one. It's been made on a video camera, not a film camera."

Summers' face tightened and the colour drained. "Er, yes, I had noticed."

Briggs took over. "So, can we clarify it is your library?"

"Er, yes, Mr Briggs, it is."

"Good. Because it just so happens we still have your diaries with us." Reilly reached down the side of his chair, placing the books on the table in front of them.

"You'll notice," continued Briggs, "that when the pornographic film was made, you were not out of town at all. In fact, the exact date and time shows us you had a meeting. At home. Doesn't say who with. Would you like to enlighten us, Mr Summers?"

Derek Summers was ashen.

Reilly noticed his hard swallow. At last, he felt he had the bastard.

"You seem to have lost your tongue. Which is a pity, because you've quite a lot more explaining to do, so you have. For example, why are four men with a taste for young girls, who worked for you, now dead? What's happened to the children who were abducted and forced to take part in the sex films? Who killed David Vickers? Who's the man with the warts?"

Both Briggs and Dawson remained silent, but the solicitor's expression was grave.

Summers bowed his head, shaking it.

Reilly slammed his hand down hard on the table.

Summers jumped.

As Reilly piled on the pressure, his voice rose. "What I really want to know is, where's my partner's son? Detective Inspector Gardener, the man with the hat. He has a son who's missing now. He went to the same school as David Vickers. Who's now dead! So too are the teenage girls in the film, I imagine."

Dawson's head bobbed up and down and from side to side as he glanced from Briggs to Reilly to Summers.

"I want to know where my partner's son is." Reilly pronounced each word and banged the desk more than once. His control went AWOL as he dragged Summers out of his chair by the scruff of his neck. "Where is he?"

Summers cracked under the relentless pressure. "No, please, stop him."

Dawson clambered out of his seat and waved a finger. "I really must protest your attitude towards my client." The agent's brow was a mass of sweat. His eyes dilated.

Briggs finally intervened. "For Christ's sake, Sean. Let him go!"

Reilly pulled Summers closer still. "You know where he is, don't you?"

"Detective Sergeant Reilly," shouted a panting Dawson.

Summers screamed like a frightened child. "Please, get him off me. I've never killed anyone."

Briggs managed to break Reilly's hold. The Irishman backed off, still blazing.

"Can I have a word in private, Sean?" Briggs asked, already walking toward the door.

Outside, in the corridor, he went on the attack.

"Jesus Christ, Sean! Have you lost your bloody marbles? In front of his solicitor, as well!"

Reilly lowered his voice. "That bastard's guilty, and you know it."

"I'll admit the evidence is stacked against him," said Briggs. "But there's still a long way to go, and without a confession, we have to keep pushing."

As Briggs went back to the door, he turned to face Reilly before opening it. "Let me take it from here."

Briggs returned to face Summers and Dawson.

It was Dawson who spoke. "That was the most appalling behaviour I've ever seen from a policeman. I shall, of course, be filing a complaint, and probably a lawsuit."

Dawson mopped his brow yet again.

"Feel free to do what you want. But until I'm satisfied of your client's innocence, he's staying in custody. Now, if you'd like to come back tomorrow, we'll resume questioning him."

"You haven't heard the last of this."

"No, I don't suppose we have," replied Briggs.

Dawson turned his attention to Summers. "I'll be back tomorrow, Derek. Don't you worry about a thing. Don't say a word to anyone without me."

Summers merely nodded, too distraught to reply.

Reilly watched as Dawson left, oblivious to the solicitor's scowl.

Chapter Seventy-one

Shortly after six o'clock, when Reilly had calmed down, he tried to contact Gardener for the fourth time. His superior's mobile was still switched off.

He called Malcolm, who confirmed he had not heard from his son.

Reilly leaned back in his chair and sighed, concerned.

He'd sent him into the city. He would have to go and retrieve him.

Chapter Seventy-two

Gardener shook himself awake and groaned. He felt rough, groggy. He struggled to focus. The pain in his head resembled a hangover. Every muscle in his body ached, especially his ribs. Gardener's mouth was dry. Remnants of a coppery taste lingered. His eyes cleared. His vision returned.

Gardener tried to raise himself, but the soreness in his ribs wouldn't allow much freedom of movement. He became aware of how tender his face was. His left cheek appeared to be housing a tennis ball underneath the skin. He touched it, wishing he hadn't.

"Keep still. You'll hurt yourself." The voice was deep and resonant.

Gardener glanced in its direction and understood why.

It must have been the man they call The Bear. At least he hoped it was. As the giant strolled toward him, he towered over Gardener. He was at least seven feet tall, built like a barn door without an ounce of fat. His chiselled features seemed to have been carved from a block of granite. He had a thick head of glossy black hair. He was dressed in a boiler suit and Doc Martens boots. Gardener's stomach turned at the sight of him. He would have given anything to run screaming from the nearest exit. Not that he could see one.

The man extended a hand towards Gardener. "Slowly. Your ribs are bruised."

Gardener glanced around, realizing it was a hand of friendship. He finally accepted the help and struggled to his feet, gasping for breath. The giant assisted Gardener over to a table and chairs.

He had no idea where he was. The room must have been underground somewhere, perhaps a large viaduct. The bricks were in good shape, and someone had taken great care to make the refuge a home. Along one wall, a blazing fire roared. Gardener noticed another vagrant roasting something on a spit. It wasn't anything he immediately recognized, and he thought better of asking. Apart from the table and chairs, they also had a three-piece suite, a couple of beds, cupboards, a drinks cabinet, a TV, and a Freeview box.

Gardener heard running water beyond a door in the wall nearest to him. He was about to ask about it when he was suddenly caught in what he suspected was an earthquake. The sound was horrendous as the whole room shook, dislodging dust from above. He lowered himself to his knees, wrapping his hands around his head, trying to block out the sound and whatever destruction might follow. It finally passed. He straightened up, wincing.

"The trains – you get used to them. Come and sit down." The giant chuckled before introducing himself as The Bear. He called to the vagrant working the spit. "George, three bowls of chicken broth, please."

As Gardener crouched to sit, he was about to ask a question when the running water stopped. He turned his head, and Bob Crisp came through the door in a bathrobe.

"Mr Gardener! I'm pleased to make your acquaintance again. Please, be seated." He glanced over at George. "Only the best china, please, George."

Bob Crisp finished drying what little hair he had and took his place opposite Gardener.

"How are you feeling?"

"Like I've been run over." As Gardener's senses returned, so too did his thirst for knowledge. "Why am I here?"

"Ah. 'One of the greatest pains to human nature is the pain of a new idea.' I don't suppose for one minute the thought of mingling with us, in order to find me, seemed like a good idea to you."

George approached the table with four bowls of chicken broth on a tray. He placed one in front of each of them before sitting with his own.

Gardener felt nauseous. He wasn't sure whether it was his apparent lack of health or state of mind. Dining with vagrants was not his idea of fun. "What happened to me?"

Bob Crisp sighed. "The underground world of Leeds is split up and run by gangs. Pretty much like any other major city in England. I'm afraid you were set upon by one of those. You took a bit of a pasting. They left you for dead. It was George who found you."

The beating explained the pain. The thought of gangs patrolling the city's streets at night, involved in underground warfare, was a prospect he found chilling. And a topic he hadn't the time to discuss.

"Look, you need to explain a few things to me. Where am I? What time is it?" Momentary panic overtook Gardener. He had no idea how long he'd been unconscious. "In fact, what day is it?"

"You must eat your food." Bob Crisp passed around baguettes. They were sealed in packets and had yesterday's date. Gardener didn't want to know where they came from.

"Please, just answer my questions. My son's life is at stake."

"Your son?" Bob Crisp stopped eating. "Is that why you're looking for me?"

"Among other reasons."

"Fair enough." He put down his spoon. "It's Wednesday. As you can see from our magnificent time piece, it's eight o'clock in the evening."

Gardener jumped up and was rendered breathless from the pain in his ribs. "Oh, Christ!"

A quick calculation told him he'd been missing twenty-four hours without contacting his family. A quick search of his pockets informed him he no longer possessed a mobile phone. Nor his wallet.

"You appear to have lost something, Mr Gardener?"

"My mobile phone, my identification, my money. Everything. What happened? How did George know who I was?"

"You were mistaken for a vagrant. We're not very well liked, you see. You've suffered head injuries and bruised ribs. George stumbled upon you, found you unconscious with your warrant card laid next to you. The gang must have realized you were not a vagrant after all. You've been out this entire time. You will need medical attention. You can never tell with head injuries."

Gardener studied Bob Crisp. He reckoned the man was in his mid-fifties from his lined, weather-beaten face out of character with his smooth, bald head. Whether it was the velvet voice with the clipped English accent, the educated manner, whatever, he felt he could trust him. That was saying something.

Bob Crisp rose, taking Gardener by the arm. They made themselves comfortable on the three-piece suite in front of the fire.

"What's happened to your son?"

The vagrant grabbed a menthol cigarette from a nearby table and lit it. Gardener sat back and told him what he knew, explaining the case in detail. Crisp barely interrupted. When Gardener finished, the well-spoken vagrant merely stared at the dancing flames.

He finally spoke, quietly. "'I should renounce the devil and all his works, the pomps and vanity of this wicked world, and all the sinful lusts of the flesh.'" He paused. "I've done you no favours, Mr Gardener. I should have spoken out sooner."

"What are you talking about?"

Bob Crisp took a drag on his cigarette and blew out more smoke. He turned to face Gardener, his eyes imploring forgiveness.

"I used to work for Derek Summers. The man you call Warthead is his son. I know nothing more. Not even the identity of his mother. From what I have gathered, the misshapen head and the warts are a genetic defect. Another story is that Summers beat the girl who carried the child, and the result is what you see."

"How were you involved with Summers?"

"I'm a solicitor by profession, Mr Gardener. Many years back I was disbarred, discredited. I now live underground in fear of my life. Hence, the reason I travel nowhere without The Bear. All because of Derek Summers. He's a nasty piece of work, sir, and you must learn not to trust a word he says. He is a depraved person.

I know nothing of his childhood, nor any family save a daughter whom, according to rumour, he abused. And the son you call Warthead. I have no idea where the blame lay for the things he does."

Gardener's flesh crawled. Could Summers be everything all rolled into one? Abductor? Paedophile? Killer?

Bob Crisp's face bore a saddened expression. He too had suffered at the hands of Derek Summers. Gardener had the impression Crisp was pursuing exoneration. As if he was guilty by association.

"Bob, can you prove any of what you're telling me? How do you know? How does my son tie in?"

"Knowledge is of two kinds. We know a subject ourselves, or we know where we can find information about it. Derek Summers makes the films himself. He makes them at home."

Gardener thought about Reilly's comment. He'd said he didn't think they'd seen the whole house. "Where?"

"He has a secret underground chamber that you wouldn't know about unless you'd stumbled across it. Like I did. Are you familiar with the house?"

"A little. Not as much as my partner."

Crisp chuckled. "'What is friendship? A single soul dwelling in two bodies.' The Irishman. You should value his friendship. He is your closest ally. Do you know the library?"

"The room beyond the study?"

"One and the same. Above one of the panels is a coat of arms. Move it and you gain entry. Down there you will find the film studio, cameras, lights, everything you need. It's a multimillion-pound industry, Mr Gardener, governed and controlled by very dangerous people. As I found out."

The Bear suddenly threw more logs onto the fire as the vagrant called George returned to the spit. Despite the roaring flames, it felt cold. Gardener felt despondent, consumed by the icy flames of defeat. How many times had they interrogated Summers, only to let him slip through the net? He couldn't believe he had let Summers go. Gardener urged Crisp. "What did you find out, Bob?"

"All I needed to know. It was late. I was in the office sorting through a lawsuit against Summers. A female client. He'd been withholding money. He said her act was substandard and she'd cost him a fortune. She claimed he'd tried to interfere with her. He beat her almost senseless when she spurned his advances. He only beats women and children.

"I left the office and went to the house. The butler said he was in the library. As I entered, I noticed the coat of arms cocked over to the right. A false wall panel lay open. I heard voices coming from a set of stairs beyond. At the bottom, I found Summers in a director's chair, behind one of the cameras. A grown man and two teenage girls were on the bed. Need I say more, Mr Gardener? Summers was also naked. Another teenager performed oral sex on him. Whether he'd been careless in leaving the panel open, I'm not sure. Whether the butler knew, I've no idea."

Crisp lit another cigarette, lost in the haunting memories. After what he'd described, Gardener couldn't blame him. He felt there was more to the story. George and The Bear paid little heed, as if they'd heard it all before.

"I was outraged, as any decent person would be. I threatened to call the police. Summers also made threats. Within a week, I'd been disbarred, discredited as a corrupt solicitor. Summers had forged documents and payments to make it look as if I had been directly involved. My own wife and child were killed in a horrific car accident. Faulty brakes, they said. The car had only passed an MOT that same afternoon. So, I know different. I can prove none of what I'm saying.

"A week later, my house had been reduced to ashes and, so too, had my life. I've been here ever since. Underground. You've no idea, Mr Gardener, what you're up against. Such power. 'Power tends to corrupt, and absolute power corrupts absolutely.' You may fare better than I, with the influence of the police behind you."

"Why have you never told anyone?" asked Gardener.

Crisp's satirical cackle echoed off every wall. "Why indeed? What is it Robert Frost once said? 'I never dared be radical when young for fear it would make me conservative when old.' I have nothing left to lose. Unlike you, with your son."

Gardener's bones chilled to the marrow.

"Go to the house tonight, for you have little time to lose. Save your son, he'll be there."

Bob Crisp rose and reached into a cupboard on the wall. "Take these."

"What are they?"

"Painkillers, of course. Your body is weak. You've eaten nothing. Not that I blame you. I, too, would have no appetite."

Gardener swallowed them down with a glass of water taken from the table.

"Here." Bob Crisp held out money.

"I can't take your money, Bob. You've done enough for me already."

"Then a little more won't hurt. We have money if we need it. Now, The Bear will escort you into Leeds. Take a taxi, go and rescue your son."

Gardener hesitated. There was so much more he wanted to ask.

"For God's sake, Mr Gardener, go!"

Gardener extended his hand to the vagrant. He had no idea how to thank Crisp for what he'd done. It had taken courage to reveal his story. Gardener doubted he could ever repay him.

Crisp shook his hand and then turned his back on Gardener, signalling the end of the meeting.

The Bear nodded.

Chapter Seventy-three

Chris spent the whole day in fear of his life, tormented by the thought of what they would do to him when they returned. Eventually, though, he'd fallen asleep. He'd woken with a start, unaware of the time or date. He was hungry. Preying slightly heavier on his mind was his survival, finding a way out of his situation.

The first thing he did was remove his boxer shorts. They smelled horrible. He left them on the floor before using the en-suite bathroom to clean up. When he was finished, Chris sat and thought about his father and the Irishman, and how they would go about changing the situation.

He figured the best thing he could do was set a trap.

He studied the room. The only thing he found he might be able to use was a small lamp on the bedside cabinet. He searched the place for something he could use to remove the plug.

When he was quite sure there wasn't anything, he decided to plug the lamp in, switch it on, remove the shade, and smash the bulb. He thought that would make it live. The next time one of those idiots came into the room, he'd give them something to think about. With a bit of luck, he might even kill the pair of them. He wasn't a copper's son for nothing.

The next thing he had to do was find something to wear. He couldn't very well stay naked.

Rummaging through a cupboard in the bathroom brought him little in the way of results, until he spotted something that didn't add up. At the back of the cupboard, underneath the towels he had pushed to one side, he could see a material he couldn't quite identify.

Chris banged on the back of the cupboard. It didn't sound right, nor was it hard like it should have been. The panel was false.

He glanced around the bathroom in nervous anticipation. Running out into the bedroom, he checked the door. It was still locked. He went back into the bathroom. He didn't care now how much noise he made. If those two creeps came to see what he was doing, he would electrocute them both.

Chris smashed his fists into the panel four times. It gave him the encouragement he needed to continue. Once he had the panel clear, he dragged out all the clothing. There were a number of school uniforms. From what he could tell, two were female and one male. Inside one of the blazers he saw the name 'David Vickers'.

He also found a pair of boxer shorts, which he recognized as his friend's. They were clean. He slipped them on.

Chris felt terrible. He tried to imagine what his friend had gone through, but his mind simply wouldn't allow it. He slammed his fists into the bathroom door, tears in his eyes. He ran back into the bedroom and grabbed the lamp. Sitting on the bed with the lamp in his hand, he waited.

Chapter Seventy-four

The night air was growing distinctly chilly. Cold enough to snow. It was after midnight. Gardener found himself momentarily suspended in the middle of a repeat performance from the previous evening. Late night revellers were clearing out of the pubs and clubs. He had chosen not to take a taxi, but to try making contact with Reilly instead. Despite his injuries, he struggled down Park Row and onto Boar Lane in search of a phone booth.

He felt conspicuous, vulnerable. In view of the beating he'd taken, he was extra careful not to stare at anyone too long. One wrong glance and he'd be in serious trouble. He was in no fit state to defend himself.

Halfway down Boar Lane, Gardener spotted his phone booth. As he drew closer, the door opened and a youth came out. Gardener stopped dead in his tracks. A chill spiralled throughout his entire body, his revulsion mounting.

For one split second, Gardener's eyes locked with Warthead's. In that fraction of time, his whole world froze.

It was impossible to describe his feelings, there were so many. Anger, bitterness, sorrow.

Above all else, Gardener's hunger for revenge was so strong, all physical impairments were forced to the back of his mind. He knew he was going to kill Warthead, despite the consequences.

Warthead took off, running down Boar Lane towards Duncan Street and the Corn Exchange.

Gardener followed, ignoring the pain in his head, his arms, his legs and, most of all, his bruised ribs. He decided not to shout at the freak, choosing instead to focus all his efforts on catching him.

Gardener heard police sirens to his right, coming across New Briggate. What happened next stunned the injured officer.

The traffic light at the Boar Lane and Briggate intersection changed to green, and the stationary car proceeded ahead.

Warthead took a chance to cross the road onto Duncan Street. Cutting across New Briggate like an atomic warhead, what later turned out to be a stolen Range Rover wasted the front end of one car, and bounced upwards in the collision. The car careened wildly out of control, taking Warthead and a portion of nearby railings straight through the plate glass window of the Burger King on the corner.

The series of explosions and shattering glass brought Gardener to his senses. He rounded the corner to confront the devastation.

A crowd milled around the Burger King so fast, he thought they must have emerged from the shadows. Most of them were okay, simply trying to figure what had happened. They were, however, ignoring the people that did need help. A number of victims had sustained cuts. Some had more serious injuries. One youth staggered around, his hand covering his right eye, blood pouring through at an alarming rate. His girlfriend was by his side, screaming at him to lay down while she found some help.

Most people had forgotten about their takeaway. Some had thrown their food right on the ground. At least six people were already on their mobiles. Only three were calling for help. Sickeningly, the others were filming.

Gardener pushed his way through the oblivious crowd. The stolen Range Rover's engine was still on maximum revs and had taken most of the customers in the fast food restaurant through the counter and into the storeroom. Dead bodies lay amongst the debris of glass, tables, chairs, and neon menus. Miraculously, two people had survived. They were staggering around with severe injuries.

The car's engine died abruptly with a crash and a clang as it seized up. The car then backfired, sending shockwaves through the crowd, most of whom were already backing away.

Gardener also retreated as the police arrived on the scene, urging people to let them through.

Before he stepped aside, he caught sight of the mangled, almost decapitated corpse of Warthead, trapped underneath the front wheel of the Rover.

Gardener turned and cursed, and slipped back around the corner onto Boar Lane, furious at the fact he'd been cheated of the chance to vent his anger on his wife's killer.

Behind him, the sirens of the ambulance service wailed as they came to deal with the dead and the injured.

In front of him, a car screeched to a halt. The passenger door opened.

"Get in, now!" Reilly shouted.

Chapter Seventy-five

Gardener stepped back, confused.

More ambulances, more squad cars, and more people swarmed the accident behind him.

"For Christ's sake, boss, get in the car," Reilly shouted again.

Gardener relaxed. A feeling of security returned. He hadn't recognized his colleague's vehicle. The last thing he'd needed was to jump into a car full of hoodlums. Once inside, Gardener closed the door. Reilly made a U-turn on Boar Lane, heading out towards Kirkstall.

"Am I pleased to see you," said Gardener.

"The feeling's mutual. What the hell's going on back there? Don't tell me you're responsible for that carnage?" Reilly glanced over. "What's happened to your face?"

"It's not just my face."

Gardener told Reilly about his previous twenty-four hours. How he'd struggled to find Bob Crisp, the beating and, finally, his eventual meeting with the vagrant and the revelations he'd heard. He also mentioned Warthead's spectacular finale.

"I knew it! I fucking knew it."

"You knew what?" Gardener was momentarily puzzled. His body had started to ache as the painkillers wore off.

"We've got Summers back at the station."

"On what charge?"

"The discs we retrieved from Myers' flat. I watched them again last night, with Briggs. We were about to leave. I'd forgotten to switch it off, and another film started on the same disc. It was an amateur video of Warthead with a teenager in the panelled library."

Gardener sighed. "How did you recognize it?"

"A coat of arms on one of the walls."

Gardener fell silent, digesting the information, quietly elated that something was finally going right.

"Well done, Sean. Bob Crisp told me about the coat of arms. If you move it, a secret panel opens and leads you down a set of stairs to another room."

Reilly left the town centre, heading toward Summers' house.

Gardener checked the clock on the dash. It was almost two in the morning. He hoped and prayed the butler had not done anything with Chris. Assuming he was being held prisoner at the house.

"I knew that bastard was guilty," said Reilly. He then told him about the incident at the station.

Gardener seethed inside at the thought of what Summers may have been planning to do with Chris. What he may already have done. "I hope to God Chris is all right."

"Another five minutes and we'll be there."

Gardener shifted in his seat. "So, we know he's a paedophile. Is he a killer?"

"I wish I could answer that question. I'd be willing to stake my career on it."

"It's always possible his employees have been blackmailing him," suggested Gardener.

"He makes the films, they all have a fallout, and he starts killing them because they know something about him?"

"Something along those lines. The problem with that is they also stood to incriminate themselves by putting him in the spotlight."

"Maybe they didn't care. But I don't hold with that one, though."

"There's a missing link here, Sean. I'm pretty sure he's in it up to his neck. But there's still one piece of the jigsaw puzzle outstanding. The curare and the plant serum."

Both men fell silent. Gardener needed Sharp's portfolio. Maybe the document would provide the final nail in Summers' coffin. He also needed to contact Fitz.

Before Gardener realized where they were, Reilly had parked the car on Summers' drive.

He eased himself out of the vehicle, pulling up on the grab handle with his left arm, comforting his ribs with his right. The silhouette of the house provided a gloomy backdrop against a clear sky.

The pruned bushes resembled a group of standing stones. Gardener was aware of an overpowering silence as the darkness closed in on him. The night had grown more chilly. A faint breeze on the back of his neck unsettled him further. Although he knew he had to go in, he was petrified at the possible outcome.

Reilly patted his shoulder. "Come on. Let's get it over with."

The front door was locked.

"Let's try round the back," said Gardener.

"Fuck that!" Reilly reached down and hefted a stone planter over his shoulder. He took a step back, ran at the door, and hurled the concrete figure through the glass section.

To Gardener, it sounded like a bomb exploded. The glass shattered, the plant stand disappeared, and, to their amazement, the house remained silent.

"No alarm? That does surprise me."

"Who cares if there is?" replied Reilly.

With the door unlocked, the two men raced through the study into the library, lighting up each room as they entered. Reilly pointed out the coat of arms and moved it.

To their left, a whole section of books glided silently inwards.

Gardener stopped at the opening, peering into the gloomy recess. He could smell leather and furniture polish. He breathed in, glanced upwards, his insides churning. "Please, God, let him be okay."

Reilly found a light switch. They both descended the illuminated stairs to the film studio.

It was exactly as Bob Crisp had described, with cameras, lights, scenery, and the director's chair.

Gardener spotted a door in the corner. He scurried over. It was locked.

"Chris!" shouted Gardener. There was no reply. He pushed against the door, but it wouldn't move. He knew he didn't have the strength to force it down himself.

"Sean, go and see if that creep of a butler is around."

As Reilly climbed the stairs, Gardener struggled to lift his leg. With all the strength he could muster, he ignored his pain and crashed it into the door above the handle. Although it didn't give, he knew it wouldn't take much pressure before it did.

Then he heard a voice. "Dad?"

"Chris?"

Chris sounded distant. Maybe the walls were thick. Perhaps he'd been woken up by all the noise. Either way, it was one of the most inviting sounds he had ever heard. If nothing else, Chris sounded okay.

"Chris, don't worry, I'm here. Stand well back from the door. I'm coming in."

Renewed enthusiasm charged through his body. Gardener glanced around the studio, noticing a fire extinguisher. He picked it up. It was heavier than he'd anticipated. He struggled with the hydrant, but seeing his son again gave him the encouragement he needed.

With every ounce of strength he had, he lifted the red canister and charged the door, shouting as he did. He misjudged his aim, running into the doorframe instead, knocking himself completely off his feet. The pain from his ribs nearly killed him.

He was barely aware of Reilly running past him and bouncing into the door with his whole body. It opened with a crash, slamming into whatever was behind. Reilly switched on the light. Chris shielded his eyes with one hand as it bathed his room. In the other he held a lamp, much like one would a sword.

The Irishman helped Gardener to his feet. Chris dropped the lamp and ran out of the room. Gardener noticed his son was dressed only in a T-shirt and boxer shorts, neither of which, he knew, belonged to him.

"Dad!" shouted Chris.

Gardener felt his son's arms wrap around him. Despite the pain, he was overwhelmed with how good it felt to see him again. "It's okay, son. It's okay. Everything will be all right."

Gardener felt Chris shaking, like a frightened sparrow he'd saved from a cat. "It's going to be okay, Chris. Trust me."

Inside the room, Reilly threw furniture around, turning the place upside down. When he emerged, he held Chris's soiled clothes.

Gardener saw them and eased Chris's arms apart. He steadily lowered himself so he came face-to-face with him. He winced as he realized Chris had a black eye and a scratch across his cheek. His son's face must have mirrored his own.

"What's happened to your face, Dad?"

"Never mind me, son. What about you?"

Chris's cheek was swollen. It was obvious he'd taken a fair punch. He remembered Bob Crisp's words, that Summers only beat women and children. The rage within Gardener was building. He was going to crucify Summers. Trails of dried tears on Chris's face increased Gardener's anxiety.

"I'm okay, honest. I was ready for him," Chris said.

"What do you mean?"

"I was ready." Chris glanced back into the room. "That lamp, on the bed, I modified it. I was going to fry them if they came near me again." He stared at the Irishman. "That's what you'd have done, isn't it?"

Reilly laughed. "I reckon I would so."

"Chris," said Gardener. "I have to ask you something." He needed an answer. But he was dreading it. "Did Summers… did he… interfere with you?"

Chris, puzzled, shook his head. "He just smacked me around when I knocked a tray out of his hand."

"That's all? He didn't touch you? You know, down there?" Gardener lowered his eyes to his son's waist for emphasis.

"No, I promise."

A wave of relief swept over Gardener. Reilly passed over Chris's clothes. Gardener could smell the overpowering scent of stale urine. He appreciated how disturbing his son's ordeal must have been, resurrecting painful memories of his own childhood. "Is this why you're wearing someone else's boxers?"

Chris didn't answer the question. "I have to show you something." He took his father by the hand into the room and showed him all the clothes he'd found in the cupboard.

Gardener stood up, seething inside. "I'm going to kill the bastard. I'm going to the cells tonight, and I'm going to kill him." Gardener's voice was even and controlled, unlike his mood.

"You're in no fit state, boss. And if we're going to do anything, we'll do it by the book."

"What? Let a jury send him to prison so you and I can pay our taxes to keep him in luxury?"

"It'll hardly be luxury when he's behind bars. You know as well as I do what happens to filthy perverts."

"What kind of a smarmy bastard lawyer has he got?"

"Not good enough to keep him out of jail."

As much as he hated the idea, he knew his partner was right. He was in no fit state to deal with Summers right now. Even if he had been, he wouldn't have managed to persuade the duty sergeant to let him. He felt so tired, he could have slept for a month.

Gardener paused and then sighed in defeat. "Take us home, Sean."

"You're both coming back to ours. Laura's running a bath, and she's calling your old man to tell him the news."

"I need to go home. The portfolio," persisted Gardener.

"I'll take you in the morning. Read it with a clear head. Then you and I can take a trip to the cells and deal with him properly."

As much as Gardener wanted to deal with Summers personally, he knew he couldn't. Sean was right again. He would read the report when he was in a better state to understand it, physically, mentally, and emotionally. He hoped to God it contained what he needed.

Gardener wrapped his left arm around Chris's neck and extended his right hand towards Reilly. "I owe you one, Sean."

"You'd have done the same for me. All that matters is that this wee lad of yours is okay."

Gardener nodded. "I take it you didn't find the butler."

"Lucky for him, no."

Chapter Seventy-six

Gardener replaced the receiver. He joined Laura, Sean, and Chris around the breakfast table. The tiled kitchen was large and spacious, coloured floor to ceiling in different shades of grey, with a black and chrome tubular-framed table and chairs. Along with fully fitted cupboards and a breakfast bar, Gardener noticed a large, full wine cooler. Strip lighting had been installed underneath the units. The kitchen opened out onto a dark wood conservatory, with a computer and a selection of prints Laura had developed during her work as a freelance photographer.

"Good news?" Reilly asked.

"I think so. Fitz confirmed the contents of the syringe were from the plants." Gardener grabbed a slice of toast and glanced at Chris. He seemed to have settled.

Both he and his son had cleaned up before going to bed. It had been Gardener's first opportunity to check his injuries. He had a swollen cheek and a cut across his forehead. His chest and stomach were covered in purple bruises, some of which had turned yellow. Laura had bandaged his battered body. Gardener had insisted he neither had the time nor the inclination to go to hospital.

He had also telephoned Malcolm, informing him that he and Chris were fine. His father had been unhappy about their decision to stay with Sean and Laura, saying that he wouldn't be settled until he saw them both for himself.

Gardener had slept with Chris in the spare double bed. Although both felt secure at having found one another, neither of them had relaxed enough to sleep soundly.

"He seems more content," said Laura.

"At least he's safe."

Reilly ruffled Chris's hair. He turned to his boss. "So, where do we go from here?"

Gardener finished eating his toast, staring out the window. The sun was up, and the garden was full of chattering sparrows. Despite being Christmas Eve, there was a distinct lack of seasonal atmosphere.

"The way I see it, Derek Summers is by far the most likely suspect. We have enough evidence against him for everything but the murders."

"What about the plants?"

"We have to start with what we know. Who we know. That means Anei."

Laura rose from the table. "I'll make another pot of coffee. Chris, would you like to come and see the fish?"

"Okay." He left the table with an understandable lack of enthusiasm.

Gardener realized his son had been through quite an ordeal. He knew it would take time to adjust. He was grateful to Laura for the diversion.

Reilly shook his head. "I'm struggling to see where Anei fits into it. I just don't think she's capable. I'm sure she's over seventy. I know she has the means and the knowledge, but she isn't strong enough."

Gardener eased back in his chair. In the other room, he heard Laura talking and Chris laughing. It was a boost to him. "I think the best thing we can do is get back home and have a look at Colin Sharp's portfolio. I'm still convinced it's Summers, and the missing link we're looking for will be in there – if Sharp has done as good a job as usual."

Chapter Seventy-seven

Gardener observed the tearful reunion between Chris and his grandfather, appreciating how close the two of them had become. He could see how relieved Malcolm was to have them both back safe and sound.

They were sitting around the kitchen table. His father had made tea. He'd given Chris a milkshake and a couple of chocolate bars. Gardener was surprised when Chris said he was going to his room to watch TV. Spook had followed. Gardener thought it best to let his son adjust in his own way.

Colin Sharp's portfolio was spread across the table before him. Gardener was impressed with Sharp's work, as usual. His colleague's dedication should be rewarded with a promotion of some description.

Gardener glanced up at his partner. "There's no shortage of material. Our only problem is the time to go through it all."

"Would you like me to help?" offered Malcolm.

"Thanks for the offer, Dad, but I wouldn't know where to start you off."

Malcolm stared at the mountain of paperwork, sifting through the small piles. As he came across a photograph, he picked it up and studied it. "I don't like the look of him."

Gardener stared at the picture in his hand. "Derek Summers. The photo doesn't do him justice, believe me. He's far worse than he looks."

"Have you found anything that links him to the curare and the flytraps?" Reilly asked Gardener.

Gardener sighed. "No, not yet."

"No, it can't be."

Gardener glanced at his father. The colour had drained from the old man's face, leaving a pale, anaemic complexion. He noticed Malcolm's shaking hand as he held the photograph.

"Dad? What's wrong?"

Reilly stood up. "I'll get him a glass of water."

Gardener reached out to steady his father's hand. "Dad, what is it? You don't look well. Is something wrong?"

"I think I know who this man is," said Malcolm, at last.

Reilly sat down, placing a tumbler of water in front of Malcolm.

"How do you know him?" asked Gardener.

"Anei once showed me a photograph of her sister Irina's husband. He was a footballer. In the photo, he was holding a trophy. There was a report underneath." Malcolm took a sip of the water. "His name was Sid Summers."

Gardener and Reilly stared at each other. Gardener's head started to spin, his mind a jumble of thoughts. "You sure about that?"

"I'm sure, son." He dropped the photo. "I'm sure."

Gardener riffled through the files. Adrenaline coursed through his veins. Paper flew everywhere. "It's here." Gardener held up a sheet for Reilly to see. "The names of Derek's parents. Sid Summers and Irina Bâlcescu." He let the paper fall. "Is this the link, Sean?"

"I'm not convinced. What about the plants?"

Gardener thought about it. "If they all grew up on a farm, had a farm shop, maybe he picked up that knowledge from his mother or his aunt."

"I'm not buying that either, son," said Malcolm. "From what I've heard, they haven't seen each other for years."

Gardener felt he was clutching at straws. His explanation was desperate, full of holes. His frustration threatened to overtake him.

Reilly's phone rang. He answered but remained in the room. "You're joking! Tell me you're not serious."

Gardener rose from the table, staring at his partner. Reilly ended the short call, an expression of defeat on his face.

"What's wrong?" asked Gardener.

"You're not going to like this."

"There's not much I do like about this case so maybe you'd better tell me."

"Summers just got police bail, with conditions."

"What? How?"

"Not enough evidence to hold him on a murder charge. Smarmy lawyer. Contacts in high places, you name it. But it was the butler who nailed it for him."

"What did *he* do?"

"Took the rap," replied Reilly, disappointed. "He's claiming it was all down to him."

"He's claiming he killed them all?"

Reilly nodded.

"He's lying, he's not capable. He's even older than Batman's butler and that's saying something," said Gardener, even more frustrated.

"*We* know he's lying, boss, but we're still gonna have to investigate his claims. All he's done is delay the inevitable and made our jobs a lot harder."

Gardener went to the sink for a glass of water, when a wave of nausea overtook him. He stopped dead in his tracks as a new thought entered his mind.

He turned, picking up the photo of Summers from the table, studying the eyes closely.

He knew immediately that he had seen them before.

Chapter Seventy-eight

Summers closed the rear door of the taxi and paid the driver with cash through the front window. As the vehicle turned and meandered back down the drive, Summers peered into the darkness at the silhouette of the house, which was anything but inviting.

His mind was a mess, full of thoughts he couldn't hold on to. Uppermost, however, was who had been responsible for killing his colleagues? He knew for a fact that Alfred wasn't, despite claiming he was. The butler was too old, too fragile and did not really have the intelligence to carry out such a plan. Apart from that, he spent most of his days tending to Summers, and pampering to his every whim. Aside from the shopping he did once weekly, the man hardly ever left the house.

So why had he taken the blame?

Originally, he had suspected one of the four Santas, but now they were all dead. What he didn't know was why. Was there any connection to him, or had they all been killed for some other reason: crossed some other person? It was possible. But he certainly didn't think that hanging around was a good idea, in case he became the next victim. No, it was time he made himself scarce, until the heat died down. If it ever would. He didn't think he was off the hook yet.

Question was, where to go: the police had his passport.

Summers climbed the steps to the front door, shocked to see one of the windows had been smashed; furthermore, whoever had done that had used one of his own planters, another possible reminder that he may be connected to the murders of his friends.

A sharp tapping sound to his left spooked him. Summers glanced around, strained his eyes but it was too dark to see anything.

Quickly, he reached into his left side jacket pocket and pulled out his house keys. Once inside with the door locked, he'd feel better. Although why, he wasn't sure. Whoever had smashed his window could still be in there.

Glancing around the house, he noticed the place was in darkness. That could work to his advantage if he had an intruder. At least he knew his own house.

Quickly rushing in, he turned and locked the front door and immediately switched on the light. Apart from the mess that the planter had caused – soil, glass and the like – nothing else was out of place.

Summers took the stairs two at a time. When he reached the landing, he switched on another light. Nothing untoward.

He crept over to his bedroom and opened the door carefully. With the light on, he studied the room. All clear. He reached up to a wardrobe and pulled a suitcase down and onto the bed. Rifling through drawers and cupboards made *him* feel like a burglar.

He slipped into the en-suite bathroom and collected everything he thought he might need for a few days.

As he stood by the bed, he strained his ears, but the house was quiet. He hadn't yet come across anything missing so, what the hell had happened at the front of the house, he had no idea.

A sudden thought hit him. Although the police may have gone through the place, he could pretty much guarantee they wouldn't have found everything capable of incriminating him. He had two separate safes hidden within the ground floor of the house that he needed to check on.

Summers dropped his toiletries on the bed and left the room, taking the staircase to the ground floor.

He ran down the passage to the back of the house, to his study.

As soon as he opened the door, he stopped dead in his tracks, shocked. Why was the study the only room in the house with the lights on?

He peered around the room. Everything was in order. He crept forward very slowly, glancing into every corner. As he reached his desk, he bent down, slowly circling the piece of furniture. There was no one squashed into the gap behind, where he normally sat.

He turned and faced the door in the corner – the one that led into the library. Creeping slowly forward, he picked up a letter opener from the desk. It wasn't much but it might come in handy.

As he opened the door, he had his second shock. The coat of arms was at an odd angle and the panel was open, allowing access to the film studio.

Summers was sweating profusely, his breathing heavier. His stomach rumbled and he considered himself lucky there was nothing in it, otherwise he couldn't guarantee how long it would stay there.

Studying the library, he realized it would be impossible for anyone to hide. He had no alternative but to take the steps down into the film studio, meaning any element of surprise was now gone.

He could always turn and flee. But it would all depend on who was waiting for him. If it was that lunatic Irishman who tried to kill him at the police station, Summers would be wasting his time. He couldn't outrun him in a month of Sundays.

No, he wouldn't do that. It was his house and it was up to him to check and see what was happening.

He strolled to the edge of the stairs. Staring down, he could see the lights were on.

"If there's anyone down there you'd better come out now."

There was no reply.

"I'm armed," shouted Summers. "The police are on their way."

The silence was deafening.

He descended the steps, the paper opener held out at arm's length, his other arm on the banister to steady himself.

It seemed like hours before he reached the bottom. When he did, he received his third and near fatal shock.

"What the hell are *you* doing here?"

Chapter Seventy-nine

The surface of the table was covered with paper. Reilly and Malcolm were standing, bent forward, reading passages. Chris was still in his room.

Gardener glanced at Reilly, pleased with Colin Sharp's dedication, disappointed by his own lack of perception.

"Got it," said Reilly. "Derek Summers started his working life with a newspaper. Seems he was quite committed. Worked his way through the ranks. Made senior editor in '79. A quick worker, by the look of things. He actually took over the newspaper in 1980. The report says he made his money by selling a couple of Van Gogh paintings."

"They would have been his father's," interrupted Malcolm. "Anei told me Sid's father had brought the treasure back. She said it was German. He obviously saw it as his insurance. I'll bet his poor mother didn't know about the Van Goghs."

"I'll bet she didn't," said Reilly. "According to the report, and the witnesses Sharp has managed to speak to, Sid Summers died of pneumonia. Sources say Derek blamed the newspaper for sending his father out to cover a story in bad weather."

"Why would his father need to work if he had the proceeds from the stolen treasure?" asked Malcolm.

"Who knows? Perhaps there wasn't as much as you think. Maybe his despicable son had managed to filter it away over the years, leaving the old couple penniless," offered Reilly.

Gardener was sitting in a chair, physically and mentally worn out. His ribs were killing him. "Does it say anything about Jacqueline?"

Reilly held the report aloft. "Not a lot. She was born in 1972, but for some reason disappeared around 1985."

"Which was obviously when she went to live with her aunt," said Malcolm.

After searching, Reilly found another file. "Wait a minute. She went to university in 1990. From there, she attended the ministerial college in Bristol. Finally, in 1997, she started her first ministerial circuit in Cornwall."

"Have we got any paracetamol, Dad?" Gardener asked.

Malcolm nodded, reached into a cupboard, passing two over with a glass of water. Gardener swallowed them. He was deflated by all the new information. He ran his hands through his hair, scraped his scalp, and then slammed them down on the table.

"Why didn't I see it? All the signs were there!" Gardener raised his head, his eyes meeting Reilly's. "It's Jacqueline." His tone was one of total humiliation, as if all the blame was his own.

"She had the access to the plants. She told me she'd studied biology. She even intimated how bad her relationship with her father was. He was a nasty piece of work. She told me a few of the things he'd done. She obviously chose to leave out some of the more emotionally distressing incidents. She was harbouring so much hate for him. I'm certain her father abused her. Perhaps the others were in on it as well. It accounts for her living with her aunt and taking the Romanian family name."

Gardener glanced at Malcolm. "For God's sake! Why didn't I see it?"

"Jacqueline... a killer?" Malcolm seemed stunned, defeated. "No, she can't be, son. You must have it wrong."

"I saw her on Monday morning in the store, minutes after it had happened. She said she was with her aunt." Gardener glanced at his partner. "Sean, ring the station, will you? Get someone to go over all the witness statements, check all the names. Tell them what they're looking for."

"There must be some mistake," said Malcolm, still refusing to accept it.

After a strained silence, Gardener heard his partner replace the receiver. "They're on to it."

"What do we do now?" Gardener asked.

Reilly's hard eyes softened. He shrugged his shoulders. "What are your choices?"

Gardener turned to his father. "They're not coming back, are they? Jacqueline and Anei?"

Malcolm sighed, his expression one of defeat. "It doesn't look like it. But if, as you say, Jacqueline's killed them all, she won't leave without finishing the job."

Gardener rose from the chair and picked up the phone. He rang the vicarage, hoping he might hear the minister's voice. No one answered. He phoned Anei. The call remained unanswered.

"Sean, grab your car keys."

"Where are we going?"

Gardener thought about that. "Could be one of two places. The airport, or his place."

"If he's on bail we'll have his passport," said Reilly, "so I doubt he would try to leave the country."

"But she can."

"Not without finishing what she started," added Malcolm.

"In that case, there's only one place to go," said Gardener, glancing at Reilly, "if he's right, they're all at his place."

Chapter Eighty

"Hello, Father," said Jacqueline, "at last, we meet again."

It was probably the first and only time in her life Jacqueline had sensed genuine concern in her father's expression. It certainly wasn't surprise.

He glanced around the film studio, probably assessing whether or not he had an advantage. He may well have, thought Jacqueline. After all, his only competition was his daughter, and her aunt Anei, who was currently sitting opposite Jacqueline, in the director's chair to his right, with her hands in her pockets.

Summers turned to Jacqueline and made a move toward her. His arms were spread openly, as if welcoming her but, as long as he had the letter opener in one of them, he would be a danger.

"Jacqueline, Anei, it's so good to see you both."

"Don't you dare come near me!" she spat venomously; a warning finger raised. From behind her back, she brought the syringe into view, pressing the plunger: the clear liquid inside jettisoned out.

Summers stepped back, maintaining his position at the bottom of the stairs, without further comment. The tension could have been cut with a knife.

Jacqueline studied her father. He had changed little since she'd last seen him, which was more than twenty years ago. His face had aged accordingly. What most people shrugged off as laughter lines could only be crevices of guilt, following a life of fraud and deception and, most likely, debauchery. He was dressed in a crumpled grey suit with a white shirt and a grey tie. He smelled of stale sweat.

"You couldn't help yourself, could you?"

Her father bore a puzzled expression. "I'm not sure I know what you're talking about."

Anei rolled her eyes and groaned.

"Don't patronize me! You didn't stop at me, did you? Raping and defiling your own daughter wasn't enough for you." Jacqueline fought to keep her emotions under control. Feelings she had harboured for years. It would be so easy to lose it now. But she couldn't allow the reptile who had claimed to be her father the satisfaction of seeing that happen. "In fact, it was just the start. You had whetted your appetite with me."

"Jacqueline, please."

Here it is, she thought, the personality change. He'd obviously decided that ignorance wasn't going to work. His next tactic would be sympathy. She knew only too well, even after all these years, that once he realized all was lost, he would become angry. Perhaps he would resort to violence.

"Jacqueline, please listen to me. You have to understand, we were drunk, we didn't know what we were doing."

"Don't you dare use that excuse on me! You knew perfectly well what you were doing."

"No, Jacqueline, we didn't..." He eased himself away from the bottom step.

"Stay where you are!"

She found it hard to believe one person could store up so much hatred for another. "You knew exactly what you were doing. Not once did you stop to think about me. About how I felt."

Jacqueline trembled with rage. She felt cold, hollow. Her insides churned. She thought she would be sick as she struggled desperately to hold on to her dignity. "I was too young to realize what you were doing when you first started. How convenient my mother's death must have been. You had the perfect excuse. You could sleep with your little girl whenever you wanted. Because your wife had died, you used your daughter for comfort.

"You insisted it would be our little secret, that we were doing nothing wrong. At first, I suppose I thought there was no harm. It was just a cuddle. It didn't take you very long to start touching, though, did it? Our little secret you said, yet again."

"Jacqueline, please…"

"Shut up! You told me everything we did was natural, that every father and daughter did it." Jacqueline shuddered. "My mother had died, and all you could do was abuse me.

"Did you ever love my mother? Have you ever loved anyone but yourself? You have no idea how I felt. I desperately wanted to tell someone. Even at that young age, I didn't think it was right. Do you know how unlucky I was? I had one friend at school."

She thought back to that day, the time when she'd finally decided to confide in Jayne. Jacqueline could still picture her friend's long, black, braided hair, the pretty blue eyes, her wide, innocent smile. How her life had almost crumbled with her friend's answer.

"Eventually, I found the courage to tell her. And do you know what she said? She told me her father did it to her.

"You disgust me! What you couldn't get from your wife, you took from me. I was ten years old. I needed comfort. I wanted reassurance that I could make it. I needed you because I had no mother. And what did you do?"

"It wasn't like that," he replied, as if her accusations were unfounded.

She noticed the expression in his eyes, realizing his mood was changing. "Well, what was it like?" She glared at him. "In fact, don't bother explaining. I've heard enough of your lies to last me a lifetime."

Her father's wrath was escalating, despite his silence. He was beginning to lose control. His mouth was a grimace, his fingers clenching and unclenching. His eyes were impenetrable.

She didn't care. There was nothing more he could do to harm her, and it only served to make her task easier.

Jacqueline's voice lowered to a whisper. "You've no idea how frightened I was the night you really decided to take control. You'd all been drinking to celebrate your takeover of the newspaper. God knows what little stunt you'd pulled to manage that one. My bedroom door shot open. I remember the light flooding in, and your slobbering, drunken silhouette filling the gap."

Jacqueline glanced upwards. She wanted to kill him now, but realized how much better it would make her feel if she could possibly instil even a portion of the fear into him that she herself had felt thirty years previous.

"You dragged me from my bed. Down the stairs. The four perverts you called your friends were all waiting for me. For their prize. I have no idea what you'd said to them, but the look on their faces told me all I needed to know. They were all dressed in Santa suits. I realized what my present was going to be. Have you any idea what I was thinking? Four men, all standing there, knowing there was nothing I could do. Nowhere to run. Did you even care?"

Her father's fists balled, ready for attack. He was no match for Jacqueline.

"I tried to run. I thought, at least if I made the effort, you might spare me." Jacqueline forced a restricted chuckle. "God, how wrong I was! All I received for my effort was a punch in the face. I remember hitting the cupboard, chipping my tooth. A constant reminder to me of that night. As if I needed one." She fought hard to restrain her tears.

"Venin," spat Anei.

"Jacqueline!" The depth of his voice carried a warning, as though, somehow, he could still control his little girl.

"Don't! Don't try to stop me!" She paused, long enough to regain her composure. Why she was explaining to him, she didn't know. Perhaps he should be made aware of her feelings, past and present. Maybe she wanted to shame him. One thing she knew for certain, she somehow had to release her own pent-up emotions.

"I was dragged kicking and screaming, onto a kitchen table. I had one of your dirty, disgusting friends down my throat... another holding my head... another sodomising me. As if that wasn't bad enough, I realized you... you... weren't drunk at all. Because you were hovering in the background. Filming everything.

"Two hours of absolute torture. I thought I was going to die. I wanted to die. My life had ended. You stripped me of anything and everything I had. And then you dragged me onto my back. You broke my finger." She held it aloft. "Then you, my very own father, raped me!"

Anei said something but the minister didn't catch it: she wasn't even sure it was a word.

Jacqueline desperately tried to hold it together. She was shaking with fear even now. Her eyes were red, swollen from the tears she could not contain. She ran her hands through her hair, wanting to leave, but knowing she couldn't. She had to see it through.

"My own father! How could you?" she shouted, spittle flying from her mouth. "You really have no idea how much I hate you, have you?"

Chapter Eighty-one

"What kind of a monster are you? Two teenage girls? David Vickers? Why do you do it?"

Out of the corner of her eye Jacqueline noticed two pairs of feet had appeared at the top of the stairs leading into the film studio. One pair of legs had casual black shoes and grey trousers: the other, jeans and brogues. One had to be Gardener. Very slowly and very carefully they descended, one step at a time, until their heads almost came into view.

"I don't have to answer to you," said Summers.

Jacqueline knew her father's anger had almost reached the point where he was likely to attack her. Luckily, she now had back-up, not that she felt she had ever needed it. She closed one hand around the syringe.

Tears welled in her eyes as she thought about Lesley Vickers peering into her son's grave, what she must have gone through. To think that the monster responsible for all that heartache was her own pompous, self-centred father.

"No, maybe not, but you will have to answer for your actions to someone. I had to bury David Vickers. Do you know how that made me feel? I wondered whether or not you were still up to your sordid little games, even after all these years. So, I investigated. I checked you out, you and your friends. Imagine my horror when I found out you were all still molesting innocent children. And you had the perfect cover. All department store Santas. You, filthy pervert!"

"So, what are you going to do about it, Jacqueline?" Summers turned and glanced at Anei. "She's hardly going to be much help to you." He turned back to face Jacqueline. "I know why you're here. You killed the others. Now you want me. But I'm neither old, fat, nor decrepit, like the others you've already taken. You're no match for me, girl."

She stared deep into her father's evil eyes. "Maybe. Maybe not. But I'm not the little girl you defiled all those years ago. When you raped me, you almost ended my life. You robbed me of my dignity, my self-respect, and my self-importance."

"You should be ashamed of yourself," shouted Anei. Jacqueline could see the hatred in her eyes. "You will go to hell for what you've done."

"Shut up, old woman," shouted Summers, without so much as a glance at her.

Gardener and Reilly had descended two more steps. Jacqueline noticed Gardener hugging his ribs. The pair whispered something to each other, but she couldn't hear the exchange.

"Between God and my aunt, I managed to restore my dignity and build a new life for myself."

"Doesn't seem to have you got you very far."

"Even your own mother hated you. Because she was your mother, though, she couldn't find it in her heart to report your actions. She believed, as I did, God would deal with you. What she didn't realize was how far your debauchery would take you. None of us did. I hope you burn in hell for what you did!"

Summers stepped forward. "I've had enough of this. If you were going to do anything to me, you would have done it by now. I don't have time to waste bandying words on you so, take yourself and this wizened old crow," Summers pointed to Anei, "out my house before I do something you'll both regret. Like I've said, you're no match for me."

"Maybe not," said Gardener, "but we are."

Summers bristled, and an expression of such evil crossed his features as his eyes narrowed and his teeth bared, Jacqueline may as well have been dealing with the devil himself. Her stomach convulsed.

But her father didn't even turn to see where the words had come from. Instead, with a speed that defied his age, he feinted to his left, slipped around the back of the chair, forced his left elbow around Aunt Anei's neck and lifted her body out of the chair, holding the paper opener to her throat.

Chapter Eighty-two

The tension in the room was palpable.

Gardener and Reilly descended the steps in a hurry and the SIO stood between Summers and Jacqueline. Reilly remained at the bottom of the stairs.

"Don't do anything stupid, Mr Summers."

"It's a bit too late for that, Mr Gardener."

Jacqueline stood by Gardener's side. "Let her go."

"What would I gain by that?" asked Summers.

"You'll gain nothing if you don't, sunshine," said Reilly.

"You're really not making life any easier for yourself, Mr Summers. You're facing charges of perverting the course of justice, kidnapping, abuse of a minor…"

"I've abused no one."

Gardener glanced at Jacqueline and then back at Summers. "I believe this lady will say otherwise. Historical sex abuse, Mr Summers, not something you can get away with these days."

"It's her word against mine, and she's a murderer; you heard her admit as much."

"And she'll no doubt face charges as well." A burst of pain shot through Gardener's ribcage, but he managed to hold it together.

"Doesn't look like you're much of a match for me, either."

"He's got me," said Reilly, "and we both know how capable I am."

"Not while I have the old woman in my grasp."

"Let's be honest here, Mr Summers," said Gardener, "once you've played your ace what are you going to do? Let's say you stab Anei, what are you going to do next? You won't be quick enough to do anything else, and there is no way out of here. You may as well put the knife down and give yourself up now."

On cue, Gardener heard the sound of sirens pulling up outside.

"Game's up, sunshine," said Reilly.

With a sudden scream that took everyone by surprise, which no one saw coming, Anei lurched backwards pushing Summers into the wall behind. Shock made him drop the paper opener. Even before it clattered to the floor, Anei brought her right arm up, forcing the syringe she had concealed in her pocket straight into Summers' neck.

Chapter Eighty-three

Summers immediately let go of Anei and slid down the wall. He brought his right hand to his neck.

"What the hell have you done to me?"

Neatly sidestepping Gardener, Jacqueline stepped over to her father as an expression of mortal fear crossed his features.

"I'm afraid you underestimated us, Father, dear." She pressed the plunger in her left hand. The clear liquid caught Summers in the face. "Pure water in mine. Looks like you chose to attack the wrong person."

Shouts and footsteps throughout the house meant that more of Gardener's team had arrived.

"My aunt had the syringe that will do the damage. Merry Christmas… *Daddy*."

Jacqueline turned and faced Gardener with her hands outstretched, as if waiting for handcuffs.

"Jacqueline," said Anei, standing near the stairs with Reilly, "don't admit anything."

"What have you given him?" Gardener asked the minister.

"Same as the others," she replied, without remorse.

"Is there an antidote?"

"No."

Gardener pushed her out of the way and bent down to Summers, whose hand still covered the syringe dangling from his neck. He was hyperventilating and perhaps going into shock.

Gardener glanced at his partner, but Reilly was already on the phone. He'd asked for an ambulance, but Gardener didn't hold out much hope of it arriving in time, nor being able to do anything when the medics arrived.

Frank Thornton and Bob Anderson appeared in the film studio. Behind them, Colin Sharp.

Thornton asked if there was anything he could do.

"Can you take these two upstairs and keep them in the study?" Gardener asked of him, pointing to the two women.

At that moment, Summers let out an ear-piercing scream and the foul odour of blocked drains permeated the room.

Gardener turned to face Summers, knowing he wouldn't have long now. His face had puffed up and his eyes were reddening. A stain had appeared around his genital area. The next step would be hideous, and he was most anxious not to watch it, having already seen what it did to Harry Clayton.

"You two," shouted Gardener to Jacqueline and Anei, "I'd like you upstairs and out of the way, now."

"What do you want me to do?" asked Sharp.

"There's not much we can do, Colin. If you go with Frank and Bob, Sean and I will stay with Summers till the ambulance arrives."

By the time Reilly had ushered everyone back up the stairs to the study, Gardener heard the sirens accompanying the ambulance. The vehicle pulled to a halt.

Within seconds, two medics appeared and bolted down the stairs. Gardener instructed them on what he knew and headed up to the study to meet his partner.

Everyone was seated. The minister straightened in hers. For the first time, he noticed how she was dressed: in a black two-piece trouser suit with a white blouse and a lilac silk scarf around her neck – no doubt ready for a trip to the airport. The sheen on her hair reflected the overhead lights. Her expression was one of defeat. He wondered what was going through her mind.

He actually felt sorry for her. A thirteen-year-old girl against the world. Raped and defiled by a bunch of bastards. But despite the fact she had every right to see the men who had violated her punished, she had gone about it the wrong way. Having gone through the ordeal she had, it would have been hard to trust any adult. But it would have been her only hope. As a mature woman of the cloth, she should have known better. There would have been channels she could have gone through. Maybe she thought the church would protect her from what was about to happen.

Her only hope would be a sympathetic jury.

Despite every thought invading his mind, she had given him absolutely no choice. He raised his warrant card.

"Jacqueline Bâlcescu, I'm arresting you on suspicion of six murders. You do not have to say anything, but it may harm your defence if you do not mention, when questioned, something you later rely on in court. Anything you do say may be given in evidence."

Jacqueline did not reply. She simply stood up, waiting for him to make the next move.

The expression in her eyes was paralyzing. He realized at that moment what her feelings were toward him: what she thought of him. She would probably have traded everything she had to be with him. He wondered briefly what would have happened had her feelings been reciprocated.

"Sean, take her away."

"Stop!" shouted Anei.

Startled, Gardener stared at the old woman.

"Don't say anything." Jacqueline reprimanded her aunt.

Reilly stepped back.

Anei stood up. "It wasn't her. It was me!"

Gardener wondered whether or not she was speaking the truth, or merely protecting her niece as she had always done.

"She did not murder those men. I did. Even if she had, who would care? People like that don't deserve to live in our society."

"Stop it, Auntie, you don't know what you're saying."

Gardener stepped forward to face the old lady. Even if she didn't kill the others, she had killed Summers only minutes ago in front of his very eyes. She would no doubt argue it was self-defence and, with a decent lawyer, not to mention a sympathetic jury, she too, may well escape any severe punishment.

Anei Bâlcescu glared at Gardener. "Can you blame me?"

Whatever her plan had been, it was beginning to unfold. Whether he could or not was immaterial. "Are you admitting to the murders of Herbert Plum, Bernard Thornwell, Frank Myers, and Harry Clayton?"

Jacqueline turned and pointed a warning finger. "I've told you, Auntie, don't be stupid. Do not throw away your one chance of going home."

"What kind of a home would it be without you?" replied the old woman.

"She's lying, Stewart," said Jacqueline, turning back to Gardener. "She's trying to protect me. I killed all of those men, and I may as well have killed my father, and I have no regrets."

"I am not lying," said Anei. "I killed those men. And you have just seen me kill another. What kind of a policeman are you? I have knowledge. I have plants. I have expertise." She was counting the reasons off on her fingers, her hand held close to Gardener's face. "You have all the evidence you need."

Gardener's head was a mess. Who the hell had killed the men? The butler, Summers, Anei, Jaqueline?

Gardener had no choice. He held his warrant card in the air once again.

"Anei Bâlcescu, I'm also arresting you on suspicion of murder. You do not have to say anything, but it may harm your defence if you do not mention, when questioned, something you later rely on in court. Anything you do say may be given in evidence."

Jacqueline almost sank to her knees. "No, Stewart. You can't. She's lying."

She turned to her aunt. "Please, tell him. You're only trying to protect me."

Tears poured down her cheeks. She addressed her aunt, who had now sat back down. They were holding hands.

"I know what you're doing," said Jacqueline. "You think that these people are going to hurt me, send me to prison. It doesn't matter. No one can hurt me anymore. Can't you see? The only people who can hurt me are now dead. I've gotten rid of them. No one else can hurt me."

She glanced at Gardener, and then back at her aunt. "I won't face this alone. The Lord will be with me. He will look after me."

Anei Bâlcescu did not answer her niece. Instead, she addressed Gardener. "I stand by my words."

After a short silence, Gardener replied. "So do I."

Epilogue

Christmas Day

"Merry Christmas, my darling," said Sarah, reaching towards him.

She was beautiful, dressed in a black two-piece suit, with a white blouse and a peach-coloured silk scarf he had bought her from Marks & Spencer. They were standing by the fireplace, in front of the Christmas tree that she had decorated. She was holding a present, reaching out to him.

He wanted to take it. When he did, she disappeared.

Gardener gasped and sat bolt upright in bed, bathed in sweat, his head pounding. The sudden movement jolted his ribs, taking his breath away.

He placed his head in his hands, going over the events of the previous evening. Both women had been arrested, detained in separate cells. The legal wheels would start turning tomorrow. It was no way to spend Christmas Day, but it was out of his hands.

He'd returned in the early hours of the morning. Chris had been in bed, but his father was still up, watching an old black and white movie on the TV.

Gardener had joined him. The pair of them had a whiskey, then another, and the rest was history.

He felt bad. He struggled down the stairs. Despite the rude awakening, the soreness in his ribs was slightly milder than it had been yesterday. In the living room, Malcolm, Chris, and Spook were all seated around the fire, listening to Christmas carols. A smell of pine filled the air.

Underneath the tree, the few presents reflected the kind of run-up to Christmas they'd had – a pretty horrendous week. He was, however, pleased with the effort his father had made with a last-minute dash to the shops.

Each of them exchanged cards, presents, and Christmas greetings. Before Gardener attempted to open any of his, he stood up. "I'll make us a cup of tea first, I think."

"I'll do it," offered Malcolm.

"No, you've done enough. Let me."

Gardener ruffled Chris's hair and stroked Spook before entering the kitchen. As he did, a box on the kitchen table was the only thing he noticed, as if he had tunnel vision. Next to the box was a card. The writing was Jacqueline's.

After making the tea, he stood at the kitchen table, smelled the perfumed card, and read the inscription. "Ma daruri si ma dragoste pentru voi. Se cu ma intotdeauna."

Carefully, he opened the box. Inside was a perfectly carved replica of the Kiss Gate. A Romanian gift, signifying true love.

"Dad! Dad! Look what I've got." Gardener raised his head to see Chris in his striped pyjamas, holding two smartphones. "Two phones! There's certainly no excuse not to keep in touch now." Gardener smiled, realizing how alike he and his father were.

Chris walked over to the table. "I want you to have one."

"I can't do that, Chris. They're yours."

"Please. You wouldn't have lost yours if you hadn't come looking for me. And besides, I haven't had the time to buy you a present myself."

He hesitated, but then took it. "Thanks, son."

Malcolm appeared at the doorway with a magazine in his hand. Gardener glanced at his father, who merely nodded and smiled. Chris ran back into the living room.

Gardener showed Malcolm the card. "Any idea what it says?"

Malcolm took his time before answering. "I'm not too sure, I'm not very fluent."

He held the card closer. "My gift and my love for you. Be with me always."

Gardener said nothing. Inside, he felt empty. His father put the card back on the table, next to the Kiss Gate. He held out a brochure for him to see.

"What's this?" asked Gardener, realizing it was the catalogue with the seats for the Bonneville.

Malcolm opened the page at the King and Queen seat, the one he wanted but didn't think he could afford. "The bloke who runs the place dropped it off yesterday. That's the one you want, isn't it?"

"I was certainly thinking about it."

"Well, you don't have to think anymore. You deserve it after the year you've had. Merry Christmas, son. But you will have to wait three months. It's being customized."

Gardener didn't know what to say. His dad patted him on the shoulder and went back into the living room to see Chris. Gardener heard his son's infectious laughter. There was a point when he thought he would never hear it again, which made him realize how important his family was. He also realized that, wrong as it was to take the law into her own hands, Jacqueline had indirectly saved the life of his son and Lord knows how many other children. For that much, he would be eternally grateful.

He studied the card and the inscription again, before sparing another thought for the minister, hoping what little family she had would be enough. On his way into the living room, a radio newsflash distracted him.

"...the perfectly preserved corpse of Wilfred Bradshaw was found in a house in Rawston. Police are anxious to trace the previous owner, a Mrs Olive Bradshaw, to discuss the mystery surrounding her brother's death. Police pathologist Doctor George Fitzgerald estimated the time of death at around twelve months ago..."

If you enjoyed this book, please let others know by leaving a quick review on Amazon. Also, if you spot anything untoward in the paperback, get in touch. We strive for the best quality and appreciate reader feedback.

editor@thebookfolks.com

www.thebookfolks.com

ALSO AVAILABLE

If you enjoyed IMPURITY, the first book, check out the others in the series:

IMPERFECTION – *Book 2*

When theatre-goers are treated to the gruesome spectacle of an actor's lifeless body hanging on the stage, DI Stewart Gardener is called in to investigate. Is the killer still in the audience? A lockdown is set in motion but it is soon apparent that the murderer is able to come and go unnoticed. Identifying and capturing the culprit will mean establishing the motive for their crimes, but perhaps not before more victims meet their fate.

IMPLANT – *Book 3*

A small Yorkshire town is beset by a series of cruel murders. The victims are tortured in bizarre ways. The killer leaves a message with each crime – a playing card from an obscure board game. DI Gardener launches a manhunt but it will only be by figuring out the murderer's motive that they can bring him to justice.

IMPRESSION – *Book 4*

Police are stumped by the case of a missing five-year-old girl until her photograph turns up under the body of a murdered woman. It is the first lead they have and is quickly followed by the discovery of another body connected to the case. Can DI Stewart Gardener find the connection between the individuals before the abducted child becomes another statistic?

IMPOSITION – *Book 5*

When a woman's battered body is reported to police by her husband, it looks like a bungled robbery. But the investigation begins to turn up disturbing links with past crimes. They are dealing with a killer who is expert at concealing his identity. Will they get to him before a vigilante set on revenge?

IMPOSTURE – *Book 6*

When a hit and run claims the lives of two people, DI Gardener begins to realize it was not a random incident. But when he begins to track down the elusive suspects he discovers that a vigilante is getting to them first. Can the detective work out the mystery before more lives are lost?

IMPASSIVE – *Book 7*

A publisher racked with debts is found strung up in a ruined Yorkshire abbey. Has a disgruntled author taken their revenge? DI Stewart Gardener is on the case but maybe a hypnotist has the key to the puzzle. Can the cop muster his team to work some magic and catch a cunning killer?

IMPIOUS – *Book 8*

It could be detectives Gardener and Reilly's most disturbing case yet when a body with head, limbs and torso assembled from different victims is discovered. Alongside this grotesque being is a cryptic message and a chess piece. A killer wants to take the cops on a journey. And force their hand.

IMPLICATION – *Book 9*

When a body is found in a burned out car, DI Stewart Gardener quickly establishes that a murder has been concealed. But with a missing person case and a spate of robberies occupying the force, he will struggle to identify the victim. When the investigations overlap, he'll have to work out which of the suspects is implicated in which crime.